THE PRETEND WIFE

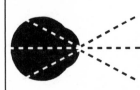
This Large Print Book carries the
Seal of Approval of N.A.V.H.

THE PRETEND WIFE

BRIDGET ASHER

THORNDIKE PRESS

A part of Gale, Cengage Learning

Detroit • New York • San Francisco • New Haven, Conn • Waterville, Maine • London

GALE
CENGAGE Learning™

Thorndike Press® Large Print Basic.
The text of this Large Print edition is unabridged.
Other aspects of the book may vary from the original edition.
Set in 16 pt. Plantin.
Printed on permanent paper.

LIBRARY OF CONGRESS CATALOGING-IN-PUBLICATION DATA

Asher, Bridget.
     The pretend wife / by Bridget Asher.
       p. cm.
     ISBN-13: 978-1-4104-2000-8 (hardcover : alk. paper)
     ISBN-10: 1-4104-2000-0 (hardcover : alk. paper)
     1. Married women—Fiction. 2. Triangles (Interpersonal relations)—Fiction. 3. Domestic fiction. 4. Large type books. I.
Title.
     PS3601.S54P74 2009b
     813'.6—dc22   2009028398

Published in 2009 by arrangement with Bantam Books, a division of Random House, Inc.

Printed in the United States of America
1 2 3 4 5 6 7 13 12 11 10 09

For Dave,
real as real can be

■ ■ ■ ■

PART ONE

■ ■ ■ ■

CHAPTER ONE

That summer when I first became Elliot Hull's pretend wife, I understood only vaguely that complicated things often prefer to masquerade as simple things at first. This is why they're so hard to avoid, or at least brace for. I should have known this — it was built into my childhood. But I didn't see the complications of Elliot Hull coming, perhaps because I didn't want to. So I didn't avoid them or even brace for them, and as a result, I eventually found myself in winter watching two grown men — my pretend husband and my real husband — wrestle on a front lawn amid a spray of golf clubs in the snow — such a blur of motion in the dim porch light that I couldn't distinguish one man from the other. This would become one of the most vaudevillian and poignant moments of my life, when things took the sharpest turn in a long and twisted line of smaller, seemingly simple turns.

Here is the simple beginning: I was standing in line in a crowded ice-cream shop — the whir of a blender, the fogged glass counter, the humidity pouring in from the door with its jangling bell. It was late summer, one of the last hot days of the season. The air-conditioning was rolling down from overhead and I'd paused under one of the cool currents, causing a small hiccup in the line. Peter was off talking to someone from work: Gary, a fellow anesthesiologist — a man in a pink-striped polo shirt, surrounded by his squat children holding ice-cream cones melting into softened napkins. The kids were small enough not to care that they were eating bits of their napkins along with the ice cream. And Gary was too distracted to notice. He was clapping Peter on the back and laughing loudly, which is what people do to Peter. I've never understood why, exactly, except that people genuinely like him. He's disarming, affable. There's something about him, the air of someone who's in the club — what club, I don't know, but he seemed to be the laid-back president of this club, and when you were talking with him, you were in the club too. But my mind was on the kids in that moment — I felt sorry for them, and I decided that one day I'd be the kind of mother not to let her children eat bits of soggy napkin. I don't remember what kind of mother mine was — distracted or hovering or, most likely, both? She died when I was five years old. In some pictures, she's doting on me — cutting a birthday cake outside, her hair flipping up in the breeze. But in group photos, she's always the one looking off to the side, down in her own lap, or to some distant point beyond the photographer — like an avid bird-watcher. And my father was not a reliable source of information. It pained him, so he rarely talked about her.

I was watching the scene intently — Peter specifically now, because instead of becoming more comfortable with having a husband, after three years I was becoming more surprised by it. Or maybe I was more surprised not that I was his wife but that I was *anybody's* wife, really. The word *wife* was so wifey that it made me squeamish — it made me think of aprons and meat loaf and household cleansers. You'd think the word would have evolved for me by that point — or perhaps it *had* evolved for most people into cell phones and aftercare and therapy, but I was the one who was stuck — like some gilled species unable to breathe up on the mudflats.

Although Peter and I had been together

11

for a total of five years, I felt like I didn't know him at all sometimes. Like at that very moment, as he was being back-clapped and jostled by the guy in the pink-striped polo shirt, I felt as if I'd spotted some rare species called *husband* in its natural habitat. I was wondering what its habits were — eating, chirping, wingspan, mating, life expectancy. It's difficult to explain, but more and more often I'd begun to rear back like this, to witness my life as a *National Geographic* reporter, someone with a British accent who found my life not so much exciting as *curious.*

The ice-cream shop was packed, and the two high school girls on staff were stressed, their faces damp and pinched, bangs sticking to their foreheads, their matching eyeliner gone smeary. I'd finally made my way to the curved counter and placed my order. Soon enough I was holding a cone of pistachio for Peter and waiting for a cup of vanilla frozen yogurt for myself.

That's when the more beleaguered of the two scoopers finished someone else's order and shouted to a customer behind me. "What do you want?"

A man answered. "I'll have two scoops of Gwen Merchant, please."

I spun around, sure I'd misheard, because

I am Gwen Merchant — or I was before I got married. But there in the line behind me stood a ghost from my past — Elliot Hull. I was instantly overwhelmed by the sight of him — Elliot Hull with his thick dark hair and his beautiful eyebrows, standing there with his hands in his pockets looking tender and boyish. I don't know why, but I felt like I'd been waiting for him, without knowing I'd been waiting for him. And I wasn't so much happy as I was relieved that he'd finally shown up again. Some strange but significant part of me felt like throwing my arms around him, as if he'd come to save me, and saying, *Thank God, you finally showed up! What took you so long? Let's get out of here.*

But I couldn't really have been thinking this. Not way back then. I must be projecting — backwards — and there must be a term for this: projecting backwards, but I don't know what it is. I couldn't have been thinking that Elliot Hull had come to save me because I didn't even know I needed saving. (And, of course, I'd have to save myself in the end.) The only conclusion I can draw is that maybe he represented some lost part of myself. And I must have realized on some level that it wasn't that I'd been missing only Elliot Hull. I must have been missing the person I'd been when I'd known him — *that* Gwen Merchant — the somewhat goofy, irreverent, seriously un-wifely part — two scoops of *her.*

Plus, did I really even know Elliot all that well? We'd met at a freshman orientation icebreaker — a dismal event really — at Loyola College, the one in Baltimore, and then, in the spring of our senior year we had an intense, messy, short-lived relationship — three weeks of inseparableness that ended when I'd slapped him in a bar. I hadn't seen Elliot Hull since a cookies-and-punch reception after the English Department's awards ceremony at graduation ten years earlier.

Regardless, I found myself feeling emotional — a welling in my throat and my eyes stinging with tears. The air-conditioning was pressing my hair flat. I stepped out of the gust and pretended that I wasn't sure it was him at all. "Elliot Hull?" I asked. I did this, I think, because I was terrified by the tide of joy in my chest. Also, I remembered enough about our relationship that I didn't want to give him the satisfaction of immediate recognition. He was the type to notice something like that and be a little smug about it.

He looked older, but not much. In fact,

14

he had the lean body of a man who would age well — who, in his seventies, might be described by the word *spry*. His jaw was more set. He wasn't clean shaven. He was wearing a faded pale blue T-shirt that was fraying at the neck, a Red Sox ball cap, and shorts that were way too baggy. "Gwen," he said, his voice tinged with sadness. "It's been a long time."

"What are you doing here?" I asked. *This is only Elliot Hull,* I tried to remind myself. I didn't remember why I'd slapped him, but I did remember that he'd deserved it. We'd been at a bar in Towson, just a few miles from this ice-cream shop, in fact.

"That sounded like an accusation," he said. "I'm an innocent man. I'm ordering ice cream."

The girl behind the counter said, "Um, sir, we really don't have that flavor? Do you want to pick a real flavor or something?" Kids today can be very earnest.

"Double chocolate with marshmallows and peanuts and hot fudge and some caramel." He leaned toward the chalkboard mounted on the wall and squinted. "And whipped cream and three cherries."

"Three?" the girl asked, disgusted by the gratuitous demands of humanity, I assume — a professional hazard.

"Three." He turned back to me.

"Really," I said. "Three cherries."

"I like cherries," he said.

"So, are you a rapper now?" I asked, pointing to his baggy shorts. This was an obnoxious thing to say. But I suddenly felt obnoxious. I'd once been an obnoxious flirt, who'd turned into a more refined flirt, but Elliot was causing me to regress — or return to some more elemental part of myself.

"I could bust a rhyme," he said. "Do you want me to?"

"No, no," I said, knowing he just might. "Please don't."

There was a lull then, and I let it lull there, lullingly. Why further engage Elliot Hull? I was married now. Was I going to become friends with him? Married women don't suddenly befriend men with whom they once ended a relationship by slapping them in a bar. But he carried on the conversation. "I'm a philosopher, actually," he said. "I philosophize. And I'm a professor, so I sometimes also profess."

"Ah, well, that fits," I said. "You're *the brooder*. That's what my friends called you in college. So now you brood, you know, professionally. Don't philosophers brood?" My father was a professor — a marine biologist — so I knew how professors could

16

be the brooding type. As a child, I was hauled to numerous potluck faculty dinners — the air stiff with all of the brooding and professing.

"I wasn't a brooder. Did I brood?"

"By the end of college, you'd really honed the art."

"Brooding hasn't really taken off the way I'd hoped — as a national trend."

"I think contentment is all the rage," I said. "Blind contentment."

"Well, there's an Annual Brooder's Convention coming up, though, and I'm keynoting so . . . What are you doing these days?"

"Me? Well, I just started something new. Sales. Interior design, kind of. It's a mishmash," I said. I had a history of swapping one job for another, something I wasn't proud of. My résumé was buckshot. I'd just quit a job in admissions at a boarding school. I claimed that I was tired of the elitism, but then I took a somewhat soft part-time job working for more rich people as an assistant to an interior designer who mainly staged upscale homes for sale. I was the one who talked to prospective clients about the nuts and bolts — quoting possible profits from staging a house before selling, using charts — while my boss, an ethereal, wispy woman in billowy outfits, would walk

17

around the house feigning artistic inspiration. Her name was Eila, but a few days into the job, she told me that her name used to be Sheila before she dropped the Sh. "Who would trust an *artiste* named Sheila? You have to do what you have to do." Then she sniffed her scarf. "Did that last place smell like Doberman or what?"

"Interior design?" Elliot said, intrigued. "I don't remember your dorm room being overly feng shui. Didn't you bolt a hammock to the walls in the minikitchen?"

"What can I say? I've always had an eye."

In the distance, I heard one of the scoopers say, "Ma'am, ma'am?" Of course, I didn't really register it, because I'm not old enough to be a ma'am. But then Elliot said, "Um, *ma'am*," and he pointed to the scooper. "Your ice cream."

"Here," the scooper said, handing me my cup of vanilla frozen yogurt.

"Thanks," I said. "A lot." I shuffled down to the register, preparing to slink away. "Well, it was nice to see you, Elliot," I said in my summarizing voice.

"Wait," he said. "We should get together. I just moved back to town. You could show me what's changed."

"I think you'll get a feel for it," I said, paying the cashier. "You're a clever boy."

He smiled at me then, his clever smile —
it was always so much a part of him that I
assumed he was born smiling cleverly. "How
about tonight?" he asked, nudging past
people so that we were side by side now. "I
could take you to dinner and then you could
take me sightseeing."

"I've got plans tonight," I said. "Sorry."

"What plans?"

I hesitated. "A party."

"You could take me. Introduce me to
people. Pawn me off on them, having done
a good deed. You were always the good-deed
type. Didn't you do a cookie drive once? I
remember buying cookies from you with
some poster board involved."

He looked so hopeful that I was suddenly
afraid he was going to ask me out. "Look,
I'm married," I told him finally.

He laughed. "Funny."

"What's funny about that?"

"Nothing . . . It's just . . ."

"Just what? Do you think I'm unmarri-
able or something?"

"You're just not married."

"Yes, I am."

"No, you aren't."

"I'm Gwen Stevens now." I lifted up my
hand, showing the ring as proof.

He was stunned. "You're really . . . married?"

"That sounded like an accusation," I said. "I'm an innocent woman. An innocent wife."

"It's just that I didn't think people really got married anymore. Marriage is so barbaric. It's like a blood sport."

"See, that's the kind of insulting thing you say that makes people slap you," I told him.

He raised his eyebrows and kicked his head back a little. "You didn't really slap me," he said. "You just grabbed my face. Very hard. It didn't do any good anyway," he said, his arms outstretched like he was some proof of a failed face-grabbing.

"Weren't you engaged to that girl, Ellen something?" I asked. Her name was Ellen Maddox. I could still see her face. "I thought you two got back together . . ."

"She left me right after college for a flight attendant, a *male* flight attendant." He said *male flight attendant* as if it was worse than a female flight attendant. "Anyway, I stick by what I said to you that made you grab my face. I stick by it, because it was the truth."

I must have looked at him questioningly. I couldn't remember what he'd said exactly, but I didn't have time to ask. One of the scoopers handed him his gargantuan cone and he was fumbling through his wallet just as Peter surfaced. "Hello!" he said, looking at Elliot in a very well-mannered way. Peter can turn on these impeccable manners — like a boy who went to boarding school in the 1950s and is now trying to compensate for a lack of parental love by asserting a chin-uppedness about life. This humility was an act. Peter was raised to be confident in all things — perhaps most of all in love.

I handed him his cone. "This is Elliot Hull. He once bought a cookie from me in college to help raise money for sea otters."

"Ah, poor sea otters!" Peter said, extending his hand. "I'm Peter."

Elliot shook it and shot me a look that seemed to say: *Look at this guy! You* are *married! And he's tall!* And then he said, "Gwen just invited me to the party tonight. I'm new to town."

"Great idea!" Peter said, and before I had a chance to clarify, he was giving Elliot directions. I was still stunned that Elliot Hull was back in my life, and that it had happened so quickly. See, it was simple. That's what I mean: I hadn't done anything to start it. I was just standing in line at an ice-cream shop one minute and then suddenly I was watching Peter make some gestures that might indicate that Elliot would have to make a turn out of a rotary, and then he pointed to his left, his arm straight out at his side, and I thought of the word *wingspan* again. Peter is tall. He has an excellent wingspan.

But there was Elliot Hull, standing next to him, and he was not tall and he was not at all impeccably mannered and he was barely paying attention. He was being Elliot Hull, thinking his brooding thoughts, no doubt. Had we kind of thought we were in love with each other a decade ago?

When Peter was finished, he said, "Got it?"

"I've got it," Elliot said, and then he looked at me. I was about to wave a non-committal good-bye, but then Elliot said, "Gwen Merchant, huh, after all these years." And suddenly it was as if I were the rare bird. I felt a little self-conscious. I might have even blushed and I couldn't remember the last time I blushed. "See you tonight!" he said, then took a bite of his abundant ice cream and walked out of the shop, one hand in his baggy shorts.

CHAPTER TWO

There's a theory about why people don't remember their infancy and young childhood. It goes like this: memory cannot exist without something to refer to. You remember something because it hooks to some earlier experience. Memories start to form not because that quadrant of the brain has finally developed, but because our lives have layers. In this sense, memory isn't a layer formed on top of experience — like a cap of ice — as much as it is formed underneath it — the way rivers can run underground.

And my relationship with Elliot Hull is like this too. For me to truly understand that tide of joy when I first saw him in the ice-cream shop and how everything else that happened followed, I need Peter. Elliot doesn't really exist without Peter — not fully. And Peter wouldn't have really existed in my life without my father — a man shaped by loss, and defined by it. And his loss doesn't exist, of course, without my mother's untimely death.

Let me dig at just one layer at a time.

I met Peter in the waiting room of an animal hospital. He'd brought in his mother's elderly cockapoo for some incontinence issues, and I was covered in blood, reading a book about the human brain. A farm dog had darted in front of me on the road that morning. I'd been on my way to an undergraduate class in psychology, even though I wasn't matriculated. I was twenty-five and had recently quit a job in marketing that had burned me out. I was working as a waitress again — happily so — and thinking about going to grad school for psychology.

I was enamored with talk therapy at the time — mainly because I had just started seeing a therapist, a very sweet older woman who wore thick glasses that magnified her eyes so it seemed as if she was looking at me intently. I wasn't used to this kind of attention, and although it made me uncomfortable, I needed her. She let me talk about my childhood for an hour every week. She let me daydream about my mother — really — and what my childhood could have been like if she'd lived. We were working through these fantasies, in hopes of getting at . . . some *elemental truth?* And what was that truth? One fall when I was just five years old, my mother died — a car accident involving a bridge and a body of water — a simple accident that shaped my life in the most complicated ways. It changed my father into someone else entirely — a cautious widower wearing Docksiders and cable-knit sweaters who devoted his life to the soniferous burblings of certain species of fish. A man who lived, for the most part, underwater. It was as if I grew up with two drowned parents — one literally and one figuratively.

What I didn't tell the therapist was that I'd been in the car with my mother — that this was a well-guarded family secret that I'd unearthed. An elderly auntie had let that information slip while she brushed my hair during a visit we made to her nursing home on a trip to Cape Cod. When we got back in the car after the visit, my father told me that Aunt Irene was fading. "She doesn't have any of the facts straight anymore." I think the therapist knew that I'd been in the car, if she was paying attention at all. But I could have gone on in therapy with her for years and never told her. I didn't care, really. She let me talk about what I wanted to. She listened. Wasn't that all anyone needed? Couldn't I help other

25

people the same way?

On the road that morning I was gliding in and out of a thick fog. I'd just inherited my father's old Volvo and was listening to tapes I hadn't played much since high school — this particular morning, the Smiths. The Volvo had an exhaust problem that made the car smell strongly of fumes. So the fog, the Smiths, and the fumes gave the morning a surreal dreaminess.

The dog was a yellow lab, the kind that makes you think of an old gym teacher — stout but still athletic. He appeared out of nowhere. I braked hard but clipped his hind leg. His body bounced off the grille and spun, tumbling down a sloping bank.

I left the car on the empty road and scrambled down the embankment. There was no one around. The dog's eyes were glassy, his chest jerking. He wore a red frayed collar with silver tags. I'd never really liked dogs. I didn't have one growing up — though, with all the lonesomeness, I should have. It might have helped. But it always struck me as odd to have a dog in the house — the notion that a beast could come lumbering through the living room at any moment.

I was afraid that he might bite me, so I introduced myself and patted the fur on his neck. Then I reached under him and hefted him up. He was heavier than I expected. But I lifted him, his tags jingling like bells, and made my way up the embankment, struggling under his weight. I put him in the backseat, laying my coat over him, and turned the car around, back the way I'd come.

Secretly, and even though I was the cause of this one, I think I'd always wanted to help in some emergency, to be a witness who helped a victim survive. I'd always wondered if anyone had seen my mother's car skid off the road into the bridge's pilings and into the lake — maybe someone driving home from a dinner party? Someone who'd just gotten off a late shift? And, of course, why was my mother out so late with me in the car?

The receptionist had gotten the dog owner's phone number off of its tags and had left a message. The dog's name was Ripken, likely after the Orioles star. I imagined Ripken's owners — two old baseball fans who'd stride in at some point wearing matching ball caps. I was already missing class, so I decided to stay with the dog to see if he would make it out of surgery. I think I already loved him. He'd looked up at me when I laid him in the backseat like he understood that I was saving him.

The surgery was taking a long time, and I tried to distract myself with some assigned reading. Lost in descriptions of the synaptic firings of the human brain, I didn't see or hear Peter walk in, so it was as if he suddenly appeared — a tall man in a crisp shirt and pleated pants, with a cockapoo in his lap.

I caught him looking at me and he glanced quickly away. We were the only two in the waiting room — aside from an aquarium and a large cage of four kittens. I looked up at the receptionist's desk to see if I could catch her eye, get an update, but she was on the phone.

Then Peter asked, "Can I help you with something? Are you okay?"

"What?" I said.

"I don't mean to pry or anything. You just look like you've been through a lot today."

I considered for the first time what I must look like — windblown, disheveled, bloody. "Oh, yes, it's been a strange day."

"And is your pet in surgery?"

"Yes, the dog's in surgery, but he's not *my* dog," I said.

"Oh."

"I hit the dog. I'm just waiting for the owners to show up. Technically, I'm the bad guy, I guess."

"But you brought the dog in . . . that's noble, and you stayed." And this struck me as a very noble thing to say. He smiled then and it was this glorious smile that revealed dimples just under the mouth.

"At least I'll have something new to talk about in therapy." I blurted this out. I was still partially in the fog, I think. I already knew that the dog would have to represent my dead mother somehow, and that this would spur a lot of discussion.

"Are you always looking for new material for your therapist?" he asked.

"I try to be entertaining. It's the least I can do."

He said jokingly, "I prefer to bury my problems. Polish the ulcer."

"That's very Hemingway of you," I said.

"Very big-game hunter," he said.

"Very running with the bulls in Pamplona."

And then the woman behind the desk called out, "Lillipoo Stevens?"

He looked at the receptionist. "Coming!" he said, and then he turned to me. "It's my mother's dog," he said apologetically.

"Sure it is," I said.

And then he asked me out for a drink.

"Ah, to polish the ulcer?" I asked. "You

know, you shouldn't ask out women who are covered in blood. I might be a murderer, depending how things go . . ."

"Well, I've never gone on a date with a murderer before . . ."

And this was old-fashioned. A date being called a date. "I'll go but only if you bring Lillipoo," I said.

I gave him my number, which entailed fumbling through my pocketbook for a pen and a receipt for something other than Rolaids or tampons — a humiliating little ritual. And then he said sincerely, "I hope it all goes okay in there."

"Thanks," I said.

He walked away then, Lillipoo tucked under his arm, her swishy tail swishing.

Peter and I dated for a year before we moved in together — and Ripken joined us. The surgery had been expensive. The owners — whom I never did meet but who still exist in my mind with their matching baseball hats — had inherited the dog from an elderly aunt who'd gone into assisted living, and they'd been letting him roam because he was flatulent. They didn't want to pay for the surgery and didn't really want him back. So I inherited Ripken — my very own old flatulent gym teacher, my first dog — minus one leg.

Peter and I got engaged a year after that, then got married. Everything was so perfectly doled out, like an automated cat-food dispenser. Instead of loving gazes, he glanced at me lovingly. There was a lazy satisfaction to it all — something that we could afford because of Peter's overriding confidence. He'd been raised by two exceptionally confident people, the kind who are usually brought down a peg or two by statistical probability — you can only live so long without encountering tragedy. And yet his parents avoided tragedy — Gail and Hal Stevens were exempt. They'd somehow found a loophole. Their own parents died with some small warning — enough to say their good-byes but not enough time to suffer. Trees fell on their neighbors' houses, metaphorically, time and again. They were churchgoers — though not deeply religious — and had gotten it in their heads that God preferred them and showed his favoritism by a lack of retardation, car accidents, cancer, suicide, drug addiction . . . They decided they weren't lucky as much as entitled, and they passed this firm belief on to Peter. And I loved this loophole, which was extended to me by marriage. I loved the air bag of entitlement, how it promised to cushion us throughout our lives. Life with

31

Peter was as safe as a brand-new Volvo.

Our period of dating and newlywed year were good. We ate bagels and drank gourmet coffee shipped from Seattle. I got a job in marketing again, because I needed to grow up. Why get a degree in psychology — all of that talk hadn't really fixed anything, had it? No. Peter had — Peter and the loophole. My elderly therapist with the magnified eyes retired, and I didn't replace her. I was relieved to get away from her gaze. People living in the loophole don't need a therapist. Plus, Peter was an anesthesiologist. So I learned to take a small happy pill, and the remainder of my restless sadness was numbed by consumerism. We got into nice tile — travertine and marble accents — and sofas and end tables and lowboys and espresso machines. We had a long-standing addiction to stemware. I learned how to make Bananas Foster, and when we had people over for dinner, I lit the dessert on fire — this beautiful blue flame.

During this time, did I ever think of Elliot Hull — how he looked at me, in the fluorescent lights of the library, lying down on the campus lawn propped on one elbow, even in the low lighting of that dank bar? I did. I indulged those memories when a certain song came on the radio, when my mind drifted to the disheveled arrangements of my past. He wasn't some airy memory, not some vague face. He was a solid presence — a figure to hang your hat on. And I remembered that he hadn't given me those love-in-glances that Peter had mastered. Not even just the magnified eyes of my therapist. No. He looked at me with his whole body. He didn't look *at* me so much as *into* me. He'd been too intense — impolitely intense. He would never have been able to comprehend how to divvy up love and dispense it in the correct dosages. He would have poured it on, if I'd let him — too much, too much, too much.

CHAPTER THREE

The night of the party, I was in the bathroom putting on mascara, wearing only a lavender bra and underwear, which made my skin look even paler. I'm not much good in the sun. I look boiled after a day at the beach and then freckled like certain kinds of trout. Better to be pale. The bright lighting in the bathroom wasn't helping. Peter and I were living in Canton, a yuppie neighborhood in the southeastern section of Baltimore, in an older apartment building that had been renovated into upscale condos. The upgrades weren't supposed to detract from the old-fashioned charm — wood floors, heavy doors — but still did. The lighting was one such example. It was too bright. I missed the dull glow of low wattage. Ripken was laying on the bath mat. He could sense when I was anxious and tended to stay close by. I looked down at him, and he looked up at me. Then he cocked his head and jiggled his stump in a phantom-limb attempt to scratch his ear. I bent down and rubbed his ear for him. I was worried about seeing Elliot again. Would I flirt obnoxiously in front of Peter? Would I become my old self again, my current self unraveling like mummy tape until I was coiled in a pile on the floor? I didn't want to have to be Elliot Hull's personal handler or get mired in some endlessly obnoxious conversation. Would Peter know to come and rescue me? "We need some sort of code," I called to Peter.

"Code for what?" Peter asked. He was getting dressed in the bedroom. I heard the jingle of his belt.

"Code for something like: *Let's* not *give this stranger directions to the party.*"

"He isn't a stranger. You two were friends in college, weren't you?"

"Not really." And I meant that we'd been less than friends and more than friends too, and there should be some name for this.

"Well, it's not my fault, Gwen," he said with a great sigh.

I stuck my head out the door. "Thank you, Saint Peter of the Excruciating Sighs." Peter, with his impeccable manners, knew how to sigh disappointment better than anyone I've ever known. His sighs were elaborate, extravagant even. He knew how to sigh whole paragraphs on how exhausting I could be. He knew how to sigh the story of our entire relationship and how we had made it to this very moment of my colossal tiresomeness. He could sigh three-part harmony or an entire Italian opera. In fact, sometimes after such a grand sigh, I would call him the Great Sighing Tenor or, simply, Pavarotti.

"Fine. But the fact is *you* invited him."

My face looked blotted out in the mirror. I'd put on too much cover-up. I do this sometimes. It's part of a disappearing instinct that kicks into overdrive when I'm nervous. I'm a nervous person in general, so I often look blotted out. "I specifically did *not* invite him. He was lying."

"Why didn't you just say, *Look, I don't want you to come to the party?*"

I didn't say this because I wanted Elliot to come to the party as much as I didn't want him to come. I was afraid of how overwhelmed I'd felt in the ice-cream shop. I thought of Elliot Hull in his baggy rapper shorts and his ball cap, with that insistently clever smile. I pictured him standing like that in a lecture hall in some fifth-rate community college, eating some insanely ridiculous ice-cream cone, while mumbling something about Heidegger, with one hand in his pocket. "I'm sure he's a fine person. He's a philosopher. I mean, do bad people go into philosophy?"

"I think bad people go into everything," Peter said. This was a little-known secret about Peter. He believed that people were inherently bad, deep down, and that they had to strive to overcome it. He always hid this jadedness from people at large, so this small comment was an intimate one. He was confessing something about himself.

"I guess they do," I said.

"Just avoid him," Peter said.

Ripken farted, then turned around and snapped at it. I'd worked hard to improve his flatulence with diet, but every once in a while he rummaged through the garbage or stole a chocolate bar from my purse and he was back at it.

I gave him a dirty look and walked out of the bathroom. Peter was wearing a short-sleeved, old-man button-down — blue and white checked with one breast pocket. "That shirt reminds me of Dr. Fogelman," I said.

"Benny Fogelman of the Fogelmans who live next door to your father?"

"Yes." My father has lived next door to the Fogelmans for thirty-some years. Fogelman's his dentist. He isn't a good dentist, however. My father is always having to have faulty caps replaced and second root canals because the first attempts weren't wholly successful. He's suffered decades of pain just because he doesn't want to hurt Benny Fogelman's feelings. Dr. Fogelman packed his basement with canned goods and bottled water and medical supplies in preparation for Y2K, then he and his wife ate nothing but canned food for a solid year after all was well. "Sometimes you have to eat your way out of a poor investment," he told me once. Dr. Fogelman is a pessimist with a dingy overbite, and Mrs. Fogelman is his trusty sidekick, his enabler, who calls him "the old turd" behind his back.

"Don't wear the Fogelman," I said to Peter. "It depresses me." I sat down on the edge of the bed, still not dressed. "It makes me feel like we're an old married couple . . ."

"Like Dr. and Mrs. Fogelman?"

I nodded and picked at the bedspread. Was this the bedspread of an old married couple?

"I like this shirt. It's retro."

It was not retro. It was stodgy. This was a subtle distinction that would be lost on him.

"Maybe Helen will like Elliot. Helen's pretty."

"She's only pretty in pictures."

"That's not possible. Pretty is pretty, isn't it?"

"I saw her in pictures, you know, when we were dating, and then I met her and she started moving around, and she laughs too loud and collapses when she laughs like one of those toys — you know, those little movable statue toys of like Goofy or something, where you press the bottom and the whole thing flops."

"Oh," I said, wondering how long he'd thought this about Helen, and why he never told me, and how many other little odd observations he'd stored away — ones about me maybe. I knew Peter didn't like my friends, but I wasn't sure I liked them either. Being friends with women has always been hard for me. I've never been good at negotiating the sudden undertow of conversations, how a conversation among women can become so unwieldy, how, in such quiet tones, there's so much freight being walloped around. Women have superhero strength in refined dialogue and I always fell for the sucker punches. Sometimes I didn't even know I'd been hit until an hour or so later — *Hey, wait a minute . . .* But by then it was always too late. Helen in particular was a sore spot. She was still single and had recently started to take it personally. Just a few years ago, she'd doled out her sympathy for us, her wifey friends, dragging along boyfriend after boyfriend to our wedding receptions and dancing recklessly on the various dance floors. But then she'd started to question her taste in men. Now she was beginning to question their taste in her. She seemed to be taking our marriages as insults, and, having perceived an attack, she was occasionally vicious. I was an easy target. She always caught me off guard, because I didn't have a guard. I blamed this on my lack of a mother figure. Certainly mothers give elaborate lessons on how to dodge and parry, and I'd missed all of that.

"Maybe Elliot likes those collapsible toys," I said. Peter didn't have any response to this. I tried to decake my face a little. "How about we rub our noses?" I said.

"Together? Like Eskimos? Why would we do that?"

"We would each rub our *own* noses. Like this." I rubbed my nose. "Our code! That way you'd know to come and rescue me in case I get cornered by Elliot Hull at the party."

"What if you have to rub your nose and

not because of some dipshit alert, but because you need to rub your nose? With your allergies . . ." Peter was always practical.

"We could rub our chins," I offered. "How often do I get an itchy chin?"

"How about we act like grown-ups instead and not like little kids who make up a pretend language of hand gestures? I'd rather not walk around parties looking like a third-base coach." As I relay this I don't want Peter to come across as good or bad. There are these little charged conversations that married couples have that, when written, sound petty and ugly. And we were, from time to time, both petty and ugly, but, beneath it all, loving.

But at this moment, did he love me? I believe he did, deeply. In fact, I think his love for me surprised him sometimes and that was one of the reasons he felt he had to keep it in check. And I didn't break him of it. Perhaps I even encouraged it. Peter's parents might have been the Loophole Stevenses, but despite all of their good fortune, I don't think many people would have chosen to be them. They had a loveless-ness to them. Peter was a better person — sweeter, kinder, more generous — but he still was their brand, their product. Is that

41

his fault?

He walked up to me, sitting there on the bed, and bent down and patted my bare knee three times. He'd done this more than a few times recently, this knee patting. It was something that the likes of Benny Fogelman would do to Ginny Fogelman if she were to get all heated up on a topic — like gay marriage — and needed some restraint. It struck me as awful. To the casual observer, it might have passed as something tender, but wasn't it really a small act of condescension? Or was it the kind of thing that I would have found funny a few years before — charmingly retro but not earnestly stodgy — but the joke had worn thin and it was now, dangerously, quickly, becoming a habit?

Peter walked out of the room and I called after him. "Are you a knee patter now? Without any sense of irony whatsoever? A nonironic knee patter?"

He shouted from the living room. "All I heard was *kneel batter now* or *feel better now* and something about irony!" And then the television clicked on and there was the sound of a soccer match — a crowd with too many horns and Spanish-speaking announcers. "If you don't get dressed, we're going to be late!"

"All I heard was breast and wait!" I shouted back. Ripken wandered out of the bathroom and laid down at my feet.

"What?" he called out.

"What, what?" I said.

The argument had officially floundered to senselessness. We abandoned it and I got up to finish dressing.

CHAPTER FOUR

Elliot Hull. The brooder. As I mentioned, we met at a freshman orientation icebreaker. It was mandatory, because it had to be. If it weren't, only the unrepentantly extroverted would have gone, leaving the rest of us, the needy, encased in chunks of ice.

There were about a hundred people in the gym, further divvied into groups of four. Elliot and I were in the same foursome. The other two — a boy and a girl — are a blur, long since forgotten. Were they nice, shy, prissy, rueful? I don't know. Maybe they were even blurry back then. Some people are. They probably went on to have perfectly lovely icebroken lives.

I only remember one of the exercises. The instructions were that someone in the group had to tell someone else in the group what to say to someone outside of the group. It was supposed to be introductory. The example was: *Go up and shake hands with that person over there and tell him you like his shoes.* I should mention here, if it's not already obvious, that I went to a fairly lifeless college, one that seemed as if it had been perfectly preserved in lava and volcanic ash circa 1954, à la Pompeii. (Will all of my metaphors about college entail being encased or preserved — in ice or lava — or otherwise smothered? They might. I'd intended to break from my father's house into the world at large, but I hadn't. I was still terrified — of what? The world at large? I don't know. In any case, I was still protecting myself and in fact, I spent my college and postcollege years perfecting my self-protection.)

What did Elliot look like back then? Like we all did. A slightly softer, pinker, shinier, leaner, crisper version of ourselves now — a condensation that's been diluted by time. This was the first thing he ever said to me: "This is bullshit. You know that?"

"It's complete bullshit," I said.

"Don't make me do something stupid," he said.

I looked at him. "I'll leave that part up to you."

"So you're funny," he said.

"No, I'm not funny," I said, and I wasn't or had never thought of myself as funny because people didn't laugh at the things I said.

"What are you then?" he asked. "Are you bookish?"

"Bookish?"

"You look like you could be bookish."

I was insulted even though I *was* bookish. I'd spent the last four years of high school pretending not to be bookish while looking forward to coming out of the bookish closet in college. "I read books, if that's what you mean."

"I can be bookish," Elliot said. "When I'm in the mood." And here he brooded momentarily, but then quickly turned to face me. "Where are those other people?" he asked. "They were right here."

"They're off shaking hands with strangers and complimenting them on their shoes."

"That reminds me," he said. "I like your shoes. They're okay. I mean, they aren't phenomenal or flashy, but they're stable but not boring. I like them."

"I don't think you're supposed to *critique* the shoes, just compliment them," I said.

"Oh," he said. "Well, I wanted to be honest."

There was an awkward pause and then I said, "I like your shoes too."

"Ah, that's the way you're supposed to do it."

"Yep."

I liked Elliot Hull immediately — shoes and all. In the end, I would still like him even though I'd kind of hate him too — both emotions simultaneously even while slapping him in that bar. I didn't like him because he was likable. He wasn't, in fact, likable in the terms that society has mutually agreed upon. But you know how every once in a while, you'll come across someone and you feel at ease with him. A lot of the time it's someone you know you'll never see again — a person in line with you in customs, in a waiting room at an insurance office, a waitress — and in one unguarded moment, one of you admits in some way that the world is full of shit, and the other agrees. A short-lived camaraderie in the world of bullshit before you sigh and move on in your different directions — except when you don't have to move on in different directions. Elliot was like that, for me, from the get-go. He was irritating, yes, but he was sincerely irritating, sincere in general, and I liked that.

"I know what I want you to do," I said.

"Okay. What?"

"I want you to pick up that girl over there.

47

Pick her up off her feet and spin her around." I pointed to a girl — a slim one, so he wouldn't have to strain. She had soft brown hair and dark eyes. I don't know why I chose this task. I was being romantic, I think. I'd seen *An Officer and a Gentleman* too many times.

He grabbed my hand. "How about *that* girl?" he said, pointing my finger to a girl in short shorts.

"No, that one," I said, pointing back at the first girl.

He nudged my finger in another direction. "How about *that* girl," he said, indicating a taller girl.

"No, that one," I said, steadfast in my original choice. "Pick her up and spin her around, like, you know, it's the end of a war or something."

"Which war?" he asked.

"It doesn't matter. Any war."

"It completely matters," he said. "I mean a World War II pick up and spin around is totally different from a Vietnam pick up and spin around. I don't think they even picked up and spun girls around after Nam."

"Fine, like after World War II."

"Fine," he said, and he walked toward the girl. She saw him approaching. I couldn't see his face, but I could see hers. She was smiling, anxiously, and he picked up speed. By the time he got to her, it was as if she knew what was coming. He lifted her up by her thin waist, high in the air, and then he spun around — like he was in fact a soldier who'd come home from World War II and had just spent the last few weeks doing nothing but picking up and spinning around girls.

That girl was Ellen Maddox. They started dating and kept dating. They dated steadily for three and a half years. I saw Elliot off and on. We had a class or two together. And he'd always bring up that orientation, thanking me for picking the right girl, or he'd simply compliment my shoes, which was our little code. And that was that.

Until one spring day of our last semester when Elliot saw me lying on a blanket in the middle of the green, studying for an exam. I was alone. A midterm was looming. I was thoroughly, openly bookish by then, wearing glasses, my hair pulled back in a ponytail — I may have even had a pencil in it. He walked up to my wide blanket and laid down on its edge. He propped himself up on one elbow and stared at me broodingly, and finally said, "You were wrong."

"Wrong about what?" I asked.

"You picked the wrong girl."

"What?"

"At orientation," he said. "You picked the wrong girl."

"Oh, really, did I?"

"Mm-hm."

"And who should I have picked?"

"That's the crazy part," he said. *"You're the right girl. You should have picked you."*

CHAPTER FIVE

Helen threw great parties. There was always some odd concoction to drink, exotic finger foods, music that was edgy but never morose (someone you'd never heard of but should have — music that scolded you for your provincialism). She had a knack for inviting a bizarre mix of people, and because most of the guests were single, her parties had an overt sexuality. She had a dominatrix friend named Vivica — a pro who worked in the city. Vivica had put Peter and me on her mailing list so we'd occasionally get those Gothic whip-wielding postcards in the mail announcing her shows with little handwritten notes on them: *Please come! XOXO Vivica.* I always thought of Richard, our postman, handling the postcards in his Jeep, reevaluating us. Richard was a hunter who was fond of Ripken. "Too bad about that leg," he always said. "That boy could have really been a good hunting dog." What did

Richard think of us? Did he go home and tell his wife about the people with the three-legged dog and the porno postcards? Were we the perverts of his route? I kind of hoped to be someone's pervert.

At Helen's party, I was clearly no one's pervert. I was never dressed right, for one thing. When I tried to wear an ironic fifties-style dress a few parties back — the kind that Helen wore with so much vamp: sharp bangs and dark red lipstick and cleavage — I ended up looking like a 1950s housewife. The pearl necklace that was so full of innuendo on Helen, stated flatly on me: pearl necklace, nothing else.

These parties put Peter in a different mood too. He toned down his manners. He drank way too much. He occasionally wanted to feed me the finger foods, which in some way he thought was sexy, but that made me uncomfortable. We became unmoored from each other. In fact, we made a pact to divide and conquer the guests. Once at the party, we'd glide in opposite directions to gather as much oddness as we could, bumping into each other only now and again to check in, and then later, on the ride home and in bed, we'd share all of our information. This way, we'd decided, we were basically living the party twice —

once through our own experience, and again through the other's. Now, in retrospect, I can see that this was a good plan in theory, especially if we'd been the type of couple who were true confidants, who knew each other intimately in every way. But we weren't. Love-in-glances only allows so much intimacy. Peter and I were perhaps looking for opportunities to become unmoored because we were both looking for something more.

So I was already out of my element, already nervous about social failure. This time, there was even more at stake. I remembered those British drawing room novels in which a missed cue surrounding the etiquette of tea could ruin your standing and mean you might be sent off to a convent. In this case, I had some inkling that Elliot Hull could unfasten my life — in a way that was a threat to my current consumerism, my bagel-breakfast contentment — and this terrified me. But what terrified me more was how much I wanted to see him again.

When we got to the party, I scanned the apartment quickly for Elliot. He was nowhere in sight.

"See," Peter said, having scanned the party himself. "He's not here. He probably won't show. It's harder than you think to come to a party alone. Luckily we can barely remember being single." This was part of our banter — how sorry we felt for single people. It was comforting.

I said, "I'm so relieved." But I wasn't. I was anxious — deflated yet still on edge.

A young woman put beers in our hands. She seemed like she'd been assigned the task. Peter drifted to the balcony, packed with idle smokers and glowing candles, and I headed for the food.

That's where I ran into Jason. He'd gotten married a year and a half earlier to a friend of mine named Faith. I'd been friends with Faith since college. In fact, she was one of the friends who'd called Elliot Hull "the brooder." She'd gotten pregnant immediately after their wedding, which was their plan, and now had a nine-month-old. It was always a little embarrassing to meet up with our married friends at Helen's parties. Our married-friends' dinner parties — including mine of the low blue flame Bananas Foster variety — stood in such stark contrast to Helen's that it was strange that we could adapt to an environment so unstifled, sexually speaking. At our dinner parties, we tried to be funny and charming and smart in front of the other couples. We tried to woo them with our good taste in imported rugs. But this was all under the radar. There was nothing that could have been called actual flirting, so all of the married-friends parties had a clamped-down suffocation — as if we were all being muffled by expensive decorator throw pillows, of which we all had way too many.

"Hi," I said. "How are you doing?"

His mouth was full. He stuck up one finger. Jason was a beefy guy who often looked baffled. I checked the front door again to see if Elliot had wandered in. He hadn't. But I spotted a new ornate mirror, a real monster, at the other end of the room. I supposed it was meant to be vertical, but Helen had it running the length of her sleek white sofa. Peter and I had recently bought a sleeper sofa in dark stripes. I'd thought it was a little overly masculine, but he pointed out how practical it was for guests to sleep on and, being dark and striped, it was also stain-proof. We could one day throw it in the kids' playroom. *The kids.* We referred to them often — our future offspring. "That'll be good for the kids." "We should bring the kids to this place one day." "I wouldn't want the kids to hear a story like that." They had a growing presence, the kids did, especially for people who didn't yet exist.

Jason finally said, "Hi." He swallowed

down the last bit of the hors d'oeuvre, then added hurriedly, "Don't tell Faith I was here."

"What do you mean? Where's Faith?" I asked, looking around.

"She didn't want me to come. She said she didn't appreciate my behavior at these galas. She wanted me to stay home with Edward." They'd named their baby Edward. This was a point of discussion behind their backs for some time, but we'd slowly worn it out, and now the kid seemed like an Edward or else Edward had changed, in our collective mind, to include him. He was cute, so that helped. "And she was going to come instead."

"But she didn't."

"No. I'm here, but she doesn't know it."

I was confused. "But why didn't you two just bring Edward like you did last time?"

"Oh, to that party Helen threw for the slutty magazine? That was weird. I mean the S-and-M girls and those two transvestites, they were all over the baby. Cooing like crazy. And then Faith didn't know where to nurse him. She said it was confusing — all of that T and A spread out on the coffee table, it felt like nursing was a perversion of the breast."

"Is that what she said?"

"Yes. *A perversion of the breast.*" He loved Faith — was proud of her odd way of putting things, her articulation. She was the one who had the white-collar job, high-level bank management, bringing in the big bucks. He lost a lacrosse scholarship and dropped out of college. He and I had a certain bond, actually, being the lesser wage-earners, the lesser-achieving of our respective couples. I stuck up for him around Faith — "He's still looking for his passion, his calling" and "We're not all on the same time clock" and "He's got a different approach to the world; why judge him so harshly?" Faith would find a way back to the specific problem at hand and away from the land mines of undiscovered passions in life, slow time clocks, and different world approaches.

"Why are you here?" I asked.

"We had a fight. I was smart enough to storm out." He smiled then, a little proud of himself. "When you have kids you'll learn. When you get into a fight, be the first one to grab the keys and storm out, or you're stuck with the baby all night." I could hear Peter sticking up for our parenting. *Hey, leave the kids out of it. You can't even comprehend how great Gwen and I will be as parents when the kids get here.* I was letting it go. I wasn't convinced of our superior parenting abilities. What did I know about parenting anyway? A dead mother, a grief-stricken father. I wasn't sure that the Stevenses loophole was multigenerational.

"Aren't you supposed to be out storming around?" I thought I saw Elliot then, just the back of his head out on the balcony. My stomach did a small nervous flip. The man turned. It wasn't him.

"I was hungry. Helen has the best food." This wasn't the reason and we both knew it. Jason had been the one holding the baby during all the cooing at the last party. I recalled a comment Faith had made about Jason using the baby as a prop. Now that I looked at Jason I could tell he wasn't dressed for the party. He was wearing Saturday afternoon yard-work clothes, and he clearly hadn't taken a shower. His hair was sticking up from the front of his head as if he'd driven over with his head out the window.

"Faith will find out. You know that," I told him.

"I figure I can buy some thinking time between now and then." He took a big swig from a glass of the night's exotic drink and made a twisted face. There was a giant punch bowl with a crystal dipper. The concoction was milk-based, creamy looking, and smelled like coconut. Jason would likely get drunk, and he wouldn't buy any thinking time, and Faith would be rightfully pissed tomorrow. This would be chalked up to Jason's infantilism, as Faith called it. His overactive id. He had a long history of squandering thinking time. He owned a take-out taco hut. "You've got to try this drink," he said. "It tastes like edible panties — tropical flavored."

I clapped him on the shoulder. "Good luck," I said. "But I have to tell you, things don't look good for you."

His mouth was full of food again, and he smiled sadly and gave a weak shrug as if to say, *Too late now.* And it was.

There were vases of fat purple lilacs on the table. They teetered lewdly over the food platters. I negotiated around them, got a plate, and filled it with all of these Middle Eastern–inspired foods — various kabobs, feta-something, tahini-something else, cheese-filled pancake-like somethings. I wondered for a moment if Helen was dating someone Middle Eastern. She was always in the process of swearing off men and then swearing them on again. Could she fall for Elliot? I wondered.

I dipped up a glass of the coconut concoction, took a sip, and thought briefly about edible panties. Would they taste like the fruit leather that was sold at the checkout of the health food store I went to every time I got hopped up on some article I read in a women's magazine about a healthier lifestyle? Would this make for edgy conversation? Could I make that funny?

That's when I saw Elliot. I was surprised to see him even though I'd been looking for him. He was so fully himself — had I been expecting only a portion? — and I loved his details. He was wearing khakis, a nice belt with a silver buckle dipping forward, some kind of black concert T-shirt, and as if just to further confuse things: a blazer. His hair was still damp from a shower. He was talking to an artistic-looking blonde wearing oversized earrings. She was gesticulating wildly, her earrings bobbing. Despite her near-hysteria, Elliot was calm. He was nodding along empathetically. He lowered his head and closed his eyes and nodded some more. Then she must have said something funny, because he smiled. He was holding a small black box that reminded me of a box I'd once used as a kid to bury a hamster. It was wrapped in a thin purple ribbon. Had he brought a present? Sitting on the small table next to him was a box like the one in his hands, except it had been opened and the lavender tissue paper had been rifled through. The gift, whatever it had been, was now gone.

I wasn't sure what to do. How long had he been here? Had he looked for me and Peter? Evidently, walking into a party alone wasn't as hard as we remembered it being. I wished that Peter was here with me now, that we were chatting vivaciously about tropical-flavored panties and laughing. I looked for him out on the balcony, but the figures gathered there were oddly lit and impossible to distinguish. I decided to busy myself looking for Helen, but Elliot caught my eye and gave a big wave. I waved back, just a propped-up hand folding twice, then looked away. But, in an instant, he was there, standing in front of me.

"Thank you," he said. "You saved me. She was a conversational vampire. Nice and all, but I think I'm now undead." Before I had a chance to say anything, he handed me the box. I remembered now that he'd once given me a sandwich in a plastic box bought off of his dining card as a gift. I didn't want to own up to the memory though. "Here, this is for you."

"Is it a small dead animal?"

"Um, no," he said. "Did you want a small

dead animal? I could run out and get one."

"No, it just looks like a . . ."

"Oh, a little casket. Right. I see that now. No. But it is a dead something. But nice dead. Open it!" He smelled like aftershave and shampoo, and I had a sudden memory of having sex with him. I remembered, fleetingly, being under a sheet, and how he was shucking his jeans, the weight and warmth of his chest on mine. Standing there in Helen's apartment, the memory made me blush.

I lifted the lid, a little hesitantly, placed it under the box, fiddled with the lavender tissue paper, and uncovered a rose corsage in a spray of white baby's breath. "You got me a corsage," I said.

"One for you and one for the hostess," he said.

"Does that mean you have two prom dates?"

"Is that not okay with you?" he said.

"So, you met Helen," I said.

"Yes."

"Did she like her corsage?"

"It made her laugh really loudly."

"She sometimes laughs loudly. But she's pretty, isn't she?"

"She's not my type." He picked up the corsage and its little faux-pearl-tipped pin.

"You mind?"

I shrugged. "Go ahead. Why isn't she your type? Is it because she laughs too loudly and flops over like one of those collapsible toys?"

I was wearing a black spaghetti-strapped dress that didn't leave him many corsage-pinning options. "Nope. Just not my type."

"Do you go around buying corsages for people now? Is that your thing?"

"I saw them in a florist window surrounded by the tissue paper inside their little caskets and, I don't know, I'd never bought a corsage for anyone. It seemed old-fashioned, gallant, but nonthreatening." He pinched the upper edge of my dress then pulled it a modest inch away from my chest so he could pin it without jabbing me. "Maybe this is why men started buying corsages for women. A chance to touch their dresses."

"Maybe so."

"Maybe this could become my thing. I thought I was saving corsages from, you know, a slow death in a florist's window, doing a good deed like your sea otters. How many did you save?"

"I think we may have saved one little paw, in the end. Maybe two."

Once secured, the corsage was a little bud-heavy. It tilted forward, as if bowing, or worse, as if it were trying to get off of me. We both looked down at it. "It's a humble corsage," he said.

"It needs to listen to some self-help books on tape," I said.

"But I'm predicting a great surge in confidence from here on out."

"On my bosom?"

"Where else?"

And then Helen was upon us. She was stunning — a perfect nose, lavish eyes, curvy lips, sharp eye teeth, a stunning jaw. Her tight dress had gauzy wings and her corsage was situated in the center of a plunging neckline, as if the dress had been designed around it. She said, "Gwen! I love this boy! Where did you find him?" She grabbed Elliot's arm — which struck me as a lovely arm, nicely tan — and put her head on his shoulder. "He's charming. He's sweet and handsome! He bought us matching roses. Who does that?"

"I don't know," I said. "He does, I guess."

"You can eat roses," Elliot said, and then he pointed to the flower vases on the food table. "Lilacs are also edible."

"And he's so scientific!" Helen said. "What do you do?" she asked.

"I teach," he said.

"He's a professor," I said.

"Oh, where?" Helen asked.

"Johns Hopkins," he said, and I was more than a little stunned by this. I'd assumed a community college — in fact a bad community college.

"Do you have to wear a tie to teach at Hopkins?" Helen asked. "I like a nice necktie."

"Nope," Elliot said. "No ties required. Only elbow patches on our jackets and tweed. But no neckties."

"Too bad," she said with a sexy pout. I was reminded of the fact that although Helen's relationships didn't ever lead to marriage, the men she dated all seemed to love her — overwhelmingly, painfully so. She tugged on Elliot's very nice arm. "Come on, I'm going to introduce you around. Where did your drink go? Let's do shots. You've got some catching up to do."

Elliot gave me a helpless backward glance. Did I mention his lashes? Dark and curly, the kind wasted on men. I felt abandoned. I did a half-turn in one direction and then in the other, and finally decided to go to the bathroom to dawdle with lipstick, wasting a little time. There was a short line. When the door opened, Peter walked out. He cupped my ear. "I'm stoned. That blonde invited me to do some blow. But I declined." He pointed into Helen's study, where Jason was talking to the blond conversational vampire, but happily so.

"Jason isn't supposed to be here."

"Oh, I know. He's doomed. He's so fucking doomed. Look at him." And we both did. He was effervescently joyful. He was pointing at the blonde saying, "See, you get me! You're like a *mind* reader!" Peter shook his head. "He's an idiot. He's stoned too. He's a dead man. It's like looking at a dead man. A stoned dead man. But I'm being so good. Minus the stoned stuff. But getting stoned isn't bad. It's just not, you know, part of our lives. What with the kids and all. We have to set a good example."

"That's right," I said.

"That's right," he repeated quietly, and then he straightened up to his full height. "Okay! Divide and conquer!" he said, and he was off.

I talked to a man about his home brewery — a minikeg in the fridge, something about hops and whatnot. I talked to a drummer briefly, until his girlfriend got a call on her cell phone and started crying. I talked to a miniaturist — a woman who built custom-designed dollhouses for the rich and famous. She was very small. I listened to a behemoth comedian who started riffing on gas prices and skinny people and how his ex-wife feminized him by making him sleep on floral sheets. I didn't have much to say to anyone. I wondered where Elliot had gone, if he would become a staple at these parties, if I'd pawned him off on Helen never to see him again. Vivica, in her studded leather, never showed up, and I missed her.

Eventually the party quieted down, and I found myself reunited with Peter, Helen, Elliot, Jason, and the blonde — whose name I never did catch — lounging around on the white sofa. I wasn't lounging. I was tense, poised. I had a plate of kabobs balanced on my knees. Having decided that I wasn't really up for the party, why not eat my way through it?

Everyone was a little drunk by now, including me. Helen was telling a story of a recent breakup. "He shut down when I gave him an ultimatum. He said it put too much pressure on him. But he doesn't know real pressure. He has no ticking biological clock. That's pressure." Unlike Peter, Helen didn't talk about kids at all — just the clock, as if having kids was some sort of time trial.

"I was engaged just two years ago," Elliot said. He was sitting there with his shin propped on one knee, holding a beer in one hand and rubbing his knee with the other, like his knee was paining him.

"But I thought Ellen ran off with a flight attendant after college," I said.

"I was engaged to someone else. Her name was Claire."

"But isn't marriage barbaric?" I asked, pressing him on this point. He had, after all, kind of made fun of me for being married. "A blood sport?"

"It is, but unfortunately I'm a barbarian."

Peter sat there puffy lidded. "A barbarian," he said. "You? That's funny."

Elliot didn't say anything. He simply leaned over the lilacs in the vase on the coffee table and ate one.

"That was very barbaric," Helen said.

"Very lemony," Elliot said, chewing.

Maybe Peter felt like he was being baited. I don't know. But suddenly he growled and slumped over onto Helen's lap and bit her rose corsage. She screamed and smacked him on the head. He reared from her, covered his head with his arms, chewing the rose.

"Did you see that?" she shrieked. "Did anyone see that?"

We all had.

I imagined telling Faith about this when

she called tomorrow to commiserate about Jason's stupidity. This was the kind of "behavior at these galas" that she was talking about. Helen's rose was just a raggedy half-rose on a stem now. The baby's breath was crumpled. I felt a little envious. No one would ever have bitten my corsage in half. I had an aura that didn't invite that kind of thing — or this is what I told myself — even from my husband. "Are roses poisonous?" I asked halfheartedly.

"I never thought of Peter as a barbarian," Elliot said to me.

"He's an anesthesiologist," I said, nibbling on my kabob. "What's the difference?" I looked at Elliot intently. I don't know that he'd be beautiful to other people — maybe a little. But he was beautiful to me. I liked the way his wrinkles were turning out even — they creased upward as if they'd all been made from laughing. I said, "Your ears are very flat to your head." This was a test, in a way. It's the kind of thing that I might have said to Peter a long time ago, but he'd simply look at me and say, "You're funny," meaning odd-funny. And I learned not to say things like that anymore.

Elliot reached up and touched one of his ears. "I was built for speed," he said.

Then Helen pressed her fingertips together and got very serious. "What happened?" she asked Elliot. "What went wrong with you and your fiancée?"

"After two years or so, I realized that I was in the middle of a conversation that wouldn't last," Elliot said.

"What does that mean?" the blonde asked.

"A marriage is a conversation that's supposed to last a lifetime. We didn't have enough to say to each other," he explained.

"That's a beautiful definition of marriage," Helen said. "Write that down," she said to me as if I were her secretary. I ignored her. "I want that read at my wedding or funeral or something."

"A lifetime's worth of material is a lot of material," I said.

"What's wrong with just being quiet together?" Peter added, and I liked when we appeared to be a united front like this. "A lot of couples are comfortable enough with each other not to talk all the time."

Jason said, "I like not talking." He wasn't as effervescent as he had been earlier. In fact, there was an eye-cutting paranoia about him now. He knew that there was a lot of talking in his near future and it was going to be unpleasant. The blonde's interest had waned too. She was holding a tissue to her nose, no longer reading his mind.

"My mother wanted me to go through with it anyway, I think. She wants me married," Elliot said.

"I despise my mother," Helen said, and she had reason to. Her mother was an alcoholic who'd been married a number of times to unlikable men. I'd always kind of wondered if Helen didn't really want to get married and have kids because she feared becoming her mother — so her relationships were always self-sabotaged. This is the kind of thing that my therapist would have said. She talked to me a good bit about self-sabotage.

"Well," Elliot said, "I love mine." And I could tell that he must be very drunk, going soft for his mother like that in front of everyone. "My mother and father had a conversation that didn't hold up, but it's worth shooting for."

I don't know why this hit me so hard, but it did. It seemed as if he was saying that the perfect relationship was out there and he, in his cockiness, was going to find it. It seemed naive and boastful, though it probably wasn't meant that way. I was going to say something in reply. I can't remember what exactly, but it was going to be vehement. Something about divorce statistics and the reality of relationships or the importance of each person in a married couple to maintain . . . what? Some privacy? Some sense of self? Some conversation that was theirs alone? (By which I meant: some lonesomeness?) I don't know. What happened instead was that I took a deep breath, and the meat — was it lamb? — in my mouth shot down my throat and lodged there. At first, I didn't do anything. The conversation went on.

Helen started in with some questions, "What was she like, your fiancée? Do you miss her?"

"I was engaged twice," the blonde said.

But then I heard Elliot saying, "Are you okay? Gwen?"

I stood up and my plate fell to the floor. I turned and could see myself in the long mirror hung behind the sofa, my eyes filling with tears and my hand at my throat — just like everyone is taught. I thought: *This is what it's like not to be able to breathe. This is what it's like to have your lungs stall. This is what it's like to drown. Like my mother did. When she was a young woman, a young mother, younger than I am now. This is what it must have been like before someone pulled me out of the car.* I'd always wanted to know, to remember, but never could, and here it was.

And then I felt arms reaching around me, a thumb knuckle digging into my stomach, then the tug of those arms — too gentle. The meat stayed put. The next tug, though, was a sharp jolt. The meat dislodged into my mouth and I spit it onto the floor. Just like that. I started gasping and coughing. I reached up, holding on to what I assumed was Peter's sleeve. I grabbed it hard. Everyone else backed away — the blonde in her platforms, Jason . . . Helen was flapping the gauzy sleeves of her dress. "Get her some water or something! Jesus!"

I turned around and there was Elliot. "You're okay," he said.

Then Peter was standing next to me on the other side, his arm around my waist. "You saved her life," he said to Elliot. Peter Stevens of the loophole Stevenses — the man who, despite statistical probability, had sidestepped all tragedy — was thrilled by this near-tragedy. He clapped Elliot on the back so hard that Elliot almost lost his balance. "That was amazing. I owe you," Peter said. "I owe you!"

And this struck me as an odd thing to say. Elliot saved *my* life. Why did Peter owe him? But no one had to owe Elliot, really. Wasn't he happy enough to have saved me? Wouldn't anyone in the room have saved me, if he could have?

At that moment the door flew open, and there stood Faith. Her hair was pulled back in a messy ponytail, and she was wearing sweatpants and an oversized T-shirt. She was holding Edward, who was wide awake and red-cheeked as if he'd just gotten off of a crying jag. She was so startlingly real that everyone froze.

Jason was the first one to move. He looked as if he was going to try to distract her. He opened his mouth and went so far as to point at me, as I was still bent over trying to catch my breath. But he must have known this would only make matters worse. He simply stood up, gave a little bow, hunched over like my corsage, and walked toward the door. Faith glared at the rest of us — with good reason. None of us had called her. None of us had sent him home. We were guilty too.

She didn't say a word. She handed Edward off to Jason. He walked out, and she gave the room one more punishing look and slammed the door.

CHAPTER SIX

What do I remember about what followed?
It started with just the three of us — Elliot,
Peter, and me — on Helen's balcony amid
the candles that had melted to waxy pools
and been snuffed out. I see us now as if
suspended by the smoky air, the balcony
itself a small cage that the three of us were
trapped in. This is where we made a fragile
pact — in large part because of Helen, who
would appear on the balcony and ignite
everything. But the strange chain of events
that was to follow required all of us, the
intricate mechanisms of conversation, so
that as a group we started at point X and
traveled, windingly, to point Y. We couldn't
have predicted how it would change things,
but each of us, even though drunk and
blurred, must have had more than an inkling
that we'd waded out into something un-
known.

Having nearly died, I'd decided to get

even drunker. Elliot and Peter got drunk along with me. They were sitting on a pair of wrought-iron chairs and I was standing at the railing. The view offered a bit of the harbor, just a bit, and only if I leaned out, which made me feel like I was on the prow of a ship. I was flushed, dizzy. The breeze was something to brace against. It was steadying in a way. There were some distant lights reflecting off the surface of the water. I closed one eye and then the other, watching the lights bounce around.

Helen was breezing around the apartment, cleaning up. There were three other guys still there. Locked in a stalemate, they were each trying to win her by simply refusing to go home. A classic move. Peter had noticed them too. "They're squatters. Look at them. Why don't they just pull up stakes already? Give up and go home?"

"How are we going to get home?" I asked.

"I can still drive," Peter said, pinching his nose, standing up tall, and sucking in his stomach as if proving his sobriety. "I'm fine." And for a moment I thought of Dr. Fogelman, who seemed as if he'd say something just like that at the end of a long party, and how Ginny Fogelman would have said, "Oh, please, do you want to kill someone and spend your life in jail?" before muttering, "You old turd." Suddenly the balcony felt like a stodgy little cage.

"I'm going to call a cab," Elliot said, but he didn't make a move to get out of his chair.

"Wait," Peter said. "We've got to get this sorted out."

"What sorted out?" Elliot asked.

"I owe you," Peter said. "For saving Gwen's life." I hated Peter a little bit for returning to this. Sometimes he got stuck on something and he wouldn't let it go. His parents probably praised him for it as a kid — they praised him for everything — calling it persistence, but sometimes it felt obsessive to me. And this felt like such a flailing attempt at a grand gesture.

"I only choked on some kabob," I said, still looking out at the harbor. "We don't have to break into a musical comedy about it."

Elliot said, "I think that repaying someone for saving your life might be true in India or somewhere . . . but not here."

"I want to know what Elliot wants," Peter said. "That's worth some conversation, at least. What's wrong with conversation?" His tone was a little belligerent and he wasn't so drunk that he didn't notice it and so he laughed, playing it off. He laughed too loudly.

"Fine," I said. I turned around quickly. Elliot's body blurred and then bobbed into focus. It was just dawning on me that I might get sick later. I was sweaty. "What do you want, Hull? What do you really want?"

Elliott looked at me and then out at the high-rises and, between them, the narrow strip of the harbor view. "I don't want anything," he said, shrugging.

"Seriously," Peter said, "you must want something." Was Peter now baiting Elliot? "Everyone wants something. It's a philosophical question — right up your alley."

"What's your alley again?" Elliot asked. "What do you do?"

"Anesthesiologist," Peter said. "I knock people out. I'm Dr. Feelgood." That's the way he always answered the question — even if a little old lady asked.

"Ah," Elliot said. "Numbness."

"You're walking away from the question. What do you want?" Peter asked again.

It was getting a little too pointed. I said, "It isn't a philosophical question. It's a personal question. What we want, what we're afraid of. You can't get more personal, more intimate. Elliot doesn't have to answer. Personal is personal."

"Would you answer the question if you were in my shoes?" Elliot asked me.

"I don't know. What do I want? Right now?" I thought about it. "I want what everyone wants."

"What's that?" Peter asked.

"To feel whole," I said.

Elliot looked at me, a little startled. I'd surprised him but I wasn't sure how. He kept watching me even as Peter started talking about what everyone wanted — 20 percent pay raises, to be rich and thin, to be famous.

When Peter was finished rattling off a litany of average American desires, Elliot said, "Okay. You want an intimate answer. The truth. What do I want?" He was taking the charge seriously now. He tapped his fingers on his thighs. "You really want to know?"

I nodded.

"I do," Peter said. "I really do."

"My mother's sick," Elliot said. "She has to take morphine from time to time now in a hospital bed set up in her living room at her lake house, and you can't fix that, so . . ."

"Morphine?" Peter said, glancing at me, confused that the conversation had taken a serious turn. "Wait. Who's taking morphine?"

"My mother's dying," Elliot stated more matter-of-factly, and then he rubbed his knee again. Was it an old injury? I watched him closely. I wanted to see what this kind of grief looked like from the outside. I knew it too well from the inside. "You can't fix that," he said, turning to me, "unless you're a cancer researcher on the brink of a cure."

"I work in sales," I said uselessly.

"I thought you were an English major."

"I think English majors go into sales," I said.

"I thought you were an interior designer," he said.

"I *work for* an interior designer. Close enough," I said. "I'm sorry about your mother." I'd learned that much from my own childhood. What you want is for someone to recognize a loss — to simply say that he's sorry. Nothing more. Just for him to say he's sorry, to give a sincere nod. One person showing another his humanness.

Helen walked onto the balcony then, picking up some errant punch glasses and beer bottles.

"Helen," Peter said. "Elliot's mother's dying." He was incredulous. He'd had such a protected life that he was stunned by things like this. He knew my mother was dead, but I can honestly say that I don't think he ever fully comprehended that she'd really once been alive — and therefore he was impatient with my father's grief, and with mine too. He let us hide it, and we were good at hiding it. He didn't even know that I'd been in the car during the crash, and that somehow I'd been saved. "Isn't that terrible?" he said, and he said this like it was an actual question, as if he wasn't sure. *Wasn't it terrible? It was, wasn't it?*

Helen stopped. "I'm sorry to hear that," she said, and she touched Elliot's head for a moment, as if giving some kind of benediction.

He nodded, then looked at the palms of his hands. The three squatters were idling in the apartment, chatting with each other now, like strangers at a bus stop, and for a minute or so, theirs were the only voices.

I've returned to this many times — the way Elliot leaned way back in his chair then and squinted up at the sky; the way he rubbed his head with both hands, as if troubled or disgusted. Did he know where he was going with this? Was he suffering a momentary hesitation? Did he know at this moment what he was really going to ask for, what he hoped would come of it? Or was he just confessing drunkenly on a balcony while a party died down all around him? I don't think it mattered. In the end, we would all have to play a role in the conversation to make all of the gears click to get from X to Y. He said, "This last visit with her, I told my mother that I'd, well, that I'd gotten married."

"Married?" Helen said disdainfully.

"You lied to your mother on her death-bed?" Peter said. The conversation made me think of my own mother. Lucky, I thought, to have had a mother on a death-bed, to have had the opportunity to lie to her.

"She was out of it, doped up on mor-phine," Elliot said, not defensively as much as explanatorily. "She was in a state; some-times when she's in these states she talks to her dead sister. It was that kind of a state."

"But why would you tell her you'd gotten married?" I asked. "I mean, wouldn't she be upset not to have been invited to the wedding and that you'd married someone she'd never met?"

"Married!" Helen said. "I mean, why not tell her you've got gangrene and have to get a leg amputated!" And then she whispered, "Marriage can kill you limb by limb. Don't you know that?" Helen enjoyed disparaging the institution of marriage in front of married people. It was a petty, almost charming kind of vengefulness.

"Well, she was in this state and she started to obsess over the fact that I wasn't married and that I'd go through life without anyone to take care of me and without anyone to take care of. She was getting more and more worked up. And so I just gave in and I lied to her. I told her I'd met someone and that it had been a quick decision — like in the old days."

"People used to do that kind of thing," Peter said. "They'd meet and get married in two weeks."

"Because they weren't allowed to have sex," Helen said. "You'd have done the same thing if you'd been in that boat, but how many years did it take you two to get engaged?" Helen pointed at the two of us.

"Three years," Peter said. "A little slice of heaven!" This was an old joke between us. We'd been to an anniversary party for a couple who'd been married twenty years and this was how the man referred to their marriage — over and over, toast after toast, conversation after conversation. By the end of the evening, it sounded like a death knell. Peter and I started to use the phrase about everything — office meetings, gym workouts, trips to the grocery store — trying to keep its awfulness at bay. We'd never used the phrase to actually describe any part of our relationship, though, and this seemed like a breach of the rules.

"My mother and my father had gotten married like that," Elliot said, "a couple weeks after they met. She respects decisions like that even though they got divorced." Everyone was looking at him now and he was suddenly aware of our eyes on him. "I don't know why I said it. It was some kind of weird impulse." He shrugged. "I didn't think she'd remember it when she calmed down, but she did."

"And now what?" Helen asked.

"And now, of course, she'd like to meet her before she dies," Elliot said, as if kind of mystified by his own predicament.

"Oh, what a tangled web," Helen said. "Tsk, tsk."

"If you met her, you'd understand," Elliot said. "She's a force. She's unwieldy. She's an unwieldy force."

"I understand mothers like that," Helen said, scratching her wrist a little angrily.

"Unwieldy like waves," I said.

"Like tsunami waves," Elliot said.

Helen turned to Elliot and looked at him squarely, taking on the stance of a lawyer.

"So you need a wife," she said, driving the point home.

"I got a call from my sister today, telling me I'd better produce a wife or else."

"Or else what?" I asked.

"I don't want to piss my mother off on her deathbed," Elliot said. "She'd haunt me the rest of my life." It was meant to be a joke, but his voice held a somberness that couldn't be ignored.

"So you do want something," Peter said. "A wife — at least temporarily."

"No, no," Elliot said, shaking his head, laughing it off. "I don't know what I'll do really. But I don't need a wife."

"But," Peter said, "we asked you what you wanted and that is what you said."

"That's not how it happened," Elliot said. He turned to me. "Is it?" And then he answered the question himself. "No, no, that's not how it went."

"Are you going to propose?" Peter asked, then he reached out and held Helen by her shoulders. "Helen, he's going to propose to you!"

"No, no," Elliot said, flustered and embarrassed.

"Always a bridesmaid, but now's your chance," Peter said.

"Oh, shove it up your ass," Helen said,

shaking him off.

"Come on!" Peter said, not letting it drop. "You two would make a delightful couple! Mr. and Mrs. Hull!"

I wanted to tell Peter to leave Elliot alone, to let it go, but I kept quiet. I liked seeing Elliot in this precarious position, and I found myself willing to put up with Peter for the moment. He goaded people when he was drunk. He could be a bit of a bully.

"No extreme measures necessary," Elliot said.

But then Helen spoke up kind of slyly. "You need a pretend wife," she said, "for your mother's sake. It would be very gallant." She turned to me. "Gwen, you should be Elliot's pretend wife."

And this is where everything turned on itself. Elliot glanced at me. His face looked stricken. I imagine now, looking back, that he was terrified. I was. I felt exposed even though no one could have known that a part of me wanted to know what my life would have been like with Elliot; and no one could have accused me of that because I was actively trying to defuse things. And maybe he was also terrified because this was what he wanted too, where he'd been hoping the conversation would go all along.

"Why me?" I asked.

"Because I'm tired of pretending with men," Helen said, and this was true. It wasn't the first time she'd said it. *Pretending* was a term she used in place of dating. "Plus, he saved *your* life, after all, not mine. Right, Peter?"

"That's right!" Peter said, not backing off of the whole idea at all. In fact, he looked lit up. "This makes perfect sense. It's so, I don't know, *European*." He had this whole spiel on how Europeans were so advanced in their definitions of marriage — especially the French. I glared at him whenever he went on this jag in public — usually after some cocktails — but he always mistook my glare for something else — a sexy leer?

"We could also just buy him a nice bottle of Cristal and call it even," I said.

"What?" Helen said, turning on me with a frenetic pitch that bordered on a stylized version of anger. "Don't you have confidence in your marriage? I mean, if Peter were against it, that would be one thing. But you? Do you really think *Elliot* here is a threat to the institution?"

"Hey," Elliot said. "Be nice." He turned to me. "I thought she liked me."

I was keeping a wary eye on Peter. "I have confidence in my marriage," I said.

"Well, then," Peter said. "Let's not be all

bourgeois about it!" *Bourgeois* was one of Helen's favorite words. I hated the sound of it coming out of his mouth — the way he squeezed a tiny bit of French accent into it. "What do you say, Gwen?"

Everyone turned and looked at me.

"I'm not a rental car," I said.

"She's not a rental car," Elliot repeated quickly, as if that settled things. He was letting me off the hook, but I wasn't sure I liked being let off the hook by him so quickly.

Helen sighed mightily.

"It's okay," Peter said. "Gwen's not the kind of person to do something like this. And that's a compliment. She's too . . ." He stopped then, weighing some options, perhaps.

"I'm too what?" I asked. I wasn't so sure it was going to be complimentary at all. Could you be *too* anything and still be complimented?

"Yes," Helen said. "What is she?"

But Peter didn't have to answer.

Elliot said, "Look, I don't need a wife. I need to grow up and not lie to my mother. That's what I need." Was this what he really wanted though — why had he brought up the subject in the first place?

"Gwen's a great wife," Helen said. "She's

88

the greatest wife in the whole wide world. She should have a T-shirt with that written on it. Do you have a T-shirt with that written on it?"

"No," I said, insulted by her effusiveness.

"She'd make the perfect pretend wife for Elliot," Helen said. "It would probably only be for just a weekend. Right? You should do it, Gwen. You should be Elliot's pretend wife. Don't be so uptight about it."

"That's right!" Peter said. I looked at him and he seemed far away, and it didn't help that he wasn't talking as much as he was shouting like he was on a beach. "Look, I'm fine with this," Peter said, almost barking. "I'm not uptight. Gwen can do it if she wants to. It's okay by me." This was the only hint that Peter might have had a tiny doubt in his mind. He lived in mortal fear of being perceived to be uptight, because he was uptight — desperately so. And he was, after all, deeply convinced of us, or maybe the institution of marriage itself, and perhaps most of all his family's legacy of imperviousness. He goaded and bullied himself too when he was drunk.

Elliot shook his head and waved Peter off. "No, no, no."

I looked down over the balcony's railing and watched a couple, hand in hand, running across the street even though there were no cars. "I think I met your mother once," I said to Elliot. "She came to the awards ceremony for English majors. There was a little punch-and-cookies thing after."

"Did she come to that?" Elliot said.

"We talked for a minute," I said. I remembered her as a woman who looked like she played tennis. She had this arched nose and Elliot's eyebrows. Elliot's parents had divorced when he was ten. His father had since invested in a new family and almost ignored Elliot and his sister, Jennifer. At twenty-one, I couldn't understand why anyone would have divorced Elliot's mother — she was so stunning. When I introduced myself to her, she said, "Oh, so *you* are Gwen Merchant," as if she'd heard a lot about me from Elliot. I remembered being complimented by that, though I wasn't sure if it was a compliment or not. By this point Elliot and I had broken up and he was seeing Ellen Maddox again. "She looked like a Kennedy," I said. "She was more elegant than the other mothers." I was a watcher of mothers.

"Gwen, you should do it," Helen whispered urgently.

I wanted to do it, and I was surprised by how very much I wanted to. I wanted to be alone with Elliot Hull. I wanted to listen to what had happened to him since I'd last known him. I wanted to know his intimate story, and maybe I wanted to tell him mine. I had a fantasy that he would fall in love with me abundantly even though I didn't want to love him in return. I wanted to be the girl at the freshman icebreaker again, starting over by shaking hands and complimenting each other's shoes, like we'd been told. I wanted his mother to say, "Oh, it's the famous Gwen Merchant again. Returned!" I wanted to bring her back to life.

"It's not every day someone saves your life," Peter said. He was aggressively chipper now. "And he said it was at a lake house. What's wrong with getting away to a lake house?"

"Is it at a lake house?" Helen said.

"Yes, but this is crazy. I shouldn't have lied. I'll just have to confess. That's all."

"It's a lake house," Helen reported to me. "Does it have a deer hanging on the wall and a wet bar? Does it have a boathouse?" She didn't wait for an answer. "You should go, Gwen."

"You've been wanting to get away," Peter added.

"I've been wanting to get away *with you,*" I said, and this was true. I'd been pushing for a weekend somewhere, but Peter always convinced me that we should invest in some household upgrade instead.

"You should just go and have fun. Talk to Elliot's mother some. Take in the sun. Take out a rowboat," Helen said, then turned to Elliot. "Are there rowboats?"

"A fleet of them," Elliot said matter-of-factly.

"Horseshoe pit?" she asked.

"Yep."

"Are there box turtles?" I asked.

"They come in herds like buffalo," he said.

"I *am* a great wife," I said, "pretend or not."

"You *are* a great wife," Peter said.

"It could be a . . . what's that word?" I asked. "That thing people used to say . . ."

"What's what word?" Helen asked.

"You know, when people do something for the hell of it . . ."

"A lark?" Elliot said.

"Exactly," I said. "It could be a lark." But when he said it, I thought of the bird — all wings, the song in its throat. I glanced at Peter and Elliot — they both looked at me expectantly.

Helen clapped her hands, tappity tappity, like a lady at an opera. "Is that a definite yes?" she asked.

I turned my back on all of them and stared at the banks of high-rise windows, the distant harbor lights, which looked soft and edgeless. I knew that I wanted it to be more than a lark, but I was trying to pretend. The breeze welled up. My black dress billowed. The corsage bobbed. "Okay, then," I said, quietly, "okay. I'll do it."

CHAPTER SEVEN

The January 1979 issue of *National Geographic* included a flimsy record inserted as one of its pages. It was a recording of endangered humpback whales singing, and had been in the works for a decade. My father had been on the project in its early stages. He was an assistant professor at University of Maryland Biotechnology Institute, where he's still a professor, and was working in conjunction with scientists at the New York Zoological Society. But he quit about six months before my mother died.

I learned early on that I wasn't allowed to ask questions about my mother. My father would admit a few things about her: She was a good mother. She loved fruits and vegetables. She'd taken dance lessons through high school. And she'd learned to knit before I was born. When she couldn't sleep — and she was a bad sleeper — she would knit. Those were the facts. That's it.

But I could ask about work, and as I grew older, I realized how much my father loved the humpback whale project, but that he'd felt that quitting it was necessary. He'd told me that it took too much time on boats. He missed his family. One time he said, "I was needed at home."

Mrs. Fogelman, who'd known my mother only a little bit — I get the impression that my mother was hard to know — has, over the years, given me some information. She knew nothing really about the accident itself, or refused to admit she did. She told me that when my mother died, my father was solid. He didn't cry. He wasn't fragile. He made his way through the funeral like an unsinkable tanker.

But the grief hit him later.

I was six years old in 1979 when the *National Geographic* record came out. It was a year after my mother's death. My father played the record constantly — the house was filled with the acoustic moans and sighs of humpback whales. For a few months, it was like living in the ocean. And I remember that my father seemed to move around the house in slow motion during that time, as if he were swimming through his life. He was finally grieving my mother's death.

Mrs. Fogelman explained, "Once you were off at school, he had time to himself. He let his guard down, and it hit him. But your father is a tough man. He didn't wallow in it for long."

I disagreed. He learned to wallow in a more private way, but he'd been wallowing ever since.

My childhood was lonesome. There were lonesome brown-bag lunches, lonesome diaries, lonesome bugs in lonesome jars, lonesome Barbies. There were lonesome holes dug into lonesome beaches, lonesome braces, a lonesome cast. There were lonesome clarinet lessons, lonesome bicycles, lonesome cereal poured into lonesome bowls. That's how I remember it. Lonesome, lonesome, lonesome.

A lonesomeness only broken by women in the neighborhood — teachers, homeroom mothers who felt sorry for me. I let them but it wasn't love. It only looked like love. It was pity. Other children treated me like I was a deformed saint — or, worse, a statue of a deformed saint. And I let them do that too, because I don't think I really knew how to be with people as a kid. My father avoided people, and I did too. It felt like a pact, as if we were protecting our loss, not allowing anyone access so that we could keep it all for ourselves. My father certainly didn't want to part with his pain.

You'd think that at home, my father and I would have had our pain in common, if nothing else. But, in truth, he could barely look at me. He loved me and still does — I'm sure of that. But I looked like my mother — my small face, my green eyes, my dark hair cupping my face. No matter how it was pinned back, it always swept forward like hers. Always.

And so I became used to love-in-glances, love with some love held in reserve, love with the background noise that is a fear of love.

And how did Elliot Hull fit into this definition of love?

Badly.

After that day when he lay down on my blanket on the green and told me that I'd picked the wrong girl at the orientation icebreaker, that instead of Ellen Maddox, I should have picked myself for him, we spent all of our time together. We rented racquets and played racquetball on the courts with their folding metal handles and glass back walls. We walked each other to class. We met in one of the conference rooms in the library basement. The conference rooms always had notes taped to their doors, reserving them for different college-sponsored club meetings. We taped up a note of our own that read: Reserved for the Albanian Student Union of Perverse Sexuality Club, scribbled in our time slot, and had sex up against the chalkboard. We traded off nights between our small campus-housing apartments, hoping not to piss off either set of roommates too profoundly. I made all of my father's recipes, and one that I'd invented — baked chicken breaded in crushed Cheerios. We didn't go out much. Late at night, we studied next to each other on bunk beds, and once we took a bath together and let it overflow, creating a small flood in the downstairs apartment.

It was too much. I felt like I was barely breathing — the way he looked at me so searchingly, the way he watched me get dressed, the way he made up songs about me. One of his favorites was about his love for me being like an ocean. I loved it but I couldn't accept it. I covered my ears every time he started up with it. But I was absorbing it all too. I was drinking it in.

We swam that spring in the university pool as soon as it opened, even though it was freezing. Our lips turned blue. I was a terrible swimmer — I still am. I remember he tried to teach me to float and that he gave up. "You're too agitated a human being to float," he said. So I stuck to my spastic swimming, whirling my arms, kicking frenetically, some sporadic breaths. "You're working too hard," he said. "Jesus, just relax. Why are you so scared?"

And I told him, standing in three feet of water next to the metal ladder, no one else around except for a few hearty lap swimmers in their rubber caps, that my mother had drowned. "Or maybe she was killed on impact before she drowned," I said. "I'm not sure." I'd left this story at home for the most part. In my hometown everyone knew about it, so I never had to explain. If there was a newcomer, someone else would whisper it to them. And when I came to college I was so happy not to be defined by it that I'd decided not to tell it at all. The few times that it had come up, in some small way, I simply said that my mother had died when I was young. I'd add, "I don't even remember her!" In any case, I wasn't used to telling the story so I didn't realize how little of it I knew.

Elliot started asking me questions.

"Was it because of a drunk driver?"

"I don't think so."

"Was it a bridge near your house?"

"North of us. An hour or so. I've never seen it."

"You don't know what bridge it was?"

"No. Who cares what bridge?"

"It's just that, I don't know, I'd be curious. I'd want to see it."

Maybe I had been curious once. But how could I have asked my father to take me to the bridge? There was no one to ask, not really, no appropriate time for such a question and so I'd let it go.

"Was she alone in the car?" he asked.

"I don't want to talk about it," I told him.

"But you should talk about it," he said.

I remember that I tried to lunge for the ladder, but he grabbed me and pulled me in close to him.

"Don't tell me what I should do," I said and I started crying.

"Okay," he said. "Then you *can* talk about it. That's all. You *can,* if you want to, whenever you want to."

This made me cry harder, and I don't know how long we stood there, but it seemed like a very long time. Finally, I started shaking because the water was so cold. We got out. He wrapped me in a towel. We'd only brought one.

Our relationship lasted only three weeks. It ended abruptly in that bar. I remember only that there'd been a fight before we went out and that we both drank at the bar. We were drunk, but I didn't accept that as an excuse. We were fighting about something that wasn't important, and then he said something in that bar, under the string of year-round Christmas lights. He said something that reminded me of my mother and my father, something provocative, something that struck me as dangerous. And I could have forgiven him. I could have easily forgiven him, but I was afraid to. He called me the next day. He called and left messages — long rambling messages, then short angry ones, then long rambling ones again. I wanted him to stop.

And then he did stop calling. It was a relief, in a way. I told myself that it was for the best. Elliot Hull was too much.

Graduation rolled around. I heard he'd started seeing Ellen again, that he'd kind of proposed and she'd said yes.

I saw his mother at the punch-and-cookies reception. She said, "So *you* are Gwen Merchant."

And then Elliot walked up, handing his mother a paper cup of some pink juice. By then we were cordial.

We wished each other luck.

That's why Peter was so attractive to me.

That's why I fell in love with him. He didn't shove love at me. He didn't lavish it on. He wasn't brimming with love. He doled it out in portions. Love wasn't an ocean — it came in packets.

And do I blame him for this?

No.

It was perfect for me when we met. In fact it was all I could have handled.

And, later, as I was learning that it was insufficient, I knew that I was asking too much of him. I'd signed on for his love in packets. And, the truth was, we'd have passed any marital test — from a psychologist to a *Cosmo* quiz. We made each other laugh. We had enough good sex and regularly so. We liked the same foods and complimented each other's haircuts and flirted enough to keep things going. We never intentionally put each other down — not with real malicious intent. We looked compatible on paper too. We had our degrees, and though I'd flopped around a good bit job-wise, he was supportive. We finished each other's sentences some, but we took turns so it was fair. We didn't squabble in public, and we barely ever squabbled at all. And we never had real fights; we aren't screamers. We both liked a tidy enough house. Neither of us were especially good dancers. We liked each other's friends, more or less. We shopped well together. He was still an inch and a half taller than I was when I wore my highest heels. Old couples smiled at us in restaurants as if we reminded them of the happy, younger versions of themselves. We were, by all accounts, lovely to be with, a sweet couple that looked nice together walking into a room.

I knew that there were many women out there who would have said: *It's enough already. Be happy with what you have.* They were right — and wrong.

CHAPTER EIGHT

The day after the party, Peter got up early to round out a foursome in golf. There was a note posted on the fridge that read:

G —
I'm going golfing with three guys from work. I'm a last-minute fill-in for the wounded. I'll be back — in golf years — just in time for your thirty-fifth birthday.
XO
P.S. Pretending to be someone else's wife? What were we thinking?

Golf years is a long-standing joke. Golf years are longer than dog years and *Monday Night Football* years combined. I've never played so I don't understand how golf — a supposed sport — can move so slowly, take so long, and still call itself a sport. Supposedly Peter's a very good golfer, which would lead one to believe he could do it faster than other golfers. But that's not how it works. If I knew Peter at all — and I did, in my way — I knew that he was using the inside golf joke to offset two things: 1. that he'd be gone for the bulk of the day and 2. that he wanted to get out of the agreement we'd made on the balcony. He'd woken up that morning and decided it was drunken fool-ishness, no longer a good idea, and he wanted to make sure I felt the same. I spent the morning nursing my hangover, and wondering just how Peter — with his impec-cable manners — was going to suggest I get out of pretending to be Elliot's wife. And I realized that I didn't want to be talked out of it.

It was a Sunday and, in keeping with my usual Sunday plans, I headed to my father's around lunchtime to check in. Sometimes Peter came with me on these quick visits, but usually he opted to stay at home. My father always asked about him when he wasn't there. Not that he took it personally that Peter didn't come; he really just pre-ferred to have Peter along to break the unsettling tension between him and me — our long history of the unsaid.

The street where I grew up lonesomely was overgrown with thick hulking oaks, bushy hedges, and tough green lawns of hearty Bermuda grass. The houses were large but tired, worn. They almost all wore the old asbestos shingles, having been built in the late sixties. Aged basketball hoops with rusting bolts were attached to their garages. The Fogelmans had a gardener who kept their yard tidy, and in addition, they worked on the yard themselves, as hobbyists. My father's house looked dejected by comparison. The roof was pale and the shingles warped. The paint on the garage doors was peeling. One shutter of an upstairs window had come unhitched and now it tilted like an errant eyebrow. It was the kind of yard that Eila would have cursed at — "This house has the curb appeal of a puckered cat's ass" — just before ringing the bell and putting on her slightly British, faux artistic accent for the prospective clients.

I was standing in the front yard, stalled there, when Lucy-Jane, the Fogelmans' cocker spaniel, trotted up to sniff my shoes. I bent down to pet her head. "Little Lu," I said, "what are you doing so far from home?" She was an older dog with sad, wet eyes. The Fogelmans hadn't bobbed her tail so it fanned out behind her somewhat majestically.

"Lucy-Jane!" I heard Mrs. Fogelman calling out and then she appeared through a stand of trees. She was wearing flowered gardening gloves and had a rubber kneeling pad tucked under one arm.

"Oh, Gwen!" she said and then yelled over her shoulder, "Benny! Come here and say hello! It's Gwen!"

"Gwen!" Dr. Fogelman shouted, and then he too was there amid the branches. He was wearing a shirt so similar to the one Peter had worn the night before that I wanted to take a picture to have some proof of the stodginess.

I hadn't seen the two of them in a few months, but they looked much older, which can happen with older people as well as with little kids — a change that takes you by surprise. Dr. Fogelman's chest looked like it had shrunk a bit, and his paunch looked more affected by gravity, and Mrs. Fogelman was hale but a little more hunched in her shoulders — like an aging wrestler. I loved the Fogelmans wholeheartedly, maybe because they treated my appearances with some of the spectacle of a celebrity spotting.

"Hi," I said, "your yard looks great!"

"Extra hours," Dr. Fogelman said. "Don't commit the crime if you can't do the time!"

Mrs. Fogelman gave him an angry glance

as if this were some reference to their marriage, then she smiled at me. "You look lovely, as always!" she said.

"Per usual!" Dr. Fogelman added.

I picked up Lucy-Jane and carried her to them. "How's the old man been these days?" I asked. They kept tabs on my father, and we talked this way about him from time to time and he knew it. He called us *conspirators*, in a joking way.

"Well, you won't believe that I invited him over to the same dinner as a single friend of mine from church. Her name is Louise. She's lovely."

"She's fine," Dr. Fogelman amended.

"She's quite lovely," Mrs. Fogelman corrected him.

"And?" I said.

"That's the end of the story," Dr. Fogelman said. "I told her not to meddle."

"I wasn't meddling. I invited two people to dinner. Is that meddling, Gwen?"

"No, I think that's nice. Is Louise interested in fish? That's the question," I said.

"No one's interested in fish like your dad's interested in fish," Mrs. Fogelman said.

"Fishes!" Dr. Fogelman added. "If I've learned anything living next to a marine biologist all these years, it's that it's correct to say fishes!"

I handed Lucy-Jane over to Mrs. Fogelman. "Well, thanks for keeping an eye on my dad," I said.

"Oh, please," Mrs. Fogelman said. "It's nothing. If I make too much soup, I bring it over. That's all." I've always wondered if Mrs. Fogelman didn't love my father a little — or was it that she saw him as a compelling tragic figure? A sad romantic leading man?

"Soup's good for him," Dr. Fogelman said. "I heard a statistic on the radio that married men live longer, but I don't see how in hell that could be true!"

Mrs. Fogelman hit him with her rubber kneeling pad.

"Talk to you later," I said.

They waved good-bye identically.

As I made my way across my father's haggard lawn, I wondered if Dr. Fogelman would outlive my father. Did wives really just feed their husbands well or did they know how to ease their hearts in some way elemental to longevity?

I knocked on the door while walking in. The house was as depressing inside as it was out. The window sills were littered with the dust of dead moths. The battered couches were arranged stiffly — not organically shifted because of actual use, but under the direction of a widower who had few guests. The dining room table had been sacrificed for my father's recording equipment so that he could listen to tracks of soniferous fishes, studying them, making notations. His current project involved working with a network of marine biologists interested in creating a National Archive of Fish Sounds in the Library of Natural Sounds at Cornell. If my father were a prospective client, Eila would have pushed for a complete move-out with 100 percent furniture rentals, plus a handyman and cleaning crew. "The entire package! Without it, my hands would be tied! And how can an *artiste* make art with her hands tied?" she'd say with a feverish lilt to her voice.

It's not lost on me that I've wandered into this job — staging homes for sale. I love the idea that you can take a ramshackle house that's been sorely ignored and nurture it back to health. "This is all about psychology," Eila had told me time and again. "We want to make a home that says: 'Here, you'll love your family. Here, you'll be love.' It isn't about art as much as it is about the definition of love."

I wondered what the house was like when my mother brought me home from the hospital. The trees were small and scrawny then — I've seen the saplings in photos. When I was younger, I asked Mrs. Fogelman if she saw my mother pushing a stroller, gardening in the yard, putting up new curtains. What did she do? Mrs. Fogelman told me, time and again, "She knit. You had hats and sweaters and blankets. She knit and knit. She could have knit that whole house, I think. She was serious about it." But I've never seen anything that looks like homemade knitting in the house — not a throw, not a scarf, not a Christmas stocking. Nothing.

Did my mother nurture this house? Was it a place that said, *Here, you'll love your family. Here, you'll be loved?* Or did it already have this air about it — this stubborn air of grief? "Sadness is palpable," Eila has said to me. "I've seen houses so sad that I think the only cure would be to burn them down."

The smell of fried bologna hung in the air. "I'm cooking!" my father called out from the kitchen. "In here!"

He always cooked for our Sunday lunches — tuna-fish casseroles, grilled cheeses, watery tomato soup, fish sticks, mashed potatoes from the boxed flakes, and bologna. On special occasions, around one of our birthdays, he'd make small, eggy fried salmon cakes from the can. That was the sum of his repertoire.

He was standing in front of the stove, cutting pleats into the fried bologna. It was an elderly gas stove with only one burner that still lit automatically. The others had to be lit with a match. He was a little stooped, aging by way of a winnowing of his shoulders and sinking in of his chest. When he saw me, he looked up from his cooking and in a moment of self-awareness, he combed the wispy hair on his head as if making an attempt to gussy up. I walked over and kissed his cheek. "How are you doing?" I said, putting my purse on the table.

"I'm fine. I spent the morning listening to a colleague's *Ophidion marginatum.*" He still used Latin names for things in the hopes that I'd learn them.

"Speak English please," I said.

"The striped cusk-eel. Great work being done in Cape Cod and New Bedford, and he's got an undergrad collecting eel vocalizations in Manhattan, right in the Hudson."

"Eels in Manhattan," I said. "Sounds like an off-off-off-Broadway thing."

"It's way-off-Broadway. I'm lending my ear, helping with identifications." He put two circles of bologna on Wonder bread for me. The mustard and mayonnaise were already on the table. We shuffled around each other, preparing our sandwiches. Then we sat down, right there, our plates set on the rubber place mats. As side dishes, he'd set out jars of pickles and olives and a bar of jalapeño cheese.

"You look a little peaked," he said.

"Peter and I ran into an old friend of mine from college. We drank too much."

"Oh, college friends," he said. "My students drink too much. They really do. I had to go to some meeting recently about binge drinking on campus — as if I can do anything about that." My father's students were good for him. They gave him a small tether to the outside world. Because of them, he'd sometimes know that a certain band had come to town, that people were wearing their pants very low on their hips, and he understood cultural concepts like date rape and beer pong.

I thought about how to bring up Elliot. I wanted to talk about him, to confide something — maybe about the way he confused me. If I had a mother, would this have been the kind of thing we'd have talked about in hushed tones while pretending to take a little tour of her new garden out back?

I knew that I couldn't say anything that intimate to my father. If I were to say that I was considering pretending to be Elliot's wife for the sake of his dying mother, my father would have taken a big bite of his bologna, nodded, and then licked one finger, using it to pick up bread crumbs on his plate. Eventually, he might say something like, "Oh, I wouldn't know anything about that." But he'd have said it so late that it would have seemed like he was bringing it back up, which would be more awkward than if he'd said nothing at all.

But Elliot was an academic and I knew that academia was safe. I said, "The old college friend is named Hull, Elliot Hull. He's a professor at Hopkins now."

"What department?" my father asked.

"Philosophy," I said.

"Ah, one of the thinkers," he said, by which he meant that Elliot wasn't one of the doers. My father had divided all of academia into two parts — thinkers and doers. My father considered himself a doer.

Lunch was brief. My father didn't believe in lingering over meals — there was too much to do as a doer. But he asked me, as he often did, if I wanted to listen to some talking fish. Sometimes I could do this, and sometimes I couldn't bear to — the constant shushing of water, the chirrups and croaks and coos, all sounded like laments to me. Sometimes it was just too hard because I would allow myself the hideous indulgence of the imagination — my mother underwater.

But today I didn't want to rush back to the apartment, to Peter and his golf bags, and his ideas on how to get out of our pact with Elliot Hull. I said, "Let's listen to some eels."

My father concentrated on fishes on the East Coast, where 150 species can vocalize. I've listened to the bumps and ticks of haddock calls, the guttural detonations of their spawning, the creaking of toad fish, the sounds of whales creating walls of bubbles to trap fish and feed. I've listened to fish all my life — buzzing, groaning, grunting, purring, honking, cooing like pigeons. My father insists that they're exchanging information about predators, that they're being aggressive sometimes and other times courtly and wooing. He believes that they throw angry fits and scold and that they even grieve. Once he told me that they talk about all the things that we talk about. I was probably ten, and I already knew that we didn't seem to talk about all of the things he claimed fishes did.

My father clamped the oversized headphones onto my head. At first, everything was muffled, and then the ocean rolled in, the movement of waves — and finally eels. Their chirrups came in rapid succession, not unlike squirrels. I looked up at my father, who was standing and pacing.

"What do you think?" he asked. "Don't they sound good? Clear? Don't they sound like they're here, right in the room with you?"

For some reason, this made me want to cry. I took off the headphones and set them on the table. "They sound happy," I said. "They sound like happy squirrels."

"I'll write that down," he said. "That's nicely descriptive."

I watched him jot in his notepad, then I turned and looked out of the old aluminum sliding door that led to the deck with its gray boards. "I want you to tell me," I said.

"What?" he asked.

"I want you to tell me something," I said.

"What is it?" he said, concerned now.

"Anything. Tell me anything about her."

He stopped then, knowing that I was talking about my mother. "I've told you a lot," he said.

"Let me tell you something," I said, still looking out the door. "I had this childhood fear that because she'd died when I was young that she wouldn't recognize me in heaven and that we'd never meet."

"I didn't know you believed in heaven."

"I know, I know. You didn't teach me to believe in things like that, but still I was afraid of that for a long time."

"You should have told me."

"No, I shouldn't have because you'd have only given me some scientist's denunciation of heaven."

He thought about this for a moment. "I'm sorry," he said. "You're probably right."

"You tell me something now." I was thinking about Elliot, what it had been like to meet him at the icebreaker, his critique of my shoes, how he picked up Ellen Maddox and swung her around, what it had been like when he laid down on my blanket on the green that spring. What was my parents' story? I didn't know anything, really. I'd come back to Elliot's phrase that marriage was a conversation that should last a lifetime. Had my mother and father had a conversation that could have lasted if it hadn't been stopped short? Did the conversation end unfinished? I didn't even know how the conversation had begun. "How did you meet?" I asked.

"We met at a dance," my father said. "People often meet at dances. I told you all that, though."

"No, I didn't know that," I said. "What

song was playing when you asked her to dance?"

"I didn't ask your mother to dance," he said. "I don't know how to dance."

"Then what did you do?" I turned around to face him.

He picked up the headphones from the table. I worried for a moment that he was going to sit down and put them on. He didn't. He just held them. "I asked her to leave the dance," he said, "with me."

I sat down at the head of the table. "That's romantic," I said.

"Your mother was romantic," he said. "She fell for it."

"She fell for you," I said.

He nodded.

"And you fell for her," I said.

"We fell and fell," he said. "That's what it was like . . . falling."

There was a twinge in his voice that intimated that the falling was both lovely and ruinous — like falling in love and falling into a dark hole. And I pushed myself to ask him, "Was that what it was like near the end, just before the accident? Like falling?"

He looked up at me, startled, as if I'd broken some code — like the chirrups of the striped cusk-eel. I felt like the boy in that picture book who had the magic crayon

and with it he could make things appear —
I felt like I'd just drawn a large rectangle
and it became a door between my father
and me, an open door.

"Yes," he said finally and he nodded as if
to say, again — that's right. He tugged on
the cord of the headphones then pressed
tears from his eyes.

CHAPTER NINE

"I sweated it all out, every last drop," Peter said, then sniffed himself. "I feel like I've been steamed and pressed." Sometimes Peter had a radio voice — like an announcer, loud, deep, fast, smooth, and worst of all, rehearsed. He was slouched on the couch, his face pointed at the ceiling, wearing a loud-striped polo, not unlike Gary's, the fellow anesthesiologist we'd seen at the ice-cream shop. His golf cleats were sitting by the door. He'd already peeled off his socks.

I walked past him and was soon banging around in the kitchen, soaking rice to put in the rice cooker, and scrubbing a pan of leftover lasagna that had burned at its edges. I was considering whether or not to tell him about my moment with my father. It was seismic really — in relation to every conversation about my mother that had preceded it, which always seemed small and brittle. I'd only seen my father cry at my high school graduation, though I saw nothing the least bit sad about it — I was so ready to leave. Even then, he'd complained about the gymnasium's dust, excused himself, and headed to the men's room in the lobby. I was afraid to tell Peter about my father's crying that day in his dining room. I was afraid that Peter would say the wrong thing. And how could he say the right thing? I'd never been able to fully explain my relationship with my father, our relationship to my mother's death — I'd never really tried. Even if Peter said something sweet, something like, "Poor guy. He misses her still," that would be wrong, and I'd get angry. It wouldn't be Peter's fault, but that wouldn't matter. Suddenly I'd find that the memory was clouded by some petty marital argument. I wanted to have it all to myself. This might seem like a small thing — like I'm thinking my way down a rabbit hole — but it wasn't. It was part of our relationship, deeply embedded, this notion that each of us kept things hidden. We had private internal lives, and that's fine, I suppose, but once two people start cordoning parts of their own lives off from each other, it's hard to know where to stop.

"Did you get my note?" Peter called. "Did you read the P.S.?"

"I did," I said.

"Jesus, we were drunk. I still smell like coconuts." He sighed.

"There's no gracious way out of it," I said, using a spatula to dig at the encrusted noodles. "You know that."

"Well, who said you have to be gracious? Graciousness is something southerners do. Your parents were raised in Massachusetts and mine were from Connecticut. We don't have to be gracious or drink mint juleps or admire seersucker. It's part of our geographical rights."

I walked around the corner of the kitchen still holding a sudsy pot. "Baltimore is technically below the Mason-Dixon line. Plus, southern or not, I gave my word."

"I don't think that's as important as it used to be." He rubbed his bare feet on the rug. He'd developed his golfer's tan — the one that concentrates on the shins and calves and leaves the feet so pristinely white.

"My word isn't as important as it used to be?" I squinted at him.

"You know what I mean. The whole concept of giving your word. It's very last century. In fact, ever since Vietnam . . ." There was no need for him to finish this thought. We both knew his post-Vietnam speeches — how the war had made it necessary for Americans to reinvent literature and politics and a sense of ourselves. It was something he'd learned from an inspiring professor he'd had in college and trotted out gratuitously.

I leaned against the doorway, the dishpan getting heavy and feeling awkward in my hands. There was a photograph of my mother on the table beside him. It was a picture of her as a young woman, before she met my father, dressed up for some formal, wearing a spaghetti-strapped dress, holding a beaded purse. She wasn't smiling at the camera; she was really laughing, her eyes glancing at someone or something off to the side of the photographer. Her teeth overlapped just slightly but they looked so beautiful, ivory, and she wore a choker with a little blue stone that sat right in the dip between her collarbones. I'd gotten used to the photograph and usually didn't register it, but every once in a while, it would catch me off guard like this, and I would think of my mother as a young woman, so alive. "I don't think that giving your word is a concept at all. It's just *giving your word.* Does everything have to be a concept?"

"But you're not a rental car," he said, smiling, holding up one victorious finger. "You said that!"

"I know," I said, turning back into the kitchen. "But I'm going."

"To his mother's lake house?" There was a pause and then finally he said, "Why? Why would you go?"

"I thought you weren't going to be uptight about this," I said, standing at the sink.

"Don't get on me with all of that uptight shit. Leave that kind of mind-game bullshit to Helen. Besides, I think she tricked you into this."

I squirted a bit more liquid soap into the dishpan, turned on the faucet, and let it fill up. The soap foamed. I turned off the faucet. "I said I'd go and I think I should."

"Oh, so people can't have second thoughts? I thought it was a woman's prerogative to change her mind."

I ignored this comment. "And, you know, second of all, let's not forget that you *wanted* me to go."

I hoped he would walk into the kitchen, to have this argument face-to-face. I know that I could have stopped scrubbing and walked into the living room and sat down and looked at him earnestly. But he wasn't doing anything in there except letting his pale feet breathe. I refused to stop what I was doing to sit with him and talk seriously. Plus, I was afraid it would give the conversation too much weight. Neither of us wanted that. "Okay, so you might not have changed your mind, but what if I have?"

I lowered my hand into the silky bubbles. "Well, isn't that a little womanly of you?" As soon as I said it, I felt bad about it. I added quickly, "There's a boathouse and box turtles and a horseshoe pit," I said. "I wanted to get away, you said that."

"You could get away with your girlfriends," he said. "Like Faith. Now, Faith needs to get away. That would be an equally good deed, getting Faith away for a weekend."

"You don't get to tell me to do something," I said, "and then tell me not to do it. You don't even get to tell me what to do in the first place." I slipped dirty plates into the dishwasher slots.

"I know that!" he said, as if this were a good-husband fundamental. "It's just that I don't think it's the best idea." There was a long pause. I suppose he was letting it all settle in. "Maybe I'm jealous."

I walked back into the living room, my hands glistening with soap. "Are you jealous?" I asked.

"Maybe," he said, putting his hands behind his head and stretching his back. It was a cocky pose. Wasn't jealousy supposed to make you vulnerable?

"I didn't know you got jealous," I said. And this was true. He seemed to be missing that genetic coding. I walked back into the kitchen. "It's just pretend. You can only be pretend jealous over a pretend thing."

"You can get out of this," he said. "Just call Elliot and tell him you can't. You're busy."

"I've already talked to him," I said, though this wasn't true. I wasn't even sure he had my phone number.

"You have? Did he call?"

"Yep, and he's setting it up. He already told his mother." I decided to let the dishpan soak. I wedged coffee mugs into the washer's upper deck.

"That fucker," Peter said.

"He called while you were golfing," I said. "Golf takes a very long time." Did I feel guilty about lying? Not really. I don't know why exactly. Maybe because when you lie out of anger, it feels more like righting an injustice. And what was the injustice? Peter was trying to tell me what to do, while pretending not to. And more important, he didn't think I was the kind of person to do something like this — and Helen was? Regardless, I didn't like to be pigeonholed.

"Did he really call — *already?*" he asked.

126

"Yep." I sprinkled the detergent into its compartments and shut the dishwasher's heavy door.

"But I still smell like coconuts," he said, more to himself than to me. "Did you set a date?"

"Not yet, but it'll be soon." I closed a few cabinet doors.

"Why do you have to rush? There's no rush!" he said, and I loved him at that moment — his voice didn't sound anything like a radio announcer. It was hitched with emotion — there was a boyish whine to it, yes, but it was an honest one. I couldn't remember the last time he'd sounded so honest.

I paused, trying to hold on to that love, trying to let it burrow down inside of me. But I couldn't. It was made of air. It evaporated. And then I said, "Elliot's mother's dying. That's the rush." I hit the start button on the dishwasher. The room filled with the noise of nozzles spraying water. I said, "She's on her *death*bed," even though I knew he couldn't hear me.

Chapter Ten

Elliot and I did eventually talk on the phone, a number of times, and although we said a lot of words, our conversations never covered much ground. He kept asking if this whole thing was okay, if it was *really* okay, with me, with Peter. I assured him it was fine. He told me again and again that I didn't have to come, that he needed to grow up, that he'd have to tell his mother the truth and that this would be good for him, like the time he was forced to eat the vegetables that he'd balled in a napkin and tried to hide in the sofa once when he was a kid. "I learned something from that. I grew as a person. I haven't hidden vegetables in a sofa for years," he said.

"The question is a philosophical one, isn't it?" I asked. "Does something that is wrong, like lying, become right if done for a good cause?"

"I could give you a semester-long answer

to that," he said.

"Do you have an abridged version that runs a sentence or two?"

"I know how to philosophize abstractly, but not how to apply it to my life. Is that short enough?"

"Very succinct," I said. "I guess I believe that the ends can sometimes justify the means. This is important to your mother?"

"It is," he said, then paused. "It was irrational that I said it in the first place. And I don't know why I then confessed it at the party. But here we are. You've said you're coming out to the lake house and I've given you every chance to back out. And so, regardless of the ends, I like the means. Is that fair to say?"

That was fair to say. I liked the means too, but didn't say so. We made our arrangements quickly after that, as if we were both afraid it would fall through if we talked about it too much. He was heading out to the lake house after his Thursday-morning graduate philosophy seminar that week. We arranged that he'd meet me at the train on Saturday around noon. Even if I was a pretend wife, there was a rush, after all. His mother was real and really dying.

I had lunch scheduled with Faith and Helen

129

midweek. We ate salads topped with goat cheese, tart apples, dried blueberries. I complained about the graphs that Eila made me show the clients. "Can you believe I have a job that involves graphs?"

Faith rolled her eyes. She was in banking.

"You should be having lunch with women who make delightful references to Jane Austen," Helen said. She was always trying to convince me to go into some other more artistic line of work, something that *deserved me,* as she put it. And even though this comment was part of a larger speech that was meant to be empowering, I always took it as a scolding. I lacked the *something* to be an artist — a specific passion? Necessary conviction? Heart? I didn't know what I was lacking, but I wasn't going to find it today, and definitely not this weekend. By Helen's definition, she wasn't lacking. Her work as a magazine editor was artistic. She said it gave her plenty of room for creativity.

"I can make references to Mr. Darcy," Faith said defensively. "If that's what you're looking for. But I'm more of a Fitzgerald girl — Daisy and her shirts, his love affair with Zelda. She burned all of his clothes in a hotel bathtub. I should try that sometime."

"I don't know that Zelda should be a role

model," I said. "Let's remember that she also went insane and did the asylum circuit."

"How's Jason?" Helen asked, sipping a glass of white wine. "Have you forgiven him?"

"He's a shit-head," Faith said. "It's who he is. As much as he apologizes for something he's done wrong, he can't really apologize for his own nature."

"That's harsh," Helen said. "But, you know . . . I hate to say this, but it's probably very wise."

"I'm confused," I said. "Does that mean you've forgiven him or not?"

"It means I've accepted him," she said, swirling her water glass distractedly. "I'm pretty sure that that's what marriage demands."

"You accept that Jason is a shit-head?" I said.

She nodded. "I knew it going into the marriage."

"Does he know this?" Helen asked.

"What? That he's a shit-head?" Faith asked. "I think that's self-evident. He does have a basic self-awareness."

"But does he know that you think he's a shit-head?" Helen said.

"It's one of the fundamental underpinnings of our relationship."

"So you don't have to have a conversation that lasts a lifetime to have a healthy marriage?" Helen asked, stabbing a cherry tomato with her fork. "That's a relief!"

"I thought you wanted me to read that at your wedding," I said.

"Ah, and this brings us to Elliot Hull —" Helen said.

"Wait," Faith interrupted, putting down her fork. "Elliot Hull? From college? The brooder?"

Faith, in her rage, hadn't recognized Elliot when she'd stormed into the party, so there was some information to fill in. I told some of the story, and then Helen took over, explaining what had happened on the balcony. Faith glanced back and forth between us, interrupting, making us back up, clarify. Between the two of us, we jerked the narration around, but every time we got things mixed up, she'd make us put things back in linear order. Faith could be an unbearable stickler, a miserable person to tell a story to. She was the kind of hyperbright person who, during a movie, asked idiotic questions that no one yet knew the answers to because the movie hadn't yet revealed all of its plot.

When we'd finally explained the story to her standards, she sat back in her chair and

132

took a deep breath. "Are you still going to be his pretend wife?" Faith asked.

"I said I would."

"It's too strange," Faith said. "Didn't you two date somewhat insanely right before we graduated?"

"Just for a couple of weeks and then he got back together with his old girlfriend."

"Now *this* I did not know. *This* changes everything," Helen said, grinning with malicious delight.

"No, it doesn't."

"Yes, it does!" Helen said, tapping her fork on her plate like a little gavel. "I must have felt that, though. I must have known it."

"Does Peter know that you two dated?" Faith asked, always a bottom-liner.

I shook my head.

"Really?" Helen said. "You haven't told him? Shouldn't you? I mean, I don't know a thing about the rules of marriage, but isn't this withholding evidence?"

"I'm not saying you should tell him," Faith said. "I just think it's interesting that you haven't. That's all."

"You should still go," Helen said.

"Why do you think she should go?" Faith asked Helen. "Enlighten me."

"Do you think life just goes around handing out really rich life experiences like party favors? Sometimes one thing leads to another, in all of these unexpected ways. And people who shouldn't really even know each other get tied together in one unexpected way or another and you should follow it out."

"Rich life experiences!" Faith said. "What's wrong with dull? What's wrong with normal? Ever since Edward was born, that's all I want. I don't want rich. I just want healthy, fine, good."

"Well," Helen said, "I don't want normal." She looked at me very seriously. "You should do it because it's interesting. And, if you want the bottom line, life isn't always interesting. Later, after it's over, you can take it apart."

"Once again, I'd like to say that there's something to be said for a life that isn't interesting," Faith said. "I like it when there isn't a lot to take apart — or glue back together."

"I'm going because I told him I would," I said. "It's a weekend at a lake house with his dying mother. That's it."

"Well, now you'll have two husbands," Helen said. "And I've decided that I'm not going to have any. I'm done."

"Again?" Faith said, with an edge to her voice. It wasn't the first time Helen had sworn off men, but still, Faith could be judgmental and not particularly adept at hiding it. Truth was, Helen and I had both confessed that we were more than a little afraid of Faith sometimes, mainly because she was usually right, and so had little experience with — or patience for — people who had to struggle toward a decision. I had the feeling that rights and wrongs presented themselves in Faith's mind automatically.

"You don't remember what it's like," Helen explained. "How many times do I have to tell the story about my mother dating my gym teacher? And do I have to cry every time? Oh, and their stories are worse! Overbearing fathers and overprotective mothers. Bullying siblings. The whole awful rot of childhood, over and over. I've decided to settle for romances, not relationships. You two are lucky."

"We found our shit-heads!" I said brightly.

"Your shit-head might still be out there," Faith said sweetly.

"Really," Helen said, "I mean it. You're lucky. Your shit-head even managed to knock you up," she said, nodding at Faith. "Just sit there for a moment, both of you, and feel lucky. Enjoy it. That's all I'm asking. Just gloat inwardly for one minute and say, 'I'm lucky.' Be thankful. That's all I ask. Please. For me." We didn't say anything. "I mean it! Do it!"

"You mean now?" Faith asked.

"Right now," Helen said.

And I thought of Peter, scrubbing his golf clubs although they didn't even seem to need it, and then I thought of Elliot on the breezy balcony. I looked at Faith, and she looked at me.

"I did it," she said. "I thought of my shithead and gloated inwardly."

"Me too," I said, but I hadn't gloated inwardly.

"Thank you," Helen said. "I appreciate that."

CHAPTER ELEVEN

Peter busied himself for the next few days. He soaked and scrubbed the heads of his golf clubs. He vacuumed the inside of his car. He took an extra shift at the hospital one night for someone who had a kid starring in a play. Everything he did was normal. Perfectly normal. There was nothing I could single out as sulking. We even had sex — good sex — twice that week, as if to say to each other, *See, all's fine.* And all was fine, more or less. Peter was busy and I let him be busy.

The only glitch was our movie group. One Friday night a month we got together with Faith and Jason and another couple — Bettina, a lispy German woman, and a guy we all called by his last name, Shweers — to watch a movie and discuss it. Shweers, who was raised in Connecticut, first name Gavin, had met Bettina in a foreign-exchange program as sophomores in college and they had been married forever. They always brought great cheese and sausages. Movie night fell on the Friday before I was to leave for the Hulls' lake house.

Peter and I chatted idly on the drive over — trying to find our normal chirpy rhythm. I told him that Helen wasn't coming. Sometimes she'd join us when she had a steady beau, but she didn't like coming alone. She always made some excuse, and often enough, they were really valid excuses — lush cocktail parties with advertisers for the magazine, art openings, dates with this new beau or that. Who could blame her for not wanting to sit around and discuss our various film picks?

"What's she got going on these days?" Peter asked, while turning onto the beltway.

"She's no longer having relationships. Only romances," I told him.

"What's the difference?" he asked.

"You know the difference," I said.

"Right," he said. "I guess I do."

"It isn't Bettina's night to pick, is it?" he asked. We'd done more than our share of subtitled foreign films. Because Bettina was German, we all felt like we owed it to her not to be so American — at least not in front of her — although we never really talked about this formally. Peter and I both dreaded the subtitles.

"I can't remember," I said.

"If I wanted to read a movie," he said, "I'd crack open a novel, for God's sake."

"Reading subtitles always make me wonder what it would be like to be deaf," I told him, and this was true. Regardless of the language, I found myself trying to read their lips.

"That's distracting."

"And sometimes, I can't help it, I spend my time looking for errors in the text. It's like being an unpaid copy editor. Plus, shit, I forgot my glasses."

The fact was that we didn't like being around Bettina and Shweers. They were one of those rare couples who were not only truly in love, but meant for each other. Soul mates, if you believe in that kind of concept. Faith and Jason had a strong relationship, but it had its massive chinks, and this made Peter and me feel better. In fact, I really enjoyed when Faith confided in me. I loved that she thought Jason was a shit-head. I reveled in it, because it made my relationship with Peter seem pretty solid by comparison. I can confess that there were times after a quiet evening at home with Peter, one when I thought that I'd have rather just been alone, reading a book, taking a shower with the shower radio tuned to the pop station, that I called Faith in hopes of hearing that her night had been worse. I hoped that her night wasn't simply lacking, but that she and Jason had bickered about how to cook a chicken or, better yet, fought and slept in different beds.

Bettina and Shweers offered no such relief. They really thought the other was funny — Bettina lisping her wry commentary, peeking out at everyone from under her squared-off bangs, and Shweers inserting a little lewd humor from time to time. They delighted in each other, always seemed to gravitate to each other, ate off each other's plates, and made little whispered asides. They were never rude or overbearing about it. They weren't sweet and gushy. There was never too much PDA. They were just simply themselves around each other.

The distinction between their relationship and Peter's and mine was so slight that it was almost undetectable — except to Peter and me. We called them "the great fakes." We had a theory that at home they turned it all off and fought over strudel portions.

I looked at the roadside whipping by and said, "Maybe they won't come. Wasn't Bettina's mother visiting from Germany or something?"

"I think that already happened and they came anyway."

"Maybe her mother caused some friction," I said. "Maybe now they have an issue."

"Actually, I think they do have issues."

"Yes, but they find them interesting. Remember when we went to their house and he put the guest coats upstairs and she put them in the office, and he said, 'I wonder what that means'?"

"It didn't mean anything," Peter said.

"That's what you told him. But, see, to them it did mean something. And it was fascinating and later that night, going to bed, they talked about it and came to some deeper understanding of themselves."

"No one can like someone else that much." This was a refrain. It wasn't that they loved each other so much that chafed us, I don't think. Love, what can you do about that? What added insult to the injury was that they liked each other so much, that they fascinated each other. I thought of Elliot's comment about a conversation that lasts a lifetime. That was what Bettina and Shweers were in the middle of, and it was painful to watch.

Faith and Jason always hosted. They had the biggest den with the largest TV and the best sound system. Jason had a lustfully high-tech side. (He'd stood in line for an iPhone when they first came out.) Plus they were the only ones with a child so it was easier for them to plop Edward in his own bed and not have to finesse any late-night transfers.

We pulled up to their suburban house. It was tall and sprawling with a wraparound porch — a two-story house with one of those entryways that goes all the way up. It made me feel especially small — all of the voices echoing when you first walk in. Though I'd never say this to Faith or Jason, theirs was the kind of house that so many of our clients had — the kind of house that already felt staged.

"Let's try to get things to clip along. I'm tired," I said.

"Yeah, you've got a big day tomorrow." This was the first reference he'd made to the upcoming weekend in days. He'd said it in an upbeat way, but it kind of took the air out of the car. I wasn't sure how to respond. Did he really want to talk about it? If so, why'd he bring it up now while we were already parked in front of their house, ten minutes late?

"I guess I do," I said. "You want to circle the block a couple times?" We were usually right on time for parties and had a habit of trolling the neighborhood until other people showed up. But he knew that I was asking if he wanted to circle the block to talk.

"No, no," he said. "Let's get this to clip along. I'm tired too."

So it seemed we were going to get through this strange thing — this Elliot Hull interruption in our lives — by trying to speed up.

We walked up to the door and gave a knock. When there was no answer, we walked in. Peter was carrying a bottle of wine and I had a box of cannolis that I'd bought at the upscale grocery store's in-house bakery.

Peter called out, "Hello!"

The house seemed empty for a moment and then Jason jogged down the stairs wearing sweatpants and a T-shirt. He was always casual but not this much. "Don't take another step!" he said, holding out his hands to ward us off. "We're under quarantine!"

"What's wrong?" I asked.

"Edward's sick. His first barf session! We're so proud," he said. "Sorry we didn't call. No time. It struck and we've been running around crazy since. Do you boil water for this kind of thing?"

"He must be confused by it," I said, imagining what it would be like to throw up without any language to explain it.

"He's pissed, actually," Jason said.

"We brought wine and cannolis," Peter said. "Can we leave 'em? Once you're off duty, you can . . ."

"I think we're pretty much on duty for the rest of our lives," Jason said.

"Ah," Peter said.

"Take 'em with you. Get drunk and eat too much! Make out in a parking lot! Live it up!" Jason said. "Faith had chosen *The Breakfast Club* for tonight. You know, we were going anti-intellectual intellectualism. She was going to ask questions like, *So, what's the feminist agenda?* It was going to be brilliant!"

And then we heard Faith's voice calling from an upstairs bedroom. "Jason! Get ice chips!"

"Duty calls!" he said, and ran to the kitchen.

On the way back to the car, Bettina and Shweers pulled up in their gas-electric.

"They love that damn car," Peter said.

"I can never tell if they're idling or off, though."

"That's the problem with them. They're stealth."

"We should tell them," I said. "Maybe unload some cannolis."

We walked up and Bettina buzzed down the window.

"Ist something wrong?" she asked. Shweers leaned over her lap and peered up at us.

"Edward has a bug," I said. "He's throwing up."

"So we've been cast out," Peter said. "How about the four of us go grab a drink or something?" This caught me off guard. I glanced at him and he smiled.

"Uh, well," Bettina said.

"We should probably head home," Shweers said. "We're both so overrun with work that we barely got here."

"We should work," Bettina said. "Ist probably for the best that we work."

"Oh, right," I said. "That makes sense. You should catch up while you can."

"You want some cannolis for the road?" Peter asked.

"No, thanks," Shweers said. "We're watching our sugar."

Bettina smiled through her gap teeth.

"Have a nice night!" I said.

"Work, work, work!" Bettina said.

She buzzed the window shut and they drove off — almost silently in their stealth car.

I looked at Peter. "Work? Work? Work?" Bettina worked in botany. I was pretty sure that she worked in a lab, cross-pollinating plants. I'd never heard her mention taking work home, being overrun.

"I'm suspicious of them," Peter said. "They probably just want to be alone together, and there's something that's just not right about that."

"Why did you ask them out for drinks?" I asked as we got into our own car.

"I was being polite," he said, but I didn't believe him. It seemed to me that as much as we didn't want to be with Bettina and Shweers, it was better than being alone. How were we going to pass the evening now that we didn't have the distraction of movie night? Were we going to have to talk? "The great fakes," he said, twisting the key in the ignition. "Maybe they're going home to finish an enormous fight."

But, suddenly, I was jealous of that prospect too.

So with our wine and cannolis, we were sent home. I ate two on the way. Peter ate three. We drank some of the wine while watching an HBO special that we'd already seen. I looked around our small living room. The room itself was put together nicely — I do

146

actually have an eye for design; even Eila had called me a natural more than once and had started to consult me on swatches and room arrangements and wall colors. But I wondered, if she was there, would she have said that there was a sadness here too that was palpable? There was a time, before we were married, when I'd sit on the floor between Peter's feet and he'd rub my head anytime he was watching sports. Like one of those bicycle-powered televisions that only play if you keep pedaling, it was a compromise, but also it usually led to a shoulder rub and then a row of kisses on my neck and, soon enough, neither of us cared what was on television. Were we sad or just tired or was this what contentment felt like — something more akin to resignation?

We went to bed early, and, with Ripken curled up at our feet, his tail joyfully padding against the mattress, Peter leaned over and kissed my forehead. "So, you're all ready to have fun with the box turtles?" he said.

"Do you want to talk about it now?"

"What do you mean? What's there to talk about?"

"You've brought it up twice, so I think there's more to say. Isn't there?"

"I don't think so. It seems settled." He shrugged.

"So you're fine with this now?"

"I was always fine with it, *really.* It's not a big deal," he said. "I'll have a nice weekend, kicking around, playing house alone. Maybe I'll invite Jason and some other work guys over."

"Take Ripken out to the park," I said. "He's been missing you." I rolled away from him but then quickly rolled back again. I'd be waking up early in the morning and we'd already decided that I'd take a cab to the train station so he could sleep in. This was our last chance to talk before I left. I wanted to ask him what he started to say about me on the balcony when he said that I wasn't the kind of person to do something like this. He'd started to say that I was too *something.* Too what? I didn't really want to know. I thought about Faith's comment — that it was interesting that I hadn't told him that Elliot and I had dated, somewhat insanely, as she put it. I said, "I thought you were jealous."

"I tried it on and it didn't fit. Too tight in the collar." He plumped his pillow expertly, like a hotel maid, and lay his head down on it so that it fluffed up. And then he added, "It's no way to live."

Chapter Twelve

The train was nearly empty. I pressed my head against the window. The seats still smelled like too many people, though — the eggy stench of commuters. I wondered whether or not I was lucky, like Helen said. I didn't believe in luck, really. I lost my mother as a five-year-old. That wasn't lucky — even if I survived the accident. If you believe that some people are lucky, you have to believe that others are doomed. That didn't seem like a fair trade.

I watched the trees until they became nothing but blurred greenery that only represented trees. What is a marriage, anyway? I wondered. It's a representation of love, but it isn't love itself. I thought of the mini bride and groom that I'd insisted on having on top of my wedding cake. I couldn't begin to remember where they might be now. Had they been a prop used by the caterer? Had Peter and I bought them? Were they packed away in storage somewhere, fitted into the box that held my gown and veil? What became of those two little representations of marriage? Surely it was a bad thing to have lost them so completely. One day, would I find them rattling around in the bottom of a dusty silverfish-infested box, having been broken into shards — a little porcelain face, a shoe, a pair of clasped hands?

The train made brake-hissing stops. People came and went. They met each other on the platforms — hugged each other perfunctorily, little gestures, representations of love — and rolled their suitcases to escalators. This made me anxious. I decided to distract myself. I pulled out my cell phone and dialed. I started with my father. I'd neglected to tell him that I wouldn't be making our Sunday brunch.

I told him, "I'm going away for the weekend with an old friend."

"The old college friend? The thinker?" he asked. It was unusual for him to have recalled a detail like that and return to it.

"He's actually worse than a thinker," I said. "He broods."

"That's what you get from the humanities," he said. "Oh, the humanities!" It was an academic's joke. My father had an arsenal of these — none of them funny.

I was wondering if he'd ask if Peter was coming along. He didn't.

"Call me next week," he said. This too was unusual. I wondered if this had to do with him having opened up to me or if it had to do with the brooder. I wasn't sure. I promised that I'd call.

I tried Faith next to see how Edward was faring.

"He's fine. Sleeping, and so is Jason. We're exhausted and on high alert. Who will fall next?" she said, ominously. "And then there were two . . ."

"I'm sure you'll be fine," I said. "Don't you get some superpowers as parents?"

"I wish. Well, you know, Jason was great last night, though. He was really together and nurturing. I feel bad about calling him a shit-head."

"He has a certain artsiness," I said.

"And what is his art, exactly?"

I wasn't sure. "The art of life?" I said weakly.

"Well, then," she said, "he's an abstract impressionist in the art of life, I guess. I wish I knew how to market that. Who would be the paying customer?"

And as quickly as that the compliment turned into an insult. I almost said, "I think you are the paying customer, Faith," but I held back.

"Wait," she said. "Where are you? Isn't it Saturday? Are you going?"

"I'm on the train."

"And so you opted for *interesting?*"

"I could get off the train and go home. It would be that easy," I said, one hand rummaging idly in the bottom of my pocketbook, playing a game of identifying objects by touch. My fingers found a cherry-flavored Chap Stick, the lone key to my father's front door.

"Do what you want to do," Faith said. "I mean, barf isn't the only way to get a rise out of your husband and find something you've been looking for in him."

"What does that mean?" I asked.

"Nothing. I'm delirious," she said. "Don't listen to me."

"Are you saying that I'm doing this to get a rise out of Peter?"

"No, no. Forget it! I was — what's that word? *Transferring.* I was transferring my relationship issues onto you. Seriously, don't listen to me."

"I'm not doing that, Faith. I'm not doing that at all."

"I think the baby's waking up," she said. "I gotta go. Please, ignore what I said. Seriously." And then she hung up.

My fingers fiddling with a half-eaten roll of Tums and a lipliner, I wondered if I wanted Peter to be jealous. I did. I truly did. Who wouldn't? But was that the purpose of this whole thing? To get a rise out of him? To find something that I've been looking for in him? I worried about this for a little while, and then slowly but surely, I worried that it wasn't true. That it was worse than that. What if I wasn't doing this to get a rise out of Peter? What if I wasn't looking for something in him? What if I was beyond all of that kind of wanting from him or knew that it was useless to try? He gave what he could. I knew his limitations. What if I was doing this for myself?

I called up Helen next. Whenever my psyche ferreted its way to some guilty sore spot, Helen was the best person to call. She loved assuaging guilt, because I think she liked to assuage her own in the process.

She was getting a mani-pedi as part of a bachelorette day for a work friend. "It's better than trying to pretend you're titillated by a male stripper dressed like a cowboy."

I laughed. We'd been to this humiliating event together about ten years earlier — faux leather chaps, a pretty but frightened guy with a lasso and a room full of women trying to pretend he wasn't gay. "I'm glad that brand of feminism is dying."

"The kind where we have to pretend we're men? Good riddance." There was a momentary pause while she talked to the manicurist, picking colors. "And so you're going, aren't you? Are you already there?"

"I'm on the train and just got into a tiff with Faith."

"Oh, well. Faith. She doesn't get it. Sometimes I think there are two kinds of people. Those who want to live life and those who just want to survive."

"She used to want to live life. Didn't she? I mean, she was pretty wild in her day. Remember when she got kicked out of that club for overly aggressive dancing and that pot dealer she dated . . ."

Helen sighed. "I think babies bring out the survival instinct. I don't blame her."

"It might strike us one day, I guess."

"What did you fight about?"

I told her the part of the conversation when she said I was doing this just to make Peter jealous or to find something in him. "That's condescending. Don't you think?"

"It's bullshit."

An elderly woman had shuffled into my car and was sitting across the aisle. She was otherworldy — from that more distinguished era when people dressed up for train rides. I lowered my voice respectfully. "It *is* bullshit. I mean, she'd said something nice about Jason and then immediately undercut it, which she always does, and this time only because I tried to tell her that he's artistic."

"Oh, that. Well . . ."

"What do you mean 'Oh, that, well'?"

"You do that."

"I do what?"

"You use Jason by trying to tell us the best parts of Jason, but, well . . ."

"Well, what?"

"You're really talking about yourself. It's subconscious."

"I am not using Jason to talk about my-self."

"Jason isn't artistic."

"Yes, he is. He practices the art of living." As soon as I said it, I felt ridiculous.

"Jason owns and operates a taco hut. He's smart and funny. But he owns and operates a taco hut, quite happily. You like to see him as something more because you like to see yourself . . ."

"As something more? Are you saying I'm not enough?" Why had I counted on Helen to lift me up? She was unpredictable at best. Sometimes she could sense weakness and would only make things worse. I felt stupid for having forgotten that she had an elaborate assortment of traps; this one would surely go under the category of *just being honest* — one of my least favorite.

"I think you're more than enough!"

"Excuse me?"

"You know what I mean," Helen said, not as ruffled by the conversation as I'd have liked her to be. "I think you're fantastic! *You* sometimes don't think you're fantastic enough."

I thought about driving Eila from house to overpriced house, carrying the briefcase she'd given me stuffed with its charts and data and contracts, how she would sometimes ask me to crank the oldies station while she sang off-key harmony to Carole King. Was I really just a chauffeur for someone who was too batty to drive?

"I've got to go. My stop's coming up."

"Don't be mad at me," Helen said.

"I'm not mad," I said.

I heard someone in the background squeal. "The bride," she whispered, "has just consented to a Brazilian wax. Oh, joy."

We hung up then, and soon the train came to my stop. Through the smeary window, I could see Elliot standing on the platform, his arms crossed. He was staring at the ground, his face knotted in thought. The train kicked up a breeze that ruffled his hair. I got up, grabbed my bag, shuffled out of my seat, down the aisle. I paused there, knowing I could pay the conductor to let me stay on until the next stop then turn around and get a ticket home. I looked at my cell phone. No messages. I could go home to Peter and feel lucky and be thankful.

But then I realized I was thankful — for this, for running into Elliot again in the ice-cream shop, for choking on the kabob, for making the agreement on the balcony.

I walked down the train's mighty steps and onto the platform, but Elliot was gone. Was he having second thoughts of his own? Had he left me there? I turned a small circle and almost headed back onto the train, but then I saw him, walking toward me, picking up speed once he caught my eye. And I was afraid for a brief moment that he was going to pick me up and spin me around like Ellen Maddox at the icebreaker. I wasn't ready for that, was I? I stiffened up. He stopped abruptly, stuck out his hand as if we'd never met before.

I shook it.

He said, "I like your shoes."

■ ■ ■ ■

PART TWO

■ ■ ■ ■

CHAPTER THIRTEEN

Elliot drove me from the train station in his mother's Audi convertible, a gift she'd gotten for herself when she retired from real estate. "She worried she'd started puttering around the house in a way she found too elderly," Elliot told me. It was a sporty coupe with five gears and a lot of kick. Elliot apologized for driving it like a teenager. His own car was a sad four-door sedan that he bought off of a friend who was trying to raise money to get to the West Coast and make millions flipping houses. "You hit the gas and about forty-five minutes later it decides whether or not it feels like going. I feel like an asshole loving this car so much. But I do. I just love it. That's all."

My hair blew wildly around my head, but I was happy to be windswept. I felt like a teenager too, though I hadn't had any convertible rides in my high school years. There's something about cars, isn't there?

Something about a man and a woman confined in a small space, rocketing along a road — it feels powerful and intimate at the same time, like sex. I couldn't get it out of my head that Elliot and I had been lovers — rambunctious young lovers, as desperate as we were clumsy. Images of the two of us amid laundry and library books, wrestling through sex, flashed in my mind.

We talked about the smell of commuters, and the old-fashioned loveliness of trains, and when he noticed my laptop in the foot-well, he told me that the lake house didn't have any Internet hookup and that they lived in the Bermuda Triangle as far as cell phones went.

"I'll check in with Peter on the landline," I said, and it felt good to say his name as some sort of clear reminder. "But I won't miss the Internet," I said and then blurted, "If I get one more piece of spam telling me that my penis is too small, I might need to go to a support group." I immediately wanted to reel the comment back in.

But Elliot laughed. "It's the Russian Internet brides that get me," he said.

"Why didn't you get one of those for this weekend?" I asked.

"The postage was way too expensive," he said. "Plus, the Russian accent is cluttered with too many rolling *y*'s. I prefer speaking uncluttered English with you." This made my stomach flip like I was a kid sitting in the backseat of a car cresting a hill at top speed.

But we were driving along a flat tree-lined country road, plastic mailboxes flashing by.

"You know, I didn't tell my mother I married *you*," Elliot said.

"What do you mean?" I asked.

"You came along after the fact. I'd already told her that I married someone named Elizabeth."

"Elizabeth?"

"Yes."

"And what does Elizabeth do?"

"We didn't get that far."

"But I met your mother once. What if she remembers me? Well, I guess it was a long time ago . . ."

"I'm hoping she'll be foggy on the details — though you haven't changed — not at all."

"That's nice of you to say," I said flatly. Of course I'd changed, especially in the last year. I'd noticed more wrinkles, freckles on my chest, and the faint blue webbing of some kind of varicose map just above one knee that I'd decided to ignore.

"It's true!" he said.

"Okay, okay," I said. "Thanks."

"Also, I should mention that there are a few wedding gifts to open. Apparently my mother was excited to share the news. They look like toasters and coffeemakers, mostly. But Jennifer knows I'm not really married to you. She knows the real story. I've filled her in."

"Jennifer? Your sister?" I'd only seen her in a series of pictures taken on a fishing trip. She'd been a sunny kid in a life preserver, about three or four years younger than Elliot.

"Her husband is on a business trip and so she's here with the kids." He'd hesitated before the words *business trip* as if this weren't quite right.

"She has kids?"

"Oh, right, that happened after I graduated. She got pregnant her freshman year of college, transferred to a school close to home. She had the baby, lived with my mother for a few years, and kept going to school. She graduated on time. She's really amazing. Her daughter is eight now. Her name is Bib. Jennifer got married two years ago to Sonny. They had a baby boy six months ago. They call him Porcupine."

"I never met your sister."

"You'll love her."

"And I'll meet Porcupine and Bib?"

"Those aren't their baptismal names," he said.

"And I'm Elizabeth."

"Right."

"And we *didn't* meet in college."

"We didn't."

"Does this mean I never slapped you in that bar?"

"You never *grabbed my face* in that bar," he corrected.

"Where did we meet?"

"We met at a monthly book club."

"Do you go to a monthly book club?"

"No," he said, "but I should. Do you?"

I shook my head.

"But now you do!" he said. "I said that I fell in love with you at the book group because of the way you fought for Nabokov."

"Well, I *would* fight for him," I said, imagining Elliot Hull falling in love with me as I gave a fiery speech to spinsters about why *Lolita* should never have been banned. "What if we get caught lying? Are you good at lying?"

"No," he said.

"I'm not either."

"I get flustered. Speaking of which, your last name is Calendar."

"Elizabeth *Calendar?*"

"There was a calendar sitting on a table nearby. I once had a music teacher named Mrs. Calendar. It's a real name."

"As long as it's someone's real name . . . I mean, I'd hate to have a fake name that also sounded fake." I stuck my hand out the window and pushed against the rush of air. "Shouldn't we have worked all this out earlier?"

"We should have. Wait," he said. He slowed down and pulled over on the dusty shoulder. The air suddenly fell still. Everything was quiet. "I'm sorry," he said. "See, I knew this wasn't a good idea. What do you want to do? I'll do anything. Do you really want to go through with this?"

I *did* want to go through with it, especially now that I was with Elliot again — alone. I didn't remember the specifics of his childhood, but I had a strong impression. He'd been a sickly kid with an absentee father, a strong, almost glamorous mother, a younger sister he doted on, some family money. Mostly it was a kind of solitary childhood, almost as lonesome as mine — a boy poking around a lake house during the long slow summer days. He'd talked about the lake house like it was an entire universe and it had lodged in my memory too as a wistful, dreamy place, bittersweet. So I wanted to see the lake house, sure. I wanted to know this part of Elliot's past. I wanted to see his mother again — always fascinated by mothers. I wanted to meet the beloved sister and her brood. But was I able to admit that I also wanted to see the life that I could have been a part of? Doesn't everyone want to believe that their lives had alternate possibilities? I must have known this on some level, because part of me hoped that the lake house would be just as billed — wistful and dreamy — but another part of me hoped that it wouldn't live up to its lasting impression. The pragmatist in me — with her boxy worldview and prim manners, hair pinned up in a tight little bun — wanted to have a look around for curiosity's sake and then, with a manageable ache of disappointment, go home to my husband — very happily, content with my life decisions. It wouldn't be this simple, of course. Nothing is. "Our intentions are good," I said. "If we get caught lying, we can always say that."

Elliot put his hand on the gear shift and jiggled it in neutral. "I'm glad you're here," he said. "It's strange that we're lying, because it seems like we aren't."

CHAPTER FOURTEEN

Elliot pulled down a long gravel driveway lined by a white split-rail fence. There was a stand of trees that opened onto a field and at the edge of the field stood the house. It was tall and lean with weathered cedar shingles and blue shutters. One of the upstairs windows was open and there was a gauzy white curtain rippling like a veil as if there were a real bride somewhere in the house.

As Elliot parked at the side of the house, I looked down a sloping lawn that led to the lake. It was a beautiful body of water that made me think of the word *body* — curving and stretching as it did from the Hulls' tall grass bank to the far side where other houses were nestled in the woods.

The Hulls had a dock wedged into the bank with orange rowboats on either side. There were two Adirondack chairs situated on the dock, facing out. Bird feeders made from gourds painted a bright yellow bobbed in nearby trees. There was an old wooden shed off to the right with a swayback roof. A fishing net hung from a hook on its front door. In the distance, motorboats were revving their engines.

I got out and stood there on the lawn for a moment, until Elliot walked up behind me. "So this is it. The famous lake house," I said.

He looked at me, surprised. "Did I talk about it a lot?"

I nodded.

"Did I overhype it?"

"No," I said. I used to imagine a young Elliot Hull mucking around on the muddy bank — one of those kids who talk to themselves while playing, acting out all the various parts. It was, in fact, a dreamy place — the expansive blue sky and blue water, the dragonflies, the yard, the grand house. "What kind of sickness did you have as a kid?"

"Asthmatic," he said. "They brought me here to air out. I used to pee off the dock."

"Everything seems so alive."

"You're surrounded by a lot of little heartbeats out here," he said. "Everything's got a pulse."

"I've been in cities for too long," I said,

looking at the rippling lake. I felt serene, like I could say anything. "I imagine you took Ellen Maddox out here."

"Ellen Maddox. It's been a long time since I heard that name. My mother didn't like her. She didn't like Claire either."

"Did she throw any engagement parties for you out here?" I pictured a few big white tents, caterers, white balloons tied to chair backs.

"Claire and I both kept putting off an engagement party, and then it was over." He shrugged. "And with Ellen, it wasn't a serious proposal. We were twenty-two. And then there was that trip she took to her grandfather's funeral out west. And the flight attendant."

"What if her grandfather hadn't died?" I asked.

"He was very sick," Elliot said, "and old. He was like ninety. He'd have died of something else by now."

"What if she hadn't met the flight attendant? That's what I mean."

"There'd have been some other flight attendant," he said. "Figuratively speaking."

"Figuratively speaking," I said. "I'm living a figurative existence right now. Everything I say is figurative. *I'm* figurative." I realized that this was one of the reasons I felt so calm and liberated. Nothing was quite real.

But Elliot was agitated. He said, "I have a story for you."

"Okay."

He looked out at the dock and then his eyes skittered across the lawn. "The other day, I ran into someone I knew at the grocery store here in town. We'd been on a summer league soccer team together. He was shopping with a kid in one of those baby seats and another kid who was pulling things off the shelf, and his cart was over-flowing. I'd come in to buy a lime. I was tossing a lime into the air and catching it. And it seemed so sad to me. A lime. One lousy lime. I wanted a gin and tonic. And he said, 'I remember when I used to come to the store to buy one thing. Don't rub it in.' And I said, 'Don't *you* rub it in.' And he didn't understand what I meant so he laughed like he got the joke."

"But there was no joke." I knew what he meant. I'd seen those families in the store too — the exhausted mothers who seemed to have a hundred arms juggling pacifiers and cans of beans and little Ziploc bags of Cheerios. I'd watched them while holding my little handheld basket of shampoo, and had felt a strange mix of sympathy and jealousy.

"No," he said.

"You felt like he was rubbing it in — the kids, the full grocery cart?"

"His mother was probably fine too. Not even close to almost dying."

"And his wife was probably real."

"Probably."

"I know how that feels," I said.

He stuffed his hands into his pockets. "I think that's one of the reasons I want you here. Not just for the lying part. But because I thought you might understand."

"Every loss is different," I said, trying to shake off the responsibility.

"I don't know about that. I mean, in the end, the feeling you're left with, it loses its particulars. I think loss is loss . . ."

". . . is loss."

We were silent for a minute and then a little girl walked around the far corner of the house. She was boxy and dark-haired, holding a bucket up over one shoulder like a pocketbook. She was wearing soccer shorts and rubber boots and a tie-dye shirt. She squinted at us as if a little nearsighted and then trudged over. She put the bucket down at her feet and said, "Mom sent away for that kit, Elliot. And it came in the mail." She turned to me. "The kit is of a mouse that an owl ate and then regurgitated its skeleton. Regurgitated means throwing up."

"Oh," I said. "That's kind of cool."

"Bib, this is Elizabeth."

"Hi," Bib said, squinting at my face for a second, then turning back to Elliot. "It's on the hall table because Mom won't let me put it on the kitchen table where there's better light." She turned to me again to explain. "I use tweezers and I wear gloves. The mouse is *fully* dead."

"Bib has a very focused mind," Elliot said.

"What's the bucket for?" I asked.

She shrugged. "I'm out looking for specimens. I pick them up with a stick though. Don't worry."

"Found anything today?"

"Not really."

"How's everything in the house?" Elliot asked, his eyes searching the windows.

"Porcupine is taking his nap. He regurgitated this morning on me." She pointed to a spot on her tie-dye. "And Grandma is taking a nap too. But I think everyone will wake up soon." She hitched the bucket over her shoulder again.

"Nice to meet you," I said.

She nodded. "We have a nesting eagle and eagles can pick up a baby sheep up to twenty pounds and just carry it away. Right up off its feet. Its *hooves.* You should be careful."

"Luckily, I weigh more than twenty pounds," I said.

"But still," she said.

"You're absolutely right."

"An eagle could lift Porcupine," she said, without much expression, as if this wouldn't be the worst thing that could happen. "Lift him right up to the sky." She walked away.

"That is Bib," Elliot said. "She goes to a school that encourages kids who are, well, hyperbright."

"She seems very smart."

"She's too smart."

"So," I said.

"So," he said.

"We should go in?"

"I guess we should. There are some gift-wrapped toasters waiting to be set loose into the world."

"Let's liberate the toasters," I said.

He shook his head and took a few steps toward the lake. "That wasn't the story I had to tell you, about the guy in the grocery store."

"It wasn't?"

"It's a story, sure. It's something I've thought about, but it isn't the story I was going to tell you when I said that I had a story to tell you." He was quiet a moment then, looking at the grass like he'd lost something there. "I saw you through the plate-glass window of the ice-cream shop. I was walking by and I saw you standing there, in line. It was like a vision and I stopped dead and my heart was pounding. I can't explain it, but it felt suddenly like I'd been looking for you everywhere for years, but I didn't know it. And then I found you. And I was wondering what to do — not about whether or not to go in but instead, I don't know, I think I was standing there waiting to figure out what kind of person I am. Weird time to be thinking about it, I guess."

I imagined him there now, watching me, standing on the sidewalk in his baggy shorts and his ball cap. Hadn't I felt the same thing, that Elliot Hull had finally shown up after all these years? But I couldn't tell him that. I was afraid of how much he'd confessed, of how much was suddenly laid bare between us. "What kind of person did you turn out to be?" I asked, fighting a tightness in my throat.

"I was so in love with you. You wrecked me for years. And I tried to fix it with Ellen Maddox and with Claire and with women in between and even with philosophy, which I thought might give me some distance from things like you, well, from you . . . some lofty distance. But it didn't. Nothing fixed it. That's what I realized standing there — I was still in love with you, that I'd never stopped being in love with you."

"What kind of person did you turn out to be?" I asked again. I didn't move. I was afraid that if I tried to take a step, I'd fall. My limbs felt like they were made of air. I watched Bib, who was walking through the reeds at the edge of the lake. There was something in her bucket now — maybe a rock. It made a hollow gong when she dropped it to her feet.

Elliot was pacing. "I turned out to be the kind of person who doesn't turn away and keep on walking down the street. I turned out to be the kind of person who goes in and says something idiotic like ordering two scoops of you and then begs my way into your life."

I wasn't sure what to say. I was afraid of saying anything that might lead him on. But, at the same time, I was exhilarated that he was the kind of person who didn't turn away. "Is this why I'm here? Did you plan all of this?"

"No! I didn't know that this would happen. I'm not a mastermind. Who could have arranged all of this?" He waved his arm with a swooping gesture. "I lied to my mother. She is dying. It wasn't even my idea that you come here." He thought about this for a moment and then shook his finger. "But I might have willed you here. Some people believe in that kind of thing, although I've never willed anything to happen before." Then he thought for a moment. "Put it this way: I'd have willed it if I could have. I'm guilty of that."

There was a nice breeze and I could see Bib squatting on the muddy bank, poking something with a stick. Was I still in love with Elliot Hull? Was that what I'd felt in the ice-cream shop? Love? If it was love, it was also mixed with fear. Elliot still terrified me. This story he was telling me — who would confess such a thing at a moment like this? I suddenly felt angry. "Why are you telling me this?" I asked, my voice rising. "Why now? Why can't you just let things progress, the way normal people do? Why can't you just . . ." Was I going to ask him to put his love in packets and dole it out incrementally? I stopped short. I knew that this would never happen. This was Elliot. This was the way he loved me.

"It's okay," he said. "I'm not asking you to really respond. I had to tell you the truth. That's all." He crossed his arms against his chest, looked at the ground and shook his head ruefully. He was conflicted and he wore the struggle openly in the restlessness of his body, his gestures. "It wouldn't be fair to ask you to go inside if you didn't know that story. It wouldn't have been fair. We can get back in the car. I can drive you back to the city if you want or put you on a train . . . or you can come inside."

I closed my eyes for a moment, and when I opened them, he was still standing there, waiting for me. "Let's concentrate on the lie," I said. "Let's just stick to that."

CHAPTER FIFTEEN

And now, we walked up the back steps of the deck and through the French doors into the kitchen. We were both unsteady, and I thought that we had a kind of nervousness that might just seem like the authentic nervousness of newlyweds who've eloped and are now introducing each other to family for the first time.

We stood uncertainly in the kitchen. Jennifer was washing Porcupine in one side of the double sink. I could see his wet head and one pink, plump arm. She hadn't noticed us yet so, not knowing quite how to start, we were glancing at each other. There was the lingering weight of Elliot's confession, the *story* he'd told me, and each glance felt like that weight was shifting between us.

Against one wall was a white sofa with bright pillows, which seemed out of place in a kitchen, but then why not have a sofa in the kitchen? Books were everywhere.

Built-in bookshelves took up one wall — where someone else might have put extra cabinets. Books were also littered on the counter and on the kitchen table, and there was a small stack on the sofa itself. Most sat, spine-up, in various stages of arrest. I could hear Eila in my mind saying, "Clutter, clutter, clutter! No one wants to inherit all of your junk, even psychically!" She was no fan of books. If there was a bookshelf, she'd take the books out and put in vases. I knew she'd fuss about the wall of family photos too. And it didn't help that they were all in different-size frames. "People have enough family! No one wants to buy your baggage along with the house!" But these photos weren't staged or even the normal frame after frame of smiling people dressed up for various occasions — the kinds of photos I've always been jealous of. My graduation photo, for example, is a lonesome shot of me and my father taken at a great distance, likely by another student, the two of us standing there next to each other, but with a damning inch of space between our boxy shoulders.

These photos were completely different. There was a picture of Jennifer holding a scratched-up knee; another with her squeezing a lanky cat. There was a photo of Elliot as a four-year-old, squatting over what looked to be a dead bird, examining it very happily, like a joyous scientist who just made a groundbreaking discovery; and another of him as a teenager, slumping in an armchair, with a look of abject disenfranchisement on his face — the brooder! There was a photo of an old woman in waders, and some old men standing in front of bushels of tomatoes. There was one startlingly beautiful picture of Elliot's mother, Vivian — almost the way I remember her — standing in this very kitchen, on one leg, trying to hitch up the slingback of a high heel. There was another photo that must have been taken from one of the upstairs bedroom windows. In fact, on one side of the photo there was the rippled edge of a thin curtain, a ghostly ribbon. It was a picture of the grassy lawn, the dock, and in the corner the little shed. It was summer. In the photo, Vivian was wearing a white one-piece and a large straw hat. Jennifer was barely walking age, wearing a ruffled skirt and no shirt, and Elliot was a scrawny boy in a white T-shirt and swim trunks. The person who took the photo must have called to them first — they were all looking up at the window. Elliot had one hand cupped at his forehead to block the sun, fishing rods sitting at his muddy feet. Vivian was pointing out the person in the upper window to Jennifer who was waving. They'd been caught in the middle of the afternoon on an ordinary day, sunstruck, beautiful. Vivian's face is slightly clouded — does she love the person in the window? It's hard to say.

I adored the photos, every one of them, and the mismatched frames — the history of quiet honest moments that they represented, the history of a real family. Eila was wrong. Sometimes people do want to inherit your junk, even psychically, and some people don't have enough family.

Jennifer, who was humming to the baby, turned off the faucet and lifted him out of the sink. Elliot bounded forward then, grabbing a thick bath towel off the back of a kitchen chair. "Here you go," he said. The baby looked slippery and fat. He had a rubbery slickness that reminded me of a seal.

"You're here!" Jennifer said to me, relieved. She wrapped the baby up in the towel and wiped her long bangs out of her eyes. She was stunning — one of those naturally rosy women who, without any makeup, look like they have on blush and lipstick. She was wearing a flower-print top that had a retro-hippie vibe and shorts. She was barefoot. I remembered the picture of her in the yellow life preserver with her tan face, streaky blond hair, and a big wry smile. She'd barely changed.

"Yep," Elliot confirmed. "Jennifer, this is Gwen, who we'll be calling Elizabeth. Elizabeth, Jennifer."

"It's so great that you came." She rushed over, propping the baby up on one shoulder. She hugged me, wet warm baby and all. I wasn't expecting it, and I almost tripped backwards onto the sofa. "Thanks for doing this," she said. "It's strange but, well, she was on a tear. She was on a real tear, wasn't she, Elliot?" I assumed she meant their mother was on a tear, but I wasn't sure what kind of tear exactly. Elliot nodded. Porcupine had found one of his ears and was playing with it, pinching it open and shut. He was a beautiful baby, big-eyed, full of chins, and drooling. "Do you want something to drink?" Jennifer asked. "Are you hungry?"

I was too nervous to eat. "I'm fine. Thanks."

"This is overwhelming though, isn't it?" she asked.

"It's okay," I said. "I met Bib. She's a very interesting kid."

"Did she warn you about the eagles?" she asked.

"She gave me a stern warning," I said.

"I think she's a little terrified of the eagles."

"Well, they can lift a twenty-pound sheep off its hooves," I said.

"That is terrifying to the smaller creatures," Elliot said.

Jennifer looked out the French doors. "She's out there with that bucket. It'll be full of who-knows-what by the end of the day."

"I heard that the regurgitated mouse came!" Elliot said.

"Oh, yes," Jennifer said, not so keen on the regurgitated mouse. "Nothing could be more delightful." She looked down at her bare feet, patted Porcupine's towel-covered rump, and then looked at me, her eyes round and wet. "I was there when Elliot invented the marriage," she confided quietly. "And when he said he was married, I was as relieved as Mom was. I didn't believe him — not in reality — but he was so convincing that part of me did believe him, wholeheartedly. And he was right. It was the right thing to do. She was on a tear about not being able to die in peace because Elliot was adrift in the world and had no anchor. It was the only thing to do. We were pretty sure that she wouldn't make it through the weekend, but then she did."

"It's strange," Elliot said to Jennifer. "Don't you think? I mean, she's been her own anchor for decades. I don't know why she thinks I need an anchor."

"You could use an anchor," Jennifer said wryly, and then she said to me, "He really did do the right thing. Thanks for being here."

"You're welcome," I said.

"Elizabeth Calendar," Elliot said, "my wife!"

I turned and looked at Elliot. He was smiling at me with his head tilted. I wanted to smile too. In fact, I think I did, just a little, but then stopped myself and tried to divert some attention from his announcement. "I kept my own name?"

"You did," he said. "You're very proud of your heritage, I think. You come from cow herders and fig farmers. And you're a true feminist."

"Am I?"

"You can be anything you want to be."

"A chain-smoking Commie?"

He shrugged. "Why not?"

"Thanks, comrade," I said. "I've always wanted to smoke Gauloises and shout 'Vive la révolution' from a balcony."

"We have a balcony," Elliot said.

"Excellent."

Jennifer rubbed the fuzz on Porcupine's head so that it fluffed like a baby chick's. "She's dozing in the living room. There was a new hospice nurse who just finished up a little bit ago. Her name's Chesa. She's really great. They're all great. I went out and got the sweet potatoes she said she wanted. We'll see if she can eat some." Her voice was suddenly a little fraught, as if she was trying to sound casual but not quite getting away with it. "I'm going to get the baby dressed," she said. "You two can have some private time with her. Let me know if she needs anything."

"We'll be fine," Elliot said.

Porcupine started arching, then wailing. "He's an alarm," Jennifer said. "Time's up!" She jiggled him a little and walked quickly out of the kitchen.

"She's beautiful," I said to Elliot. "And Porcupine is very fuzzy."

But Elliot didn't hear me. He'd walked to the edge of the kitchen and was leaning against the doorway. I followed him and looked where he was looking — at the hospital bed situated in the warm sun streaming through a bay window. I could see his mother lying there, a thin body covered with a pale blue sheet, her head turned to one side, her eyes closed. Her hair was white and smooth, blending into the pillow.

"She doesn't look like a Kennedy anymore," Elliot said. "I barely recognize her until she talks . . . and then I know it's her. She has a way of putting things . . . But from here . . ." And for the first time I saw the depth of Elliot's sadness. He loved his mother. He was heartsore and he wasn't going to hide it. Elliot was here, in the pain of it. And Peter? Was it even fair to compare him to Peter? It wasn't fair, but it's what my mind did, naturally. I'd never seen Peter really sad. It was the difference between seeing a map and seeing the land itself.

"Let's go in," I said.

As if she'd heard us, Vivian opened her eyes and looked at us. She raised her hand, just a bit above the sheet, and waved us forward.

We both walked to her bedside. She pushed a button on the guardrails and the bed buzzed into a seated position.

"Mom," Elliot said. "This is Elizabeth. And this is my mother, Vivian."

She was weary but there was still brightness in her eyes, and she had the most elegant nose and long neck. She held out both of her hands, palms up. I put my hands in hers and in that small gesture, I felt like I was handing over some essential part of myself. It was so intimate and quiet. I trusted her immediately.

She squinted at me, as if reading my face, not unlike Bib. In fact, there was a brief moment in which I could see Bib in her distinctly. And then she took in my face and said, with strong conviction, "Oh, look! He found you." For a moment, I wondered if she recognized me — Gwen Merchant — from the cookies-and-punch reception over ten years earlier. I felt a whirl of panic in my chest, realizing that maybe it was already all over, that we'd been caught. I looked at Elliot. His eyes darted to me too, and he pursed his lips, poised to correct her, but then she almost sang, "*Elizabeth. Elizabeth.* I've been waiting for you to arrive." She turned to Elliot. "Get my glasses off the side table. I want to see the ring."

Of course she would want to see the ring, but for some reason I hadn't thought of it. She put on her glasses, tilted her chin up, and gazed down at my hand through her bifocals. "Oh, it's beautiful. You picked this out? My stripes-and-plaid son?" she said to Elliot. "I've never thought of you as having fine taste in jewels."

"I have *some* taste though," he said.

"I helped pick it out," I said, and I had,

this was true. It was unromantic, but Peter had been practical about it. *You're going to have to wear this for the rest of your life,* he'd said. *So let's make sure it's something you actually like.*

"And nicely done," Vivian said, and then she took off her glasses, folded them up, and laid them on her frail chest. "I'd like to get down to brass tacks," she said. "I'm no longer interested in the breezy conversations of the healthy, wasting their time with idle banter that plods and piddles, amounting to nothing but vague weather reports." Elliot was right. No one quite spoke the way she did — not just what she said but how she said it. She'd emphasize this word and that, in ways that honed the meaning, but there was also some lingering speech impediment that I couldn't put my finger on. It could have been that the meds she was on — morphine for one — were causing her muscles to go a little slack, but it also seemed like her mouth had been trained to work around some difficult *s*'s or *r*'s. But the old problem would sometimes creep in and make a consonant sound thicker, fuller than it should. She spoke succinctly and elegantly. I assumed that she spoke this way because maybe the books were all hers and she'd read them. The living room too was lined with bookshelves. There were armchairs and standing lamps — all of which seemed to invite someone to sit and read.

And almost every surface was covered with flowers. There was a fireplace in the living room and its brick front was blocked by tall vases. Arrangements with notes sticking out of them on plastic stalks were sitting everywhere except the bedside tables, which were devoted to medical essentials — pill bottles, ointments, tissues.

"I don't think we need brass tacks just yet," Elliot said. "How about icebreakers?"

"That's what I don't have time for, Elliot. You know that."

"Brass tacks," I said. "That's fine. What do you want to talk about?"

"You," she said.

"What do you want to know?" I glanced at Elliot nervously.

"Do you want to have kids?" she asked.

"See, now that seems kind of personal," Elliot interrupted.

She looked at Elliot sharply. "I want to know if I'll have more heirs one day. I don't think that's too personal!" And then she turned to me and said, "Is that too personal?"

"I do want to have kids," I said. I'd always wanted kids, even though I hadn't really

190

liked being one. I was afraid of them, from the anxious way infants seemed to crave their parents, if only by scent, to the way Helen, for example, talked about her own mother, the disappointment of a maternal failure. But I wanted kids nonetheless — babies to wash in sinks and kids who poked things with sticks. "Maybe two or three," I said.

"Children are our worthwhile murderers, and I mean that in the best way, Elliot."

"I already know this speech," he said to me. "I almost have it memorized. The 'Worthwhile Murderers' speech."

"But it's true," his mother said. "And should be devoid of guilt on either side. We pour all of our energies into our children in hopes of raising our own replacements. Elliot is better than I am. Jennifer too. So I've done my job."

Something about this struck me as so candidly loving, I was afraid for a moment that I might cry. I thought of my mother. She hadn't had the opportunity to pour all of her energies into me. Would she have said I was a good replacement? "My mother died," I said quickly. It was the kind of thing I'd only ever admitted when it was impossible not to and so I surprised myself by volunteering this. "When I was young. I don't really remember her."

It didn't seem to surprise Vivian, though. She said, "I'm sorry, dear. I'm very sorry to hear that. How old were you?"

"Five," I said.

"Do you love your father or at least respect him?"

"Yes," I said.

"And do you forgive your parents?" she said.

I wasn't sure what she meant. "For what?"

"Everything," she said.

"I think I have forgiven my father," I said. "I think so." But I really wasn't sure. Didn't some part of me hate him and his talking fishes and our awful Sunday lunches and the barren house and the dead moths? "No," I corrected myself. "Maybe I haven't."

"Every child has to go through some reconciliation with their parents. I think that your mother's death doesn't make her exempt from needing forgiveness, does it?" She glanced at Elliot. "That's a perfectly fine question. Don't even start."

"Maybe Elizabeth doesn't want to talk about these kinds of things," Elliot said, gently urging his mother to stop. "She might not want to."

But I stuck to the conversation. "I've never

really thought about whether or not I forgive my mother," I said. "Forgive her for dying? I don't think I've even blamed her yet."

"It isn't really necessary," she said. "There's time for all of this. It will make things easier, though, once you've forgiven your parents for their flawed humanity, their lack of fortitude and virtues, their warped egos." She looked at Elliot. "Have you forgiven me yet?"

"For your flawed humanity or your warped ego?" he asked.

She shook her finger at him in a mock scolding.

"I'm trying," he said. "I might need some therapy down the line."

She whispered to me, "He adores me actually. A little therapy would do him good. But don't let him get lost in the couch. Some people get lost in the couch and can't find their way out."

"I'm not going to get lost in the couch," Elliot said.

"Your father did," Vivian said. "You have a genetic tendency to want to go over your own flawed humanity with a fine-tooth comb."

"My father got caught up in therapy in the seventies," Elliot explained to me. "But that was the thing to do back then. A fad — like Valium."

"I preferred Valium," Vivian said to me, smiling, and then she asked, "Do you believe in God?"

"Can we at least warm up to religion and politics?" Elliot said. "This shouldn't feel like the Spanish Inquisition." He sighed and looked at me apologetically.

"What's a little talk of God?" Vivian said. "Do you find God offensive, Elizabeth?"

"No, I don't mind," I said. "I believe that there's something beyond us that's a greater force," I said. "A force for good. I can't believe that this is all that there is. But I was raised by a man of science so I do my best." I felt like I was revealing too much of my own life now. Should I lie a little more to play Elizabeth more convincingly?

"Then do you believe that this force enters into our existence? Does this force meddle? Will it get you a good parking space when you're late for an appointment at the bank? Do you believe in miracles, for example?"

I wanted to say yes. It seemed like the right answer to give to someone who would live only by a miracle, but there was something so frank about the way she asked the question, so frank about the way she said everything, that even though my presence in the house was based on one enormous lie, I was sure she'd have no tolerance for anything but the truth. "I'm afraid of miracles," I said.

"Ah," she said, nodding, as if this were the first interesting answer I'd given. "That's good. Fear. But you can't let it steer you." She closed her eyes. "I believe in miracles, but that's only because I have no choice in the matter." She fell silent and, with her eyes closed and her nearly instantaneous calm, I wondered if she had dozed off. But then she opened her eyes. "Do you have a working definition of love?"

I looked at Elliot and then back at her. "Um . . ." I was stumped. "I think . . . that true love should be a conversation that lasts a lifetime."

She squinted at this answer. "Elliot," she said, in a scolding tone, "are you using my material?"

"I learned from the best," he said.

"Sorry," I said.

"For what?" she asked.

"Recycling good lines," I said.

"I consider it a compliment," she said. "Where were you born?"

"Ohio." Couldn't almost anyone be from Ohio? This was a bland lie, and that's what I was going for.

"What do you do for a living?"

I didn't want to say interior design. I didn't want to say something that involved the sciences like my father. I thought of my mother next. What did I know about her? Not much. "I knit," I said. "I design things to be knitted. I'm a designer." And because that sounded too vague, I said, "I knit hats mostly."

"Hats," Vivian said a little dreamily. "I like hats. Is Jennifer making sweet potatoes? I can smell them."

"She is," Elliot said. "You promise to eat some?"

"I don't make promises anymore," she said, and then started. "Oh!" she said. "We almost forgot!" She reached for a glass on her bedside table. "Hand me that spoon," she said to Elliot. She then clinked the spoon against the glass. "I missed the wedding and the reception!"

"We didn't have a reception," Elliot said nervously.

"Ah, but I like this tradition. Old people can tap their glasses and young people kiss. It makes no sense, but I like it because it seems primitive."

Elliot looked at me, and I looked at him. We were husband and wife — we had to kiss. I gave a small shrug and he dipped in quickly and pressed his warm lips to mine. My cheeks flushed and I felt heat flood my chest.

"Love," Vivian said, "is unmistakable." She set the glass down on the table, lay back, and closed her eyes.

"Should we let you rest?" I asked.

"Pull up a chair. Read to me while I close my eyes."

I looked at Elliot. I pointed to myself and mouthed *Me?*

He nodded.

"What do you want me to read?" I asked.

She waved her hand as if to say, *It doesn't matter.* "I don't care whether it's highbrow or lowbrow. Pick at random."

Elliot handed me a book from the bedside table that had a bookmark in it. It was a novel by Elizabeth Graver, *Unravelling.* I'd never heard of it. I opened it to the marked page and I started in. "A girl showed me how to do the drawing-in, her hands as quick as barn swallows darting in and out of the walls of thread that hung from a giant spool in the ceiling . . ." I sat and read a good chunk of the novel, which was lyrical and captivating. And while I read, the kiss would sometimes return — the soft give of Elliot's lips on mine — and I would blush all over again. It was just a little kiss, I told myself, but still it kept returning, a sensation of soft skin.

This house wasn't at all what I expected. I was surprised to realize that I'd had expectations, that I'd been steadying myself for a dying mother without knowing I was doing it. Had I been preparing myself to enter a house filled with the sad songs of humpback whales? To find a man in a cable-knit sweater trapped in a pair of headphones? Had I been expecting the blunt contraction of grief that I always feared when I walked into my father's house — the conversation that always loomed but never arrived?

I wasn't unnerved by Vivian's questions, not as much as Elliot was, not at all. I felt relieved. I've never been very good at breezy conversation or idle banter, as Vivian put it. Breezy conversation has more traps and mines than the big stuff.

At some point, I heard Bib talking to Jennifer in the kitchen, the clatter of pans, and Porcupine's occasional grunt, and I lifted my head from the book. Elliot was sitting in one of the armchairs, his head propped by one hand. He was gazing at me in the way that I remembered from college, a kind of steady gaze that used to make me look at my shoes. But there was more complexity to the gaze now — an unrelenting sadness riding below the surface. Something about that sadness resonated with my own — the sadness that seemed to have been built into my foundation. The sun was still dousing the room with light. His mother's breaths had settled into the deep rhythm of sleep.

He said, "You're really here."

And with that I felt as if my heart were pitching forward, toward Elliot. I looked back at his mother, the slight inward curl of her thin hand. I thought of my father. He didn't hide his sadness as much as he'd created a fog from it and had learned to hide within it. People might not know why he seemed so distant — his very voice was tinny and hollow, in a way, as if speaking through tin cans from very far away. He was far away. "You're really here too," I said, and I meant that this household was occupied by people who were foreign to me and this home wasn't anything like the place I'd called home, or even the home I'd made with Peter, because everyone was so present, so close, so here.

It was like returning to myself — as if I'd been lost so long I forgot I was lost, gone so long I forgot I had a home once, but then found myself walking around a familiar corner, saying to myself, *I remember this place* — my heart picking up speed in my chest. Like pausing to put my hand on the trunk of a familiar tree, walking to the next corner with my eyes closed, picturing what I thought might be there, and then opening my eyes and finding it — my home, my yard, my fruit-heavy orchard trees, as if it had all just risen out of the ground to meet me.

Does this sound too outlandish? Too far-fetched? Was I crazy for letting Elliot make me feel this way? All I can say is that at that time I didn't question it. For the moment, it was too simple to question: Elliot Hull — home, yard, orchard.

CHAPTER SIXTEEN

It's hard to say if I fell in love with Elliot first or his family or both at the same time. I loved the way his mother turned conversations into something that rose up and out of the everyday into something charged — or strangely holy. I loved the way Elliot and Jennifer bickered in the kitchen and drank from whatever wineglass was sitting on the table and picked off each other's plates; the way they pointed at each other and laughed when one of them said something funny, and how they listened to Bib when she told long stories about things she'd poked with her sticks. I loved the way Porcupine was passed from one person to the next — including Bib, who held him in his tubby middle, his legs dangling the way a cat's would if held like that — and how he was passed without comment even to me, how he'd land in my arms and stare at me, his toothless mouth open, eyes wide.

Elliot spooned his mother sweet potatoes while Jennifer and I stood in the kitchen boiling shrimp, their dark gray bodies pinking and rising to the boiling surface. Jennifer told me about her wedding to Sonny in a park. Bib had worn a blue dress that she and her grandmother had made together with the sewing machine in the attic.

Elliot walked in and found his place in the conversation. "And they made my tie out of the same material. It was crooked, but perfectly crooked."

"The tie was Bib's idea," Jennifer said.

"We were matchers! Weren't we, Bib?" Bib was walking by with her pellet box.

"Yes," she said, a little shyly. "And we danced a lot. We got really sweaty. It was a sweaty wedding."

"It was. Wasn't it?" Jennifer said.

"Too bad we didn't know Elizabeth back then. She'd have made us matching knit hats!" Elliot said.

"I panicked," I said. "I don't know what came over me."

"It was fine," Elliot said. "Turns out, my mother has always loved hats."

I asked Jennifer more questions about Sonny. He was a drummer who was on tour with a band that had a small cult following in the folk world. Jennifer said, "I found him in a lost and found, literally. He'd lost a wallet, and Bib had lost a journal at a concert. Neither thing showed up so we got married as a consolation prize."

"You found what you were supposed to find," I said, thinking of Elliot ordering two scoops of Gwen Merchant and getting more than he'd asked for.

Sometimes the only thing that would make Porcupine stop crying was if someone took him outside to pace. Jennifer had to help her mother to the bathroom, and Elliot was fixing a salad, so I was in charge of Porcupine and Bib, who was already out on the deck wearing latex gloves and a face mask. Tweezers and the owl pellet were sitting on a flattened paper bag in front of her. I was holding Porcupine and pacing, as instructed.

"What are you going to do?" I asked.

"Find the mouse bones," Bib said. Porcupine was still fussing some, little complaints really. "You should sing," Bib said.

"Sing?"

"Porcupine likes the song about the screen door."

"The screen door?"

"You know: The screen door slams and Mary's dress sways. He likes that song."

" 'Thunder Road'?"

Bib shrugged.

"Does the pellet stink?" I asked.

"Not much," Bib said, still leaning over the pellet.

Porcupine fussed some more so I started humming Bruce Springsteen into his pink ear.

"Are you here because my grandma is going to die?" Bib asked.

"Um, no," I said.

"People come by a lot because she's going to die. She's my other mother," Bib said. "I have two."

"You're lucky," I said, "to have two mothers."

"And now I've got a father too. Sonny." Bib still hadn't touched the pellet. She was just staring at it. "Do you think that someone will open Grandma up when she dies? She's giving her body to science."

"I don't know," I said. "But that's a nice thing to do."

"We're just bones and stuff."

"But there's more to us than that," I said and I squatted next to her pellet. "We're imagination and love and dreams. Aren't we?"

Bib looked up at me. I hadn't realized it but she'd been crying. Her face was streaked with tears. "I can't cut open my pellet," she said.

"You don't have to," I said. "You know, we are bones, and the bones can be used by scientists, or they can fade away. But all of the other things that we are — imagination and love and dreams . . . that lives on even after we die."

Bib looked at Porcupine's dimpled knees and squeezed one of them with her gloved hand. "Where does it all go when we die?"

I pointed to her heart. "Inside the people we've loved."

She wiped her nose on her sleeve. "Barn owls have very good hearing. They can hear animals that are under the snow. Females lay four to seven eggs at a time." Porcupine started to cry. We both looked at him. "You stopped walking and singing," Bib said.

"You're right."

I stood up and paced and sang "Thunder Road" while Bib put the pellet back in its box with the tweezers, the mask, and the gloves. Porcupine rested his fleshy cheek on my chest. His body went slack with sleep. Bib and I sat on the edge of the deck, and I distracted her with stories from my childhood, growing up in a yellow house on Apple Road with the climbing tree over the driveway and the crazy Fogelmans next door, and my father who believed in talking fish.

"Talking fish?"

"Yes. They have languages. We just don't understand them."

"Maybe everything has a language we don't understand."

We sat there and watched the fireflies blink in the grass and told each other what we thought they were saying.

"That one's saying *Come here! Come here!*" Bib said.

"And that one's saying, *Can't you see I'm busy?*" I said. "Oh, and that one there is saying, *I miss you! Why are you so far away?*"

"That one's saying, *Stay with me forever at the summer house. Stay, stay, stay.*"

And I loved that firefly. I wanted to stay, stay, stay.

CHAPTER SEVENTEEN

Later, we all ate dinner in the living room gathered around Vivian's bed — Jennifer was sitting in an armchair balancing Porcupine, Bib was sitting cross-legged on the floor, and I was standing. Elliot was feeding her sweet potatoes.

"Open the wedding gifts!" his mother said.

"Not now," Elliot said. "We'll do it later." I already felt guilty about the gifts and didn't want to open them either.

Elliot and Jennifer started talking about a childhood prank — taking the rusty water from the toilet at an old ski lodge they used to go to and trying to get other kids at the lodge to believe it was iced tea and drink it.

"You drank it once," Elliot said to Jennifer.

"I never drank it," she said. "That other kid did. What was he? Canadian?"

"I'd never drink toilet water!" Bib said.

"I'd never even try to make Porcupine drink it!"

"Of course you wouldn't, Bib. *You* are the perfect child," Vivian said with a placid smile. "Those two had to learn to be good. You were born that way."

They talked and talked while Vivian took small spoonfuls of sweet potatoes. Finally, she lifted her hand in a gesture of *no more.* She tugged on Elliot's sleeve and he leaned down so she could whisper in his ear.

"Okay," he whispered back, nodding. "Okay." And then he ushered us all from the room. He put his arm around Jennifer and started to talk to her about morphine levels, and they drifted away from me for a few minutes.

I cleaned up the kitchen while Jennifer talked to hospice on the phone while nursing the baby, and Elliot put Bib to bed.

When he walked back downstairs, he looked like he'd almost fallen asleep himself. His hair was mussed and his eyelids heavy. I was drying the shrimp pot. Jennifer had gone in to talk to her mother. He was exhausted but he was smiling — a soft, tired smile.

I pointed to the photo of him on the wall, the one of him as a sulking teenager. "Look," I said. "Proof!"

"Proof of what?" he asked.

"Elliot Hull, the brooder."

He laughed. "Look at that hair, and those madras shorts. What was I thinking?" He shoved his hands in his pockets, looking distracted.

"Are you okay?" I asked.

He smiled. "I promised you a fleet of rowboats. Do you want to go for a night ride?"

"Does Jennifer need you?"

"Not now," he said. "I asked her if we could disappear. I reminded her that we're newlyweds."

I remembered the kiss again, the sweet tenderness of his lips and how Vivian had said "Love, it's unmistakable." I felt like a newlywed — anxious and flushed. Was love — real love — unmistakable? "Can anyone deny newlyweds?" I said.

"Not in good conscience," Elliot said.

The lake was quiet except for a couple of kids on a far-off dock holding sparklers. Elliot sat facing me in the rowboat, the kayak paddle resting in his lap. We were so close that our knees overlapped, my knees inside of his. The rowboat was drifting. The lake reflected a bright fat moon.

"You have a good family," I said.

"They are good," Elliot said, looking up at the sky.

"Did you ever reconcile with your father?" I asked, remembering how hurt he'd been in college, realizing for the first time that he was angry at his father and had good reason to be. As far as I could remember, he'd left the family for another woman and barely played a bit part in Elliot's life after that.

"I wrote him a letter a few years out of college, and I told him what a shit he'd been, but that I still loved him."

"Did he write back?"

"Yes," he said, nodding his head roughly. "He was very cordial. It was a nice letter. We still don't really speak."

"I'm sorry."

"It's okay," he said, and then he looked at the kids on the end of the dock, spinning their arms around so that the sparklers made lit-up hoops in the air. "You surprised me in there with my mother, answering all of her questions. You didn't like answering questions like that in college."

"I didn't?"

"No, you didn't," he said, sounding a little put out with me.

I thought of the two of us standing in the freezing shallow end of the university pool. Elliot had asked all of those questions that I didn't have answers for. "You asked difficult questions, and I was just a kid. I wasn't ready."

"Are you ready now?"

The question sounded loaded. I wasn't sure how to answer. "I don't know."

"Should I ask you again?"

"Ask me what?"

"Ask you the question that made you grab my face in the bar and stop speaking to me?"

"I don't remember the specific question," I said, but my heart started beating more quickly, as if some part of me did remember, if not the words then the feeling — like the time my apartment was robbed before I met Peter and was living alone: not so much frustrated that things were stolen as much as feeling invaded, imagining the thief going through all of my things.

"You don't?"

I shook my head, glanced up at him and away again.

"Do you want me to tell you?"

I didn't, but I couldn't admit that I still wasn't ready — for what, I wasn't sure. "Tell me," I said. The breeze off the lake was cool and I wrapped my arms around myself and tucked my chin to my chest.

"Early in the day, while we were lying in

bed, it dawned on me that you were in the car when your mother got in her accident. I don't know how or why, but it just struck me as the reason why you were so afraid in the water, why you'd cried in the pool. I pushed you on the subject, and you got mad. You finally admitted that I was right, but told me not to talk about it anymore."

"And then you talked about it in the bar." I remembered this now. We'd gone with a group of people, but as was usually the case, we'd ended up alone, in a corner talking, just the two of us.

"Today my mother asked you if you'd forgiven your mother for dying. But I didn't think of it that way. You didn't act like someone who couldn't forgive your mother. You acted like someone who couldn't forgive yourself."

"What does that mean?" I asked, holding on to the side of the rowboat, which seemed like it was bobbing now more than drifting.

"You really don't remember any of this? Do we have to have the argument again?"

"I guess we do," I said. "Because I don't know what you're talking about."

"I asked you if you felt guilty, like it was your fault your mother died."

"How could I have felt guilty? It wasn't

my fault. I was five years old. I was a kid in a car."

"That's what you said then too. You said, 'Five-year-olds don't feel guilt about something like that. They don't understand.' And I said that you got smarter, though, and one day you did understand, didn't you? You had to have understood."

"Understood what?" I asked, still gripping the rowboat.

"That you lived and she didn't, that someone came in and saved you — a stranger, a driver on that same road, and he saved you first, and ran out of time to save her. He had to make a decision and he picked you."

Elliot was right, and I knew it as soon as he said it. I thought of his mother's speech — that children became a parent's worthy murderers. It struck me as honest because it was true. In my case, it had seemed literally true. After the trip to the nursing home where the elderly auntie had let it slip that I was in the car with my mother at the time of the accident, and after I'd had that confirmed by Mrs. Fogelman next door, a few months went by as this new truth settled in through my skin, into my bones. And then there were a few years when I would imagine the stranger who saved me as I was going to sleep. I remembered the version of that stranger now, stopping his car and running into the water, and then finally diving underwater to save me — but not my mother. I was quiet.

"Gwen," Elliot said. "Are you okay?"

The kids had new sparklers now, two in each hand. They seemed to be shaping letters in the air, but I couldn't read them. I looked at Elliot. He touched my hand still holding on to the lip of the rowboat, trying to keep my balance. "And what did I say to that?" I asked. "Go on."

"You said, 'Fuck you.' "

"Ah, well, I was quite the wordsmith back then," I said, but we were beyond this kind of lightness. "What else? Finish the story."

"You said to my mother this afternoon that you haven't forgiven your mother because you haven't started to blame her yet. Why is that?"

"I don't know. What's it to you?" I thought of the owl suddenly, the barn owl responsible for making Bib's pellet. I thought of the mouse being swallowed whole and alive.

"Is it because you're still blaming yourself?"

Elliot's eyes were wet and shining. Mine too felt teary. The breeze was coming up quick off the lake. "Tell me the rest of your story," I said. "At what point did I slap you?"

"You didn't slap me . . ."

"When did I grab your face?"

Elliot looked down at his hands. He was reluctant to go on with the story. He put a hand on each of his knees. "You said you were fine with your mother's death and I should be too. You told me not to fucking psychoanalyze you. But I said you weren't fine with it. And you weren't. Are you fine with it now?"

The rowboat had made a slow half turn. I could no longer see the kids on the dock — only the black expanse of the lake. I had never been a very good swimmer. I wondered if the rowboat tipped, would I be able to make it back to the Hulls' dock? How had I gotten all the way here with Elliot Hull in a rowboat? I had a tidy life in which no one asked any important questions, no one pushed me to reveal anything that I didn't want to reveal, no one went rooting through my past to find out why I was the way I was — no thieving, all safety. "When did I grab your face?" I said again.

"You asked me why I was going through all this," Elliot said. He was almost whispering now — his voice hushed and pained and strangely tender. He looked beautiful, the dark lake at his back, the wind rippling his shirt. "You asked me why it was so fucking important. I told you it was so fucking important because I wanted to know you better than I knew myself, because I wanted to spend the rest of my life with you because I love you like that."

I looked at Elliot. That was the part that I hadn't been able to withstand, that had been so unbearable, so unforgivable. It wasn't that he had rifled through my childhood, my psyche. No. The reason behind it all — his love, his bold-faced confession of his love for me — that is what I couldn't accept.

I grabbed Elliot's face — gently this time. I held his face in my hand and then he leaned forward, jostling the rowboat, and kissed me, and I let him kiss me and I kissed him back — the rowboat turning slow circles in the lake.

CHAPTER EIGHTEEN

I woke up in the morning in Elliot's bed from his childhood summers, alone. I'd slept there, fitfully, alone too. Elliot and I had kissed in the rowboat on the lake, but those were our rules at sea. When we reached the Hulls' dock and we'd gotten back on dry land, he said, "I'm sorry. We shouldn't have done that. I know that it has to end here. I know that."

But, of course, it couldn't really end. Elliot was in love with me and I was in love with him, although we hadn't said it aloud in uncertain terms. This was our predicament, and it was worse than having an affair, wasn't it? Although it wasn't as wrong as an affair, maybe, because what we felt for each other was out of our control, it made everything more complicated.

And when I woke up in Elliot's bed from his childhood summers — Elliot having slept in one of the armchairs in the living room so that he could tend to his mother if she needed someone in the night — I felt the compulsion to run, the instantaneous guilt and dread. I knew that I had to go home as soon as possible. I had to see Peter and return to my own life, and try to make the best of that life.

The room was spare — some soccer trophies, a desk, a bureau — but it did have a landline and an old rotary phone with its spiral cord. It was nine o'clock in the morning. I dialed my home number, and looked around the room as it rang. There were books in here too, of course, adventures and fantasies and a few that seemed schoolish, math especially, as if he'd been forced to bring some work along in the summers to make up for a deficiency.

Peter didn't answer. I listened to my voice on the answering machine. I'd have to change it. My voice sounded too automated, too cold, as if I didn't really care whether people left a message or not. I hung up on myself.

I dialed Peter's cell. It went straight to voicemail. I wondered if he'd picked up another shift. I said, "Hey, Peter, there's no good reception out here. I'm going to be home by midafternoon. I don't want to waste the day. I hope you're around. We could go out to dinner maybe? That Thai place? Okay, talk to you later."

I got dressed quickly and walked downstairs. Bib was in the small den, watching *Sponge Bob.* Porcupine was in his Excersaucer nearby, pulling on a red plastic flower. The house smelled like bacon. Jennifer was in the living room, filling a glass of water from a pitcher, talking to her mother. Jennifer looked up.

"Good morning!"

Vivian faced me. *"Elizabeth, Elizabeth,"* she said. "Will you please come and open these presents! They're taunting me."

"Yeah, when are we going to free those poor toasters?" Elliot said. He was standing at the end of the hallway, holding a spatula. He read my expression, which must have been anxious, and added, "This afternoon, maybe! I've got bacon to burn." He dipped back into the kitchen and turned on the fan. I could hear its loud, low whir.

"Just a minute," I said and I followed Elliot into the kitchen. "Elliot," I said in a quiet voice.

He was laying bacon on a plate covered in a folded paper towel. "You can't go," he said.

"I have to."

"Nope. I've already decided that you

should stay through dinner, at least. Take an evening train."

"I have to go. Your mother will understand."

He stopped, put down the spatula, leaned against the counter. "I'm not worried about my mother right now. I don't want you to leave like this."

"Like what?"

"Like running away," he said.

"I have a *real* husband. A *real* marriage."

He picked up the spatula and tapped it nervously. "But, see, I've been thinking. We could . . ."

I cut him off. "I can't destroy a marriage because of a kiss on a rowboat."

"It was more than that. This isn't the beginning. This is the middle. You know that."

"I know that?"

Jennifer walked into the kitchen then, filling a vase with water. "She's out of it today. She wanted more morphine, but this is what it does to her."

Elliot nodded. "She was talking to her dead sister all night." And I realized that Elliot hadn't slept. He was wearing the same clothes from the night before.

"I have to head out early," I said. "I'm so

sorry. This is hard, but there's something at home."

"Oh," Jennifer said, glancing at Elliot. "Well, this is more than we could have hoped for anyway." She opened a packet of flower food and sprinkled it into the vase. "If it's easier, I can tell Mom. I can explain. She's so out of it, she may not understand. Don't worry."

"I'll go in and say a proper good-bye."

"Okay." Jennifer walked toward the living room. "I'm sorry you have to go," she said. "It's been great having you here, to have someone's new energy, a distraction from . . ." She didn't finish the sentence. She smiled. "Don't worry about it." And then she walked out.

A few minutes later, I had my bag and I was sitting in the chair pulled up to Vivian's bedside, telling her that I was needed at home. Elliot was pacing in the background and Jennifer was standing by, holding Porcupine.

Vivian was restless. Her eyes were closed. She said, "If I lived in Japan in the good old days, I'd have walked up a mountain to die in the snow, like a good old useless person by now." And then she shook her head. "Ice!" And I thought she was correcting herself — as if she'd meant that she should have died in the ice by now, not the snow. But I was wrong. Jennifer repositioned Porcupine and scooped up an ice chip from a glass and slipped it into her mother's mouth.

"I'm glad we got to talk yesterday," I said, and I slipped my hand through the guardrails into her hand. She grabbed my hand tightly and looked at me, surprised to find me there. Then she waved her kids out of the room. "Go!" she said. "Leave us alone."

Elliot and Jennifer paused. Then Jennifer put down the cup of ice chips and said, "Okay, Porcupine, let's go find Bib." She walked out of the room and Elliot reluctantly followed.

Vivian was coherent now, but struggling. She stared at me as if trying to see me through a dark tunnel. She said, "What's true is true."

"Yes," I said.

"I've always felt sorry for newlyweds. Doom, doom, doom. I was a damaged girl and I made a damaged decision in a mate . . . back in the Stone Age. But you and Elliot have found each other. It's a thing beyond luck, beyond wisdom."

"Thank you," I said.

She appraised me then and looked suddenly angry. "Oh, you've no idea! I cannot stand how young people waltz around with no conceivable idea!"

"I-I . . . I'm sorry," I said, unsure of how to read her anger.

"Listen to me," she said. "Let me put it thusly. Bib is afraid of the nesting eagles."

"I know," I said, assuming she was half-dreaming.

But then she gripped my hand. "You don't know!"

"I'm trying to understand," I said.

"If you let fear make your decisions for you, fear will make good decisions — but only for its own sake, not yours." She shook her head, as if to start again, more calmly this time. "Bib is afraid of the nesting eagles and doesn't want to stand in the field because she thinks they'll have a good eye on her and they'll take her from us. Right off the land. I tell her that one day she'll need to be brave if she wants to marry the man she truly loves."

This took me by surprise. I wasn't sure what to say. "Bib is a brave girl."

"And I tell you to stand in the field with a big rake and not be afraid of the nesting eagles." She stared at me — her eyes suddenly steely. I wondered if she'd confused me and Bib in some strange way, but I also knew that she hadn't. This is what she wanted to tell me. Her eyes were so sharp, so tightly trained on mine. "What's true is true," she said. "Right?"

I nodded.

"Marriage is a crock!" she said. "But love isn't. What's true is true," she said again and then closed her eyes.

"What's true is true," I said.

She nodded and loosened her grip on my hand. I stood and picked up my bag.

She said something so softly I couldn't hear it.

I leaned forward. "What did you say?"

She whispered again hoarsely, "I'd recognize you anywhere." She opened her eyes and stared at me.

I felt off balance and grabbed the back of a chair. I was sure that in that moment, she knew exactly who I was. "Excuse me?"

She blinked a few times in quick succession, as if clearing her mind. "Stay," she said. "Just a few more days. I'm dying, for God's sake."

CHAPTER NINETEEN

We seem to think that things in life are clearly labeled as right and wrong, as if the world's been divvied up by someone with a giant ink pad and two rubber stamps. We're deeply invested in the notion that when we choose to do the wrong thing, it's because we're weak or lazy or compelled by our desires or our overriding ids. Because, if this is the case, then we can blame those who do the wrong thing and pin on them the suffering that wrongness causes. And, if the world comes clearly labeled and people fail to do the right thing because of their own shortcomings, then we can believe that doing wrong is easily avoidable. We can believe that we can do right and we can be good.

I used to believe this more or less, because there is some truth in it, somewhere. But this theory sells life short. The world isn't that simple, and the labels of right and wrong, if they exist at all, get smeared to the point of illegibility. And then where are you? Or, more pointedly, where was I?

I was staying. At the time, I thought it was wrong because I felt like I was giving in to something and I've always associated that feeling of giving in with weakness. I thought that it was all wrapped up in Elliot. I think I wanted to believe that I was using Vivian's plea for me to stay as an excuse to linger here in this house, stricken as it was with so much grief and love, to linger in my role as Elliot's wife. But it wasn't that simple. It had to do with Vivian herself. It had to do with this woman, this mother, and the fact that I needed something from her. Of course, I barely understood any of this at the time.

I walked back into the kitchen carrying my stuff. Elliot had the restless air of someone in a doctor's waiting room — he looked at me expectantly, his arms crossed, his eyes wide. Jennifer was holding Porcupine and waving to Bib from the open French door, leading to the deck. I could see Bib in her waders, waving back like a sailor on a ship.

"I'm staying," I said.

Jennifer turned around. "Oh, good," she said, relieved.

"How did she do it?" Elliot asked, referring to his mother.

"I don't know," I said. "She's a force. An unwieldy force."

"I warned you about that," he said, and then he smiled broadly. "I'm glad you're staying."

"Me too."

First, I called Eila. I used the rotary phone in Elliot's bedroom, and was pretty sure that I was timing the call after Eila's tai chi class, in hopes of getting her at her most subdued.

"Eila!" she said, as if shouting her own name were an acceptable way of answering the phone.

"Hi, it's Gwen."

"Gwen," she said, letting out a full breath. The fact that it was only me meant that she didn't have to put on the whole show — maybe just a quarter of the show. I always wondered what the real Eila — or, well, that would be Sheila — was like.

"I have a sick relative. I came for the weekend and they need me to stay longer."

"A sick relative?" she asked. "What kind?"

I wasn't sure what she meant — what kind of sick or what kind of relative — so I answered both. "My mother-in-law has cancer."

"I'm so sorry," she said, although neither

sincerity nor empathy were her strong suits. "How is Peter taking it?"

I was surprised that she remembered my husband's name. "Better than I thought he would."

"When will you be back? The Westons, the Murphys, the Greers."

"I'm hoping just a few days," I said. "Hopefully, I'll be back for the Greers, Wednesday afternoon."

"Let's make that essential. The Greers on Wednesday. I *need* you, darling!" And then she started talking to her dog, Pru, and hung up.

Peter was next. I wasn't sure what to expect from him. I dialed our home number on the rotary, sat down on the edge of the bed, and waited for him to answer. On the bedside table, I noticed a small boat — the kind that would normally sit in a bottle. I picked it up. It was light as if made of balsa wood. I was expecting the answering machine to kick in, but Peter answered at the last moment, a little breathless.

"Hello?"

"It's me," I said.

"How are things with you, Mrs. Hull?" he said jokingly, and I kind of wished he hadn't sounded so chipper.

"Not perfect," I said, thinking that I could

tell him — right now — about having kissed Elliot on the lake. I set the little balsa wood boat down on the night table. "Where have you been? You sound like you're out of breath."

"I was doing sit-ups with the music cranked and almost didn't hear the phone."

"Do you crank the music while I'm not home? Is that why the neighbors give me dirty looks?"

"AC/DC," he said. I imagined him suddenly in a different life — a beloved bachelorhood — a life where he had the time to acquire his perfect abs, but he'd have a stagnant taste in clothes and hair products and music and pop culture references. Hadn't I kept him up-to-date, refusing to let him stagnate in an era, as bachelors so often do? I was good for Peter, I decided. He needed me, but, in the same moment, I wondered if he needed me in a way that really mattered. "So what's going on?"

"I have to stay a few more days." I saw Vivian in my mind's eye, the way she looked at me when she'd said, *I'd recognize you anywhere.* The moment she'd said those words to me, my heart felt full and taut, and now just thinking of them, the feeling was back. My chest filled with pressure. I closed my eyes for a moment and took a deep breath.

"Really?" Peter said. I couldn't read his tone — was he just surprised or was he enjoying his faux bachelorhood and cranked-up AC/DC?

"Don't act too bent up about it," I said.

"No, no," he said. "You just caught me off guard. What's going on?"

"She's doing badly," I said. "And I feel like I'm helping some, an extra pair of hands." I felt guilty now. I hadn't really helped much. I hadn't done the dishes even. I added quickly, "I think I'll make my vegetarian lasagna tonight and do the Mrs. Fogelman deep-freeze standbys." When I was twelve or so, Mrs. Fogelman had been the head honcho of community outreach at her church, and she and my father made a deal that I would help her out every time she cooked for charity. I learned how to make every casserole known to man, how to divvy it up in single portions and store them in freezer bags. When I went to a few conferences as a communications director, I loaded the freezer for Peter just so, but overestimated my time away and we ended up eating from the Ziploc bags for months.

"It's your forte," he said, although he pronounced *forte* as *fort*. It was a joke of my father's, one that's only funny if you don't intend it to be. "Stay and help."

"I called Eila," I said. I put my finger on the top of the balsa wood boat's sail. It was on hinges so the sail lowered down. "She was okay with it. I caught her right after tai chi."

"Smart thinking."

There was a lull in the conversation. I wondered if he was trying on jealousy again — if he was feeling tight in the collar. Or maybe we both knew that if I started to talk about what was going on, it would open up a longer, darker conversation.

"I miss you," Peter said.

And I knew that he was wrapping things up. "I miss you too," I said.

"Keep the updates coming," he said.

"And you take it easy on the neighbors."

"I will," he said. "Scout's honor."

I hung up the phone — the earpiece was so heavy that it was satisfying, in a strange way, to settle it in its cradle. The little boat caught my eye again. I pushed its sails up and down and back up again, wondering what had happened to the boat's bottle. I assumed it was broken — an errant football being tossed across the room knocking it off a shelf — but the boat with its airy body and its light frame survived intact, a little artifact of Elliot Hull's childhood. What did that mean, metaphorically? A waterless, bottleless boat?

Vivian was dozing and Jennifer was exhausted, so Elliot and I offered to take Porcupine and Bib to the grocery store with us while I shopped for the fixings for Mrs. Fogelman's deep-freeze standbys. In the driveway, Elliot and I tried to figure out the complex straps of Porcupine's car seat.

"That way," I said.

"Nope. I think it's this way," he said.

We jiggled the straps and crisscrossed them and laughed. Finally, Bib got too impatient and did it for us. "See!" she said. "It's easy!"

"For you," Elliot said.

"She's a child prodigy," I said.

"I have a very high IQ," Bib said.

"Do they test that in school?" I asked.

She shrugged. "I don't know."

Elliot drove Jennifer's minivan. "I feel like I'm at the helm of the *Proud Mary*," he said, squaring his strong shoulders. "This thing is massive."

"Who's Proud Mary?" Bib asked from the backseat.

"To explain Proud Mary I'd have to start with the steamboat industry," Elliot said. "Then move to the sixties and Credence

Clearwater Revival, and then I'd have to go over Ike and Tina Turner," he said.

"And you'd have to explain what it's like workin' for the man every night and day," I said.

"It's really hard to work for the man," Elliot said.

"Who's the man?" Bib asked.

Elliot didn't answer. He just started singing the song. I kicked in some backup — a few low *rollin's* and some *hoo, hoo, hoo, hoo,* which seemed to amaze Porcupine. We were pretty terrible, but distracting, and that was our overriding mission. I wondered when I'd tell him that his mother knew the truth. She'd *recognize me anywhere.* Why did those words strike me so deeply, even when my mind just gave them a glance? I couldn't explain it, but I knew that Elliot would have a theory. I wasn't sure that I was ready for his theories, though, about me, about mothers. He knew me so well, but I wasn't sure how it was possible. Had I once been brave enough to hand over that much of myself? I was young then. I didn't know any better, but I did know better now, didn't I? We came to a red light and I had to fight the urge to lean over the seat and kiss him. He was so kissable.

In the store, we cruised the aisles. Porcupine was now in one of the shopping cart's baby seats and Bib was asking about every odd item she couldn't immediately place — coconut milk, saffron rice, dried black-eyed peas, a pumice stone, headless fish laid out on ice chips. We did our best taking turns explaining, while trying to gather stuff for multiple recipes at once. Porcupine started to cry so I held him and bounced and pointed out things with my elbows and sandals. "Some of that," I'd say. "Um, no, no, the bigger size. That one." And there was Elliot, looking at my legs, my pointed toes. "This one? Or this one? This one here? Or that one there?"

When we got to the check-out line, Porcupine was asleep and he suddenly seemed to be made of rocks. My arms were burning, and Elliot remembered that we were missing bread, of all things. He and Bib went running off and left me at the checkout.

"They'll just be a minute," I told the cashier.

"It's a good thing your husband helps out. You've got your hands pretty full," the cashier said.

I almost corrected her, saying that he wasn't my husband and these weren't our kids, but Elliot was supposed to be my husband, so I just smiled and nodded and even threw in a tired shrug as if to say: *Oh, well, this is the way it is!*

When Elliot and Bib reappeared in view, I was relieved to see them. "Here they come!" I said, but it was more than a simple kind of joy. I felt like they were racing back to me, for me. I remembered Elliot's experience a few days earlier, running into the guy he'd known in high school with his full cart and his kids. Right now, taking long fast-walking strides, like a cross-country skier, he seemed to be gliding. He seemed happy. This was what he'd wanted, wasn't it? Bib looked happy too, swinging two bags of bread in her fists.

"Here we are!" she yelled. "Here we are!"

Here was this beautiful simple moment — this sweaty baby, this kid still wearing her rubber boots, Elliot and me in a grocery store being mistaken for a family. My childhood had suffered a gaping hole. I'd never felt absolutely in my element in any job. And had I ever felt truly and deeply myself with Peter? In this moment, pretending to be someone else's wife, being mistaken as the mother that I wasn't, I felt like I was where I was meant to be.

CHAPTER TWENTY

I cooked the rest of the day — lasagnas, squash casserole, quiches, a thick potato soup. Elliot chopped vegetables. Bib measured and stirred. Jennifer moved in and out. And Porcupine's face was sometimes bobbing over her shoulder, sometimes over Elliot's, and then sometimes I'd find him on my own — my hands dusted in flour or gritty from potato skins. At one point, I remembered what it was like to be bustling around Mrs. Fogelman in her kitchen on a Sunday afternoon, preparing meals for people who'd just had a baby or who were coming home from surgery or who'd suffered a loss. There was a feeling of greater purpose. Dr. Fogelman steered clear, and Mrs. Fogelman and I became a well-oiled machine, gliding around each other, cracking eggs, whisking, setting up various timers for different dishes. Sometimes I would pretend that she was my mother. I would refuse to look at her face, concentrating instead on the middle of her body, her pale, freckled arms, and the apron tied around her waist. I loved it most of all when it was quiet except for a radio she had set up on the back of a counter. I thought I almost knew what it was like to have a mother, but then eventually she would say something and I would look up and it would be Mrs. Fogelman, not my mother at all.

I couldn't remember ever having cooked with Peter. We'd shared a kitchen from time to time. He'd be fretting over one dish and me over another. But we never cooked together. This was different. Elliot and I swatted at each other and took time out to say, "Smell this fresh mint." We brushed past each other in the small space between the counter and the island and the stove. I'd never been so aware before of the sexy physicality of cooking — the bending, the balancing, the whisking, the urgency of the dinging bells keeping everything speeding along and then slowing down, the dipping and straightening, the bowing to the food again and again. With Elliot in the kitchen, cooking wasn't just a service. It was more of an art, something you could infuse with love and attention to detail. It was sensual.

I thought of Bettina and Shweers. Was this

the way life was for them? Was everything — even the simplest drudgeries of drying dishes — richer because they were together? I felt like my body wasn't just my own. Instead it seemed to stretch out to include Elliot. I was aware of him at every turn. I could feel him shuffling behind me or reaching in front of me. Elliot Hull in his baggy shorts, after all this time. Sometimes it seemed as if I'd known him forever.

Eventually I used up all of the Hulls' Pyrex dishes and pots and pans. I'd filled all of the pie crusts. The counters were lined with food set out to cool. The kitchen was hot and steamy, but it smelled good.

"She can cook!" Jennifer said.

"Turns out she can cook a lot," Elliot said.

"But is it quantity or quality?" Jennifer asked, sidling up to the quiches.

"Only one way to find out," I said.

We ate some from each dish, leaving most of it for the freezer. We also had saffron rice and coconut milk, things we'd picked up at Bib's request. Vivian was still dozing. An early dose of morphine had only taken the edge off. She'd asked for more and the second dose had knocked her out. I'd hoped to feed her, to have made something that she was hungry for, but it still felt good to see everyone gathered around the table, eating and mmm-ing and reaching across each other to refill their plates.

After dinner, Bib suggested a game of Pictionary.

Jennifer bowed out — Porcupine was fussing. "It's time for the night-night routine."

I offered to sit with Vivian. "To keep her company," I said.

"I'm a master at Pictionary," Elliot said to me. "I once drew a gazebo in four seconds. You might miss some true artistry."

"I once drew a carrot and Uncle Elliot thought it was a surfboard," Bib said. "And he just kept telling me that it was a surfboard when it wasn't."

"And then I pouted," he said. The kiss in the rowboat flashed in my mind. His lips. It made my stomach flip. Outside, it was growing dark. I wondered if we'd find ourselves alone again, and, if we did, what would happen?

"Keep all the drawings and fill me in later," I said.

"Our *masterpieces*," Elliot corrected. "Right, Bib?"

She smiled sheepishly. "Right."

The head of Vivian's hospital bed was elevated. Her eyes were closed. Her hair had flipped onto her face as if she'd been sleeping restlessly. I wasn't sure what to do. I knew that I wanted something from her. *I'd recognize you anywhere.* I wanted her to say those words again or something, anything, that would make me feel like I'd been found. How long had I felt like a child lost at the beach holding a pail that knocked against her legs, disoriented by family after family huddled under beach umbrellas. Out of all of the women who could have been mother figures for me — Mrs. Fogelman had done her best; Eila would never work out; Peter's mother was too cold and had never liked me much — I wished, in this moment, that I hadn't pinned all of my hopes on this one woman. She was dying. I wouldn't have enough time to absorb all of the maternal love that I was lacking.

I sat in the recliner across the room, afraid I'd wake her if I got too close. But she seemed to sense I was there and soon enough her eyes were open and she was looking at me. "Giselle," she said. "I saved them in the middle of the night."

"I'm not Giselle," I said, crossing to her bedside so that she could see me by the light of the lamp on the table. "It's me." I wasn't sure what to call myself — Elizabeth or Gwen — so I just said again, "It's *me.*"

I put my hand on hers and she gripped it

tightly. Her face was stricken with anger. She said, "Tell him the truth." And then she pleaded. "Promise me that much!" I understood that Giselle must have disappointed her in life, many times over, deeply. I felt like a traitor — as Giselle and as myself.

"I promise," I said. "I'll tell him."

Her hand relaxed. She closed her weary eyes. Tears slipped from them into her hair. "Fix my hair. It's all a mess," she whispered. "Fix my hair."

I pulled away a few wisps that were touching her cheek and then stroked her hair with my fingers and then my whole hand, again and again. Her hair was fine and soft. Oddly, now I felt like I was her mother, taking care of a fevered child, but that felt right too. Don't the roles of mothers and daughters turn on themselves so that daughters become mothers? The roles are supposed to be fluid, one teaching the other to be a mother so they can, one day, be tended to like a child. I hadn't realized that I would miss out on this too, tending to my mother in her old age. She would never grow old, not even in my mind's eye. Even in my dreams, she was young and looked like she did to me when I was a kid. "Vivian?" I whispered. "Is there anything I can get for you?"

She opened her eyes and then gazed at me. "They don't know," she said, "and I don't want them to. Can I tell you?"

"Of course, anything," I said.

"He left me for her," she whispered. "My sister. Giselle."

I wasn't sure how to respond. "Your husband?"

"She came here to stay after living with some guy in Burbank. She was heartbroken and then I caught them together. He loved her, but she didn't love him."

"I'm so sorry," I said.

"She didn't know how much she wanted to destroy me. She tried to steal everything from me. She was young. She loved me too, just as much as she hated me." She pinched her eyes closed. "She's dead now. A motorcycle accident out west. When you're about to die, everything comes flooding back. It comes back disguised and strange. Her mice . . . I could feel them in my hands."

"It's the morphine," I said.

"It's the death," she said. "Don't tell the children."

"I won't."

"They think it was a woman from town. Why change the story now?"

"What's the truth," I asked, "the truth you wanted her to tell him?"

"You promised," she said, raising one finger. *"You* promised to tell him the truth — not Giselle. *You."*

"But I thought you didn't want me to tell Elliot about this," I said, confused.

"Tell him *your* truth," she said. "A promise is a promise."

In a few moments, Vivian's breathing became soft and slow. She was asleep again. I wasn't sure what to do or what I'd just promised. I wanted to tell Jennifer or Elliot, but of course I wouldn't. She was sleeping peacefully now. I set her hand down on the bed sheets and took my seat in the recliner.

Tell him now, I thought, watching the thin curtains puff and billow in the breeze. *Tell him the truth. Promise me that much!*

I wondered about her husband, Elliot's father, the affair with Vivian's sister. How long had she carried this secret? Had she never told anyone before? I wondered if, on my own deathbed, I would want to tell some long-kept secret. I thought of my own men. Which one needed to be told the truth now? Peter or Elliot? And what was the truth? How could I tell anyone the truth if I didn't know it myself?

CHAPTER
TWENTY-ONE

After Porcupine and Bib were both in bed, I found myself sitting on an Adirondack chair on the deck overlooking the lake. There was a cool breeze and the rippling water caught the moonlight. By the dock, Bib's white buckets seemed to glow. Elliot was inside. He'd taken over my watch of Vivian though she was sleeping soundly. Part of me hoped he'd fall asleep in the recliner and we could avoid being alone, avoid any more conversation. The day had been strangely wonderful — the grocery store trip, the steaming kitchen, the feeling of family, even if it was family brought together by this sadness. I didn't want to dismantle it, but at the same time, I wanted to be alone with him, of course, more than anything, back out on the rowboat, spinning slow circles on the lake. Jennifer appeared with a bottle of red wine. She filled two glasses, handed me one, and sat down on the chair beside mine. "I know that you're leaving things behind to be here," she said. "I hope that's okay with everyone."

I assumed she was talking about my marriage. "I think it's fine," I said. "My husband was cranking the AC/DC last I checked, pretending he's twenty again."

"I think men can regress pretty easily. It doesn't take much." She smiled. "It must be a pretty good relationship if he's letting you disguise yourself as someone else's wife. I don't think Sonny would go for it, even if it was for a good cause. And drummers are supposed to be really laid back."

"Peter doesn't seem to mind," I said, not indicating a good relationship or a bad one. I could tell she was fishing, maybe for Elliot's sake? I wasn't sure. "Your mother mistook me for Giselle," I said, changing the subject.

"Was she talking about Giselle again? She always gravitates to her when she's in her dream states. It's her younger sister. They were very close as children and didn't get along well as adults. She died thirteen years ago."

"And your father," I asked, "where is he these days?"

"Arizona. She won't let him come. She doesn't want him to see her like this."

"Did she really love him, you know, deeply?"

"I don't know." Jennifer stared into her wineglass. "After the divorce, he stayed away mainly, I think, because she made him feel so ashamed. She has that power. Her rightness and how sure she is of it, how *convinced.* It's her worst trait."

I listened to the chirruping frogs. "She still believes in love, though," I said.

"Very much so, but not for her. Not men. She took the loss so hard. Maybe that's what's made her a true romantic. She hates to see love go to waste."

"She's made me promise to tell the truth," I said, smiling. "What truth? I don't know. It was a general promise."

Jennifer squinted across the lake. There was a dock, strung with lights. "I don't know if there is a truth." She looked at me then. "Do you think that there are truths when it comes to matters of the heart? Absolute truths?"

I shrugged.

"You love someone or you don't, but do you think life dictates the rest or can love dictate life?"

I wasn't sure whose life she was talking about now, mine or her mother's. "I don't know," I said.

She sat back in her chair, swirled her wine. "Well, now you know how Elliot felt."

"In what way?"

"When he told her he was married. He had to. She has a way of making you say what she wants to hear." She pulled her legs up to her chest. "Did you play along?"

"I guess I did."

"When she asked you to promise to tell the truth, you did promise, didn't you?"

"Yes," I said. "I did."

"And are you?" she asked, looking at me very frankly.

"Am I what?" I said, pretending to be more confused than I was, hoping she would let the question evaporate.

"Are you going to tell him the truth?"

"Which him? Which truth?"

"Any him," she said. "Any truth."

Did she want me to tell my husband that I was in love with another man? Did she want me to confess to a kiss on a lake? Did she want me to tell Elliot how deep this ran and risk the perfectly good life that I had? I thought about Helen in the restaurant making us close our eyes and be thankful for just one minute for what we had. I had a good life and Peter was a good man, and who was I to want more? Did I feel like I deserved more than that? I didn't believe in being entitled to the good life. Life was life. It handed out its sorrows randomly. You took what you got and you found something in it to be thankful for — that was your job as a human being.

Jennifer must have sensed that I was riled. In fact, I felt a little goaded.

"I'm sorry," she said. "I'm overstepping."

"It's okay," I said and I meant it. We were just two women talking by a lake, drinking wine. These kinds of conversations have always made me uncomfortable — like a foreigner who speaks only a pidgin version of the language of women. But things happen between women in quiet conversations like these, important things. And, honestly, I knew that she was right to goad me. I needed it. I wasn't one to goad myself. "You're right. I think I have to tell the truth to someone," I said. "A promise is a promise."

Some time passed — I don't know how much. Jennifer gracefully redirected the conversation toward safer subjects — Bib's experiments, the baby's toes, which seemed to overlap strangely, the singer-guitarist whom hospice was sending over in the next few days to make a house call. "My mother's never liked those people who just suddenly whip out a guitar and start a singalong. She claims that they've ruined church, and she said, and I quote, 'It's one of the reasons the seventies fell flat.' "

I talked too, about work, trying to describe Eila and our clients in their überposh, stuffy, dismal homes, a greedy bunch, and how they always ended up clinging to Eila's artistic gauziness. "It's like they know what's lacking in their lives and she knows how to lend it to them." She asked me some decorating questions and I did my best to think of what Eila would suggest.

After a lull, she asked me what song I would crank to pretend that I'm twenty again. That's when Elliot arrived.

"I have no idea," I said.

"No idea about what?" he asked.

"I'd crank up some Van Morrison," Jennifer said. "I was kind of nouveau hippie in my twenties."

"What would you crank up to remind you of being twenty?" I asked Elliot.

"Is that the question you can't answer?" he asked me.

"I just can't think," I said.

"You liked Smashing Pumpkins and I liked Pearl Jam, and you had a crush on Howard Jones and loved all of those theme songs to John Hughes films. And INXS, you

were hooked at a young age."

I blushed, not just heat in my cheeks but down my neck and across my chest. "Right," I said. "Howard Jones. He was elegant."

"How's Mom?" Jennifer asked.

"She's sleeping soundly."

"And no peeps from upstairs?"

"None," he said.

"I'll go in, check on everyone." She picked up the empty bottle of wine. "Good night!" she said over her shoulder.

"Good night," I said.

And she disappeared into the house.

Elliot walked to the deck railing and said, "You liked The Pretenders' 'I'll Stand by You,' and Pat Benatar, and although you'd never confess to it in public, you had the radio in your car — the little sputtery Toyota — set to the easy-listening station. And you had a clichéd side. When you were really pissed, you'd turn up Alanis Morissette, like every twenty-year-old girl back then. And Johnny Cash — you knew all of Johnny Cash and you blamed that on your father. And you also liked Rickie Lee Jones and you loved Carole King. You knew all the words. I assumed that your mother had those albums."

"How do you remember all of that?"

"Each time I hear one of the songs I associate them with you. It all comes back. Every time." He sighed. "From *'I feel the earth move under my feet,'* to *'No one is to blame.'* When I hear 'Pretty in Pink' on the radio, I have to listen to the whole thing — out of respect for you."

"I'm so sorry," I said. "You've been brutalized all these years."

"I'm chivalrous. What can I say?"

"You know," I said, walking to the deck railing and standing next to him. "I'm curious. People ask you what you do, and you have to tell them you're a philosophy professor. What do they say to that? I mean, it must be kind of . . ."

"Embarrassing?"

"No, it's just that . . . I guess you could say you're a philosopher. But then . . ."

"They'd imagine me wearing white robes and eating grapes."

"Or you'd just be dead."

"Right, and I'm not dead yet."

"So, what do you do?"

"Most philosophers usually lie about this. On a plane or something, I tell them I sell life insurance or Amway. I ask them if they've ever considered how Amway might improve their life."

"Can Amway improve my life?"

"Absolutely." The wind had made his eyes

water and they were shining in the porch lights. "Look at me!"

And I did look at him. I knew that I was going to have to go home at some point. This wouldn't last, and I'd have to remember little moments like this — his bare feet, the frayed hems of his jeans, his shining eyes. My hand was an inch from his. He stretched his pinky and touched my pinky with his — like a sixth-grader.

"I like you," he said.

"Really?" I said. "I had no idea."

"Actually," he said, leaning in to whisper. "I don't like you. I like-you like-you. This is serious."

"You liked Otis Redding," I said. I remembered a mix tape he had and how he listened to it in his Walkman.

"Shout Bamalama!" he said. "Otis, my man."

"You were right about Carole King and Rickie Lee Jones. My mother didn't have a lot of albums, but I knew that those were her favorites, and I went through a phase in middle school, playing them over and over and over. My father must have known what was going on, that I wanted some kind of connection to her, and he never complained. They became our background music." I thought about that for a moment. "It must have been hard for him. I never looked at it from his perspective before, but he let me do what I needed to."

"I wonder what the fish are talking about tonight," he said.

"If only my father were here to translate," I said.

"He's still talking to fish?"

"Everybody's got to have someone to talk to."

He turned and looked at me and I loved the way he looked at me, drinking me in, running his eyes over all of my features, lingering on my lips. "I don't know what to do."

"I didn't think you did."

"I just thought I'd be honest. Just in case you thought I had a master plan that I was working out here. I don't."

I said, "Your mother knows that it's me."

"You?"

"She knows that I'm Gwen Merchant, not Elizabeth."

"She told you that?"

I turned away from the lake and crossed my arms on my chest. "I've had this fear since childhood that since my mother died when I was so young she wouldn't know me in heaven because I'd changed so much, and we'd never find each other. It was a stupid fear," I said. "But your mother said to me: *I'd recognize you anywhere . . .*" I started to cry — a quick gasp and then a sob. I covered my face with my hands. "That's what I've been wanting to hear — for as long as I can remember — from my own mother." Elliot reached over and stroked my hair. "It wasn't my fault," I said.

"Of course it wasn't your fault, Gwen. Of course it wasn't," he said. "Guilt doesn't have to make any sense."

I wiped the tears from my face and looked at him sharply. "But this guilt does make sense. Our guilt, being here together."

He didn't have a response for this.

"Don't you think I'd like to be like you?" I said. "Don't you think I'd prefer to be able to tell people the way I really feel and take in, you know, really accept the way they feel about me? Don't you think that I'd love to be that way?"

"You can be that way," he said.

I shook my head. "I am who I am."

"Does that mean I can't tell you that I love you still?"

"You can shout it, if you want to, but I just can't take it, not the way you want me to. Don't you know that about me by now?"

He laughed and pounded a fist on the railing. "That's the sad part," he said. "I even love that about you too."

Across the lake, there was a pop — like champagne being uncorked — and then a chorus of voices rose. "Someone's having a party," I said.

He put his arm around my shoulder and pulled me to his chest. He smelled good, like aftershave and the food that we'd cooked that day. He said, "Let's pretend it's a party for us, and we've wandered away to be alone."

A woman's laugh rippled across the lake. Drunken men started singing some kind of college fight song. A dog barked. Another champagne bottle popped open. He held me like that on the dock while the voices kept echoing.

CHAPTER
TWENTY-TWO

The next two days passed quickly, even though I tried to hold on to every moment. I was put on kid duty, for the most part. Jennifer taught me how to use the baby sling, and I took the kids to a berry patch where we were given a bucket and paid for our harvest by weight.

Bib and I played croquet in the yard, where she proved to be a vicious competitor. When Elliot joined us he made up extra rules — style points — for playing only on one leg, using a British accent, spin moves. He held Porcupine, which he claimed upped his handicap. Bib delighted in all of this. My accent was wobbly, but I was great on one foot and my spin moves weren't shabby. Elliot played barefoot and, while trying to knock me out of the game, hit his own foot with the mallet. There was bright sun and a grassy lawn filled with wickets and Elliot dueling with Bib — their mallets on guard.

When Porcupine went down for his nap, Bib took me for tours of her pollywogs swimming in buckets. The water was murky and the pollywogs flicked their tails wildly or held them pin-straight. She pointed out a mosquito larva.

"There," she said. "See it!" But it moved so fast that she kept having to point it out, its two minuscule paddles spinning madly. She pointed out the American bullfrog, which was smaller than the others.

We stole lettuce from the fridge, boiled it, and fed it to them, their bulbous heads rising to the leaf, munching away almost imperceptibly. "They're so alive," I said.

"That's because they are alive," she explained patiently.

We ate from the meals I'd prepared, plus blueberries and cream for dessert. Vivian was doing no better, pain-wise, and she'd edged off of the morphine so that she could be more alert. It was a constant battle between how much pain she could endure and how much time she couldn't spare. I sat with her on Tuesday night.

"You're leaving in the morning," she said. I nodded.

"At least open my gift," she said, pointing to the wedding gifts huddled on a far table. "Do me that favor?"

"Sure," I said. "I'll get Elliot."

"No, no," she said. "It's for you. There's an overpriced cappuccino maker in there from me too. But that was before I knew you." She pointed to a gift the size of an *Encyclopedia Britannica* wrapped in silver paper embossed with bells. "Sorry about the paper, left over from the holidays. I had Jennifer wrap this for me."

I picked up the gift. It was lighter than I expected. I sat in a chair next to the bed and let the gift sit in my lap. I felt giddy.

"I feel like a little kid," I said. "I'm not sure why I'm suddenly nervous."

"Open it," she said. "You're making me nervous."

I pulled off the taped edges, being careful with the paper.

"Rip it," she said.

I paused and then ripped the paper right in two. And there was the framed picture, the one of Vivian in her white swimsuit and Elliot and Jennifer, just little kids, on the grassy lawn by the deck, the one taken from the upstairs window. "How did you know that I love this photo? From the moment I saw it . . ." I couldn't go on. The words stopped in my throat, which suddenly went tight with tears.

"Elliot said he'd seen you looking at it.

I've always loved it too."

I ran my finger along the see-through curtain along one side of the frame. "It's like someone's been keeping watch over you."

Vivian reached out, her arm painfully thin but still elegant. I leaned forward, knowing she wanted to touch my face. Her hand was soft and dry. "She is, love. She is keeping watch over you." Of course, I hadn't consciously been thinking of my mother, but this is what Vivian meant, that my mother was still with me, that I could never be a stranger to her — she'd been with me all of these years, keeping one loving eye cast on me and my life and the people in it alongside me. My eyes welled up, tears slipped down my cheeks.

"Thank you," I whispered. "Thank you." I knew that I was changed in this moment in a fundamental way. If I could never be a stranger to my mother, then she couldn't remain a stranger to me — not any longer. I knew that this meant that I would have to confront my father and try to find out the truth, once and for all.

Vivian nodded. "You," she said, "I wish I had more time with you. You're a good daughter. And Elliot is lucky." She looked at me with watery blue eyes. "Be good to him."

That night, I couldn't sleep. The one thin sheet was stifling, and when I kicked it off, I was chilled by the breeze through the window. It was getting gusty outside, actually. The leaves were rustling, and when I went to the window to shut it, the moon was lost in quick purplish clouds, and the trees seemed to be swaying. The sky looked burdened, heavy, the air tensed for a storm.

The photograph sat on my bedside table. I picked it up and looked at it again, noticing the slight bow of Elliot's knees, the sag of his swim trunks, the curly lumps of his hair. He was a beautiful kid with a wry smile, some freckles, a wise look in his eyes, taking it all in — a little philosopher already. I sat on the edge of the bed and then stood up and paced. I needed something to drink — a glass of milk to help me sleep.

I padded down the stairs in a blue tank top and shorts and slipped into the kitchen. I poured a glass of milk and then looked out the French doors to the view of the lake, the tall grasses bending deeply in the wind. I let my eyes wander down to the water, and that's when I saw something white shifting at the end of the dock. At first I thought it was a crane or some large white bird, but then I saw that it was a shirt. Elliot was sitting at the end of the dock, alone.

I walked out onto the deck and watched him for a moment. He leaned back, his hands on the dock, his elbows locked. I walked across the lawn, which was cool and wet on my feet, and down the dock. The wind was so loud now that he didn't hear me until I said his name. "Elliot."

He turned around, startled. "What are you doing out here?"

"I could ask you the same thing."

"I'm here for the light show." He pointed toward the far corner of the lake. "The lightning will start over there then it will tear across the lake. It'll likely pass right over us and end there." He drew a line over the lake, stopping above some distant roofs.

I looked up at the sky, the breadth and dark, arching blueness of it.

Elliot scooted over and patted the dock. "Sit."

I sat down beside him. The dock was old, its edges soft.

"When I was a kid, I got caught in a gustnado," he said. "In a sailboat, right out there."

"A gustnado?"

"It's like a tornado, but it's a gust of wind that comes up from nowhere. It filled the

261

sail of the boat I was on — a neighbor's boat — and lifted me and the boat into the air, just a few feet, but still it was so strange. This bubble of air rising up out of the blue. It was this kind of weather, but during the day, just before a thunderstorm. I told my father about it but he didn't believe me. I really wanted my picture in the paper."

"Did you tell your mother?"

"She believed me. She called me Gus all summer long. She called me *her little survivor.* It was the summer before their divorce and she was looking for reasons to get me to believe that I was tough, that I could make it through anything. She knew what was coming."

"She's smart," I said. "She's really very smart."

"You like her," he said, lifting his eyebrows. "I thought you two would like each other."

"I can't explain it, but she's done a lot for me. This short visit. I don't know how to put it, but I'm different. She's made things shift for me."

"In a good way?"

"In a good way."

There was a distant rumble. I looked toward the corner of the lake where he said the lightning show would start, but he kept his eyes on me. I could feel his gaze. I closed my eyes. "She told me to be good to you," I said.

"She did?" He leaned forward and glanced up at me hopefully. "And?"

"This might be all we ever get."

His face was lit up softly by the far-off lightning. The wind flipped my hair across my face. He brushed it back with both of his hands and held my face. Then he kissed me — a soft kiss that quickly turned passionate. I imagined it — having sex with him on this dock, the lightning rising up, the wind churning around us, the rain. It was all I wanted in that moment.

But he pulled back. He said, "I don't want this to be the thing swept under the rug."

I was breathless. "What?"

"I don't want this to be all that we ever get. And if we go through with this, it becomes something else. An affair, something we'll have to sweep under the rug."

"I can't leave my husband," I said.

"Yes, I know that. I understand," he said. "But I don't want to become something you feel guilty about, something to be ashamed of."

He stood up. I heard the rain starting across the lake. It moved quickly, and in a matter of seconds, it was pouring down on us. But neither of us moved.

"I remember what it was like, to be with you. I remember the feel of your ribs and your hips. I remember the birthmark on your upper thigh. Don't think this isn't killing me," he said and he pushed back his wet hair. "I'd give anything to have sex with you again," but then he corrected himself. "*Almost* anything." He looked beautiful, rain dripping off his lashes, his skin shining wet. "I learned, growing up, that things can fall apart. My parents were together and then it was over. I learned to mistrust my heart. But when I look at you and when I see the way you look at me, I know that I'm right to love you. I trust myself again." He wiped the rain from his face. "I love you," he said loudly over the rain. "It's simple."

I stood up, feeling breathless, ran my hand down his soaking shirt, and gripped it for a second. This was anything but simple. Then I loosened my fist, letting go.

CHAPTER
TWENTY-THREE

I hoped that the good-byes would be as quick as I could make them. I walked into the living room. Vivian was staring at the bookshelves. I sat in the chair beside the bed. "I'm taking off now," I said.

Her eyes drifted around my face. She said, "Come and see me again soon." I wasn't sure if she knew exactly who I was now or if she was being automatically polite. But then she patted my hand. "Thank you for doing this."

"Doing what?" I said, feigning ignorance.

"You know," she said. "You didn't have to."

I leaned down and kissed her cheek, but I couldn't say a word. My voice was lost in my throat.

Elliot was holding Porcupine, waiting for me on the lawn. I could see him through the window in quiet conversation with the baby. I couldn't erase the image of his face in the pouring rain, the way his shirt felt in my fist, the wind, the lightning, and how he'd been the one to leave first. He'd turned and trudged back to the house, his black hair shiny and wet.

"I don't know how to be good to him," I said to Vivian. "And still be a good person."

"You are good," she said. "You *are*." She sighed. "The person who took the photograph I gave you — it was my sister. I love the photograph because I think, in that very moment, she loved us. She loved us too much and didn't know how to tell us, how to express it. She ended up trying to destroy us. But I've always wondered what would have happened if she'd been able to just say how she felt and really listen. There's more to all of that than people think."

"Did you love him?" I asked.

"I did," she said. "I still do." She smiled then and touched my cheek with the back of one hand. "You *are* good," she said. "You hear me?"

I closed my eyes and gave a nod. I knew that I had changed, and that I would go home and change the life I'd built around me — a life of breezy conversation and idle banter. I wasn't sure if Elliot Hull would fit into this new way of life — this new construction — or not. But I knew I had no choice. I was different now. I hoped only that I wouldn't lose my nerve, that Vivian had given me enough of her own precious strength to see me through. Would I be able to stand in a field with a rake and not make decisions based on fear? "Thank you," I said. "For everything. For more than you can imagine."

"You're welcome," she said.

I stood up feeling strong and sure, but also with a whirring sadness in my chest. I wanted to say that I would see her again soon, but I couldn't make that kind of promise and neither could she. And so I picked up my bag, paused for a moment in the doorway, and walked out of the room, the house.

Bib was running across the yard. She got her foot hooked in one of the wickets and fell hard to the ground, which was still wet from the rain. She called for her mother, who appeared from the driveway where she'd been talking to a hospice nurse who'd just arrived.

Jennifer was walking the hospice nurse to the house, Bib clinging to her side. Jennifer looked at my bags. "Oh, no! It's really true." She grabbed me and hugged me. "Don't go!" she said and then immediately added, "I know, I know. I'm just being selfish!"

Bib hugged me too around my hips. "You're going to come back!" she said. "So I won't get sad about it."

I patted her back and mussed her hair.

Elliot handed the baby to Jennifer. "So, we're off," he said, and he picked up my bag. I followed him to the car.

On the way to the train station, it was still overcast so Elliot kept the top of the convertible up. The air felt trapped and dry.

"How are you going to handle this? You have your own life waiting for you too," I said. "Don't you have to teach still?"

"I had some people covering for me. My colleagues have been great. But I'll have to start commuting. Monday through Wednesdays there, and the long weekends here. Jennifer's husband will be coming in soon. His band's tour is coming to an end. They'll be local for a while and he's a huge help. You'd like him. A wild man but a sweetheart too."

The car was quiet. It seemed like there were so many things to say that we couldn't possibly make a dent. When he pulled up to the train station, I told him not to walk me to the platform. I sat in the car with him for a moment though. How was I going to carry this time here with Elliot and Vivian, Jennifer and the kids with me into my life?

Finally Elliot said, "Everyone thinks that I can't settle down, that I can't commit. I thought that was my problem too. But the fact is, when I saw you in the ice-cream shop, I realized that I hadn't been able to commit because I was already committed — to you. And that doesn't have to make sense either to anyone but me."

What if I stayed here with Elliot? What if I never went home? Eila would hire someone else within a week. Would Faith and Helen tell me that I was crazy? Would my father drive out to give me some awkward counsel? Would Peter show up and try to get me back? I'd never seen him in any kind of real crisis. I had no idea how he'd react. I thought of the fireflies that Bib and I had translated: *stay, stay, stay.* It was a fleeting fantasy. There was no reality in it. I knew that I was going home. "You know, we can't see each other anymore. It would be excruciating. I couldn't . . . I have to fix my own life." I felt a lump rise in my throat. I didn't want to cry in front of him.

"Are you asking me for a divorce? We didn't even open all the presents yet." He was trying to sound light.

"I'm only asking for a pretend divorce," I said. "They're less barbaric."

"I refuse to sign the papers."

I looked at him. "This is serious."

"You don't have to tell me it's serious," Elliot said. "I want the overflowing grocery cart with the snot-nosed kids, and you, forever."

I picked up my bag from the foot well, unzipped it, and reached inside, feeling for the edges of the photograph his mother had given me. I picked it up, stared at it for a moment — the family that was the three of them, the ghostly ribbon of the curtain, the rippling water at their backs. It wasn't mine. I handed it to him.

"No," he said. "She gave it to you."

"But it doesn't really belong to me."

"Yes, it does."

"You'll want it," I said, "later, after she's . . ."

"It's yours," he said with finality. "She wanted you to have it."

I sat the photograph in my lap. What would I do with it? Where would I put it? Could I set it up in the living room next to the photograph of my mother wearing the spaghetti-strapped dress and holding her beaded purse? What would Peter think of that? For now, I simply put it back in my bag. The truth was that I wanted to keep it. I'd hoped he'd refuse to take it back.

"I want to know . . . I want you to give

me a call when the time comes . . . when your mother passes. I need to know." I wanted to tell him that she'd told me to stand in the field with a rake and not make decisions based on fear. But I couldn't.

He nodded.

I climbed out, shut the car door, and walked quickly to the train station — its bank of windows fogged by the mix of humidity and air-conditioning — and there I saw a reflection of myself walking in fog.

■ ■ ■ ■

PART THREE

■ ■ ■ ■

CHAPTER
TWENTY-FOUR

I decided on the train ride that I had to toughen up. And, in the face of loss, who was tougher than my father? I would remove myself emotionally. I would observe marriage. I would look scientifically at this thing that Peter and I had. I would approach it the way my father would a chirruping trout off of Cape Cod. I would start from scratch, asking simple questions to find simple truths: What is marriage? How does it operate in private, in public? What's its role for the individuals involved and in society at large? And, of course, what I really wanted to know was what marriage had to do with me, personally, what did it want from me, what did I owe it, and what did it owe me in return.

The only glitch in this plan was that my father was no longer my only model on the subject of loss. My conversations with Vivian rang in my head. In my quest to find simple truths, I knew that I would have to confront my father. And in a larger though hazier way, I knew that from now on, I wouldn't be able to simply let fear make my decisions for me. Though I wasn't sure what this really meant, this new way of living would require a kind of bravery that I wasn't sure I had in me.

I wasn't ready to live this bravely. Not yet. Elliot had come back into my life like a windstorm, and I'd lost my bearings. Couldn't I wait to be brave until I at least had some idea of where I stood in my life? I granted myself this reprieve.

I knew this was cowardly and wrong, but I hoped that Vivian's wisdom and the charge she'd given me to live a life not ruled by fear would return to me when I needed it most.

For now, still feeling windswept by Elliot, I focused on trying to put my things back in order.

When I got home, Peter was asleep on the sofa, curled toward the television, which was on with the sound off. He had a throw pillow wedged under his head and a fist balled up by his chest. I sat on the sofa at the space by his shoes — he still had them on. I assumed he'd stayed out late and fallen asleep hard and fast — maybe a little drunkenly.

Because of shift work at the hospital, his natural internal clock had eroded and he slept when he was tired, instead of by any set pattern.

Ripken was pawing at me to take him out. I patted his knotty head. "Okay," I said. "Okay."

When I stood up to get his leash, Peter rolled to his back and stretched. "You're home."

"I'm home," I said. Already thinking as a scientist, I decided that marriage had much to do with home. The two concepts overlapped in so many ways that maybe it was possible to mean one and say the other and no one would notice.

He propped himself up on his elbows. "How was it?"

I thought about this for a moment. "It was sad. They're losing their mother, and she's a wonderful person. And it's hard to lose someone you love."

"Yes, that's true," he said, as if this hadn't dawned on him. "I meant, I guess, how was it pretending to be someone else's wife? How was that part?"

"Oh," I said, picking up Ripken's leash from the ceramic bowl we kept it in. "That was strange. I'm not much of a liar. I told her that I knit hats for a living. Does anyone knit hats for a living?"

"Old women who live in Bulgaria?" Peter offered. "I think the correct term is milliner, not someone who knits hats." He often corrected me on things like this. I'd called his mother a piano player for a year or two before he finally blurted, "Pianist! She's a pianist! Piano players work in honky-tonk bars or wedding bands."

"Too bad you weren't there," I said. "You'd have smoothed out all my lies for me." I clipped the leash onto Ripken's collar. I looked at my watch. "I have to meet Eila at a client's house at three-thirty," I said. I had about an hour to get the dog walked, shower, dress, before I had to take off. Ripken was bouncing around in joyful circles now. "Come with us," I said.

"I've got to take a shower," he said, then he walked up behind me and put his arms around my waist. He whispered into my ear, "But, tell me, seriously. What was it like? Did anyone clink wineglasses so that you had to kiss?"

"It wasn't a wedding," I said.

"C'mon, you had to have held hands, at least, to be convincing," he whispered.

"Would that be some kind of weird turn-on?" I asked.

"No," he said, dropping his hands. "I just

want to know what happened." And now I could tell that he wasn't curious as much as he was jealous.

"I thought you weren't jealous — that you tried it on and the collar fit too tightly."

"Hey, I'm just trying to get a picture of how it all played out. That's fair."

"Well, I talked to his mother a lot and his sister, who has two kids, and Elliot. And they all seemed to be doing the best they could, under the circumstances. This isn't really a happy time for them. I'm here. I'm back."

He sat down on the sofa. "What's that supposed to mean?" he asked.

"What?"

"Forget it," he said. "I can see that I'll just have to ask Elliot how it all went. He'll give me a straight answer."

"Elliot? Don't bother him with this." I thought of Elliot with his stark honesty. I walked to the front door with Ripken.

"I've been meaning to ask him to go out golfing with some of the guys, introduce him to a couple of people."

"He doesn't have time to golf. He's at the lake house with his mother every weekend and juggling teaching." What would he spill to Peter during an interminable golf game?

"I'll ask him to do a weekday morning

round with the ladies. He's a professor. That's barely a job," he said, and then he leaned forward. "Why don't you want me to ask him any questions? Any reason?"

I shrugged. "Ask him anything you want," I said. "It's fine by me!" I opened the front door and walked out, Ripken trotting ahead of me.

I felt more than a little panic-stricken. Once outside, I flipped open my phone, but I had no idea whether I should call Faith or Helen, both or neither. In my last conversation with Faith, she'd accused me of trying to get a rise out of Peter, trying to make him jealous by being Elliot's pretend wife. And then Helen told me that I tried to boost up Jason because I wanted to boost up myself, that I didn't think enough of myself. I didn't particularly want to talk to either of them. But the fact was that I had to learn to overcome these kinds of things if I was going to have long-term friendships with women, and because I have no sisters, I needed these friendships to keep me grounded. It's just the way it is. Good friends say what they have to say. If it isn't that kind of friendship, then it isn't worth it. I needed more honesty in my life, not less.

I called Helen and got her voicemail. I wasn't sure how she did it — the voice in her outgoing message was professional but also sexy. The words *I'm not in right now* seemed to have a double or even a triple meaning because of the nuance of her tone, but there was nothing you could call her on. On the surface, it was the same as everyone else's outgoing message. Regardless, I felt blindly flirted with. After the beep, I suggested the possibility of getting together that night for a quick dessert at a creamery not far from Faith's house.

I called Faith and she answered immediately. "How did it go?" she whispered. She was obviously somewhere she really shouldn't have been picking up. I kept it as short as possible: "The situation calls for emergency ice cream."

"That bad?"

"Where are you?"

"I'm about to give a speech about something I know nothing about. Have I mentioned I'm faking my way through life?"

"Should I try that?"

"I think we all already are."

At work that day, Eila and I were trapped in someone's living room. The couple — an uptight pair, nouveau riche, one with adult braces — had excused themselves to argue the finer points of their dedication to Eila's total vision for their staging. They'd shut themselves up in their granite-packed kitchen. Eila caught me staring absently at the tan Berber carpeting.

"What's wrong?"

"Oh, nothing," I said, giving her an over-bright smile.

"I know something's wrong. Spill it."

"I don't know," I said. "I'm trying to hold my life together, I think."

"Oh, right. You're still so young. I forget that about young people." She patted my knee. "Listen, when you get older, you'll realize that your life isn't held together to begin with so trying to hold it together, well, that's a myth. An impossibility."

The voices in the kitchen rose feverishly. Something was slammed down on granite — a nouvelle cuisine cookbook? Then there was quiet.

"Listen to them in there. They still think they're holding it together. Ha!" she said. "It's disastrously tragic."

By the time I got to the creamery, I was about fifteen minutes late. Our clients' kitchen argument had lingered after they reemerged, and every joint decision was a slow, agonizing process of grunts, glares, angry gestures, accusations, and the wife throwing her hands in the air at regular intervals and saying, "Whatever!" Faith was already eating frozen yogurt at a table in the back. She'd brought Edward and he was dozing in his car seat next to her. There was a line of tween girls in full makeup with hair plastered into ponytails. They were wearing matching dance outfits, blue leotards with spangles, but they had on sneakers and windbreakers.

"I'm so sorry," I said. "I thought that Helen would be here at least and you two would start chatting without me."

"She called a minute ago and said she would if she could but she can't. I think she might be in love or something and too embarrassed to tell us that she's fallen so quickly after swearing off men again."

"This would be a new record."

"Would it? I'm not so sure. She likes to swear off men so that she can tempt herself. It's a cycle."

I shrugged and sat down. I didn't want to deconstruct Helen, not without her here. That wasn't worthwhile. Plus, I was in need of deconstruction myself — some clarity. I picked at a thread on my pocketbook and then stared out the plate-glass window.

"Order something."

"I can't eat," I said.

"I thought this was an ice-cream emergency."

"I've been with a squabbling couple for the last three hours. They jangled me. Maybe in a minute," I said. "Plus, there's a line."

"They appeared out of nowhere," Faith said, pointing her cone at the group of girls. "I'm scared of them. It goes way back. A primeval fear." They were loud and nervous, poking each other, whispering then roaring with laughter. "They're like a herd of unpredictable animals."

We watched them for a minute. The lead girl was obvious. She had the best hair and she wasn't loud at all, but everyone seemed to swirl around her. Two of the mothers were with them, trying to take orders and present them, as clearly as possible, to the woman behind the counter, scribbling notes.

"We were once that young," I said.

"It seems impossible."

"How's Edward feeling?" I asked. "One day, you know . . ."

"Completely fine. He's a trouper. And he's agreed never to be an adolescent. He's going to skip it," she said, then leaned forward on her elbows. There was a lull and she knew that I was stalling. I didn't know where to start. "Tell me what's going on," she said.

I sighed. "Something happened," I said, meaning that I'd changed, that something deep inside of myself had taken a turn.

"Did you have an affair with Elliot?"

"No," I said. "Well, there was a kiss. But it's worse than an affair."

"Oh," she said, sitting back, knowing exactly what this meant. "It'll pass," she said. "Everything will be fine."

"Somehow, this trip, it changed me," I said.

She looked at me quizzically.

"His mother gave me a photograph of Elliot and his sister and herself, standing in the yard, and it's blocked off a little by this bit of curtain. I can't explain it," I said. "But the photograph moved me. It was such a gift. It made me feel better, stronger, more taken care of. It's like I realized I'm being watched over . . . It's like she understood . . ."

"Understood what?"

I couldn't do any better than that. I didn't know what else I meant. "Nothing. I hid the photograph in the top shelf of my closet." I looked at her. "Don't worry. I'm not going to wreck my life. I'll fake it, right?

I'll fake my life even better than I have been. But, between you and me, I don't want it to pass," I said. "I don't want *fine.*"

She nodded. Edward stirred at her feet. She jiggled the car seat and he shifted again and then let out a soft purr and was back to sleep. "I'm sorry," she said. "I can't imagine."

"The problem is that Peter wants to take Elliot golfing. He wants to introduce him around, insinuate him into our friendships."

"That would be a disaster."

"I know."

The girls were clumping at the different tables now — the seating arrangements were highly ritualized and hierarchical. They buzzed around each other, stood up, moved over, sat down again, the combinations coming together, falling apart, rejoining in different constellations.

"You just have to go cold turkey," Faith said. "Don't let everything fall apart."

"What if life isn't held together to begin with, so trying to hold it together is impossible?" I asked her.

She laughed. "Life *is* held together," she said. "It might only be held together with a bunch of rigged-up ropes, but we keep checking the knots, making sure that everything's holding. We have to."

■ ■ ■ ■

After telling Elliot just that morning not to call me, not to have any contact at all except on the occasion of his mother's death, I called him. I was on my way home from the creamery — I'd ordered a scoop of ice cream and it sat melting in its waxy cup. I pulled over into a development of boxy 1940s-style houses to make the call.

"Hello," Elliot said. His voice was deep and soft and a little frayed at its edges. I thought of his mouth and his white teeth and his jaw. It happened that quickly, his whole body appearing in my mind.

"Hi, it's me."

"I thought we were under strict orders . . ."

"Peter is going to ask you to play a round of golf with him and some of his buddies."

"That's thoughtful of him!" Elliot said, as if unaware of the possible awkwardness.

"I want you to be busy."

"I might be busy. What date is he looking at?"

"I'm not calling as his scheduling secretary."

"Oh? Really?"

"Really." I fiddled nervously with some

papers, picked up a stack, and tapped them into order.

"You want me to decline the invitation."

"Yes," I said definitively. "But no!"

"Which one? Yes or no?"

"You can't decline outright, because that would be suspicious."

"Declining outright would be suspicious, how exactly?"

"He thinks something happened."

"Something did happen."

"Listen! Just say you'd love to and then later say you can't."

"This is complicated. How about I just go?"

"Do you even play golf?"

"I did a few times in high school. My friend, Barry Mercheson, his parents were members of this club and he caddied. We drove the carts around, mostly. It was before I had my driver's license so . . ."

"This isn't funny," I said.

"How about I go," he said. "And just have fun and play some golf."

"Okay," I said. "Fine. Play golf. Just don't do that thing where you're so earnest."

"I'll try to play a dis-earnest game of golf."

"Promise!"

"I promise. I'll be completely lacking all earnesty. And by earnesty should I mean

288

honesty?"

"Keep both of them in your back pocket."

I paused a moment. "How's your mother?"

"Can I be earnest now?"

"Yes," I said. "And honest too."

"She's still alive, but I already miss her."

Chapter
Twenty-Five

I was on edge, yes, and watchful, observant. I was in my life and taking mental notes on it at the same time. I was waking up in the morning, opening my eyes to the sun, and then realizing that I was awake, that I was a woman in a bed, a wife. This was my foot, touching my husband's foot. I would floss and see a wife flossing. I would say good morning to Peter in the kitchen, and he would be talking about grain cereals versus sugar cereals and the obesity epidemic, and corn syrup, and I'd see how I responded, nodding, agreeing, pouring milk into grain cereal, wishing it were soaked in corn syrup. He'd say something funny and I'd say something funny. It wasn't the same as cooking with Elliot. This was merely banter. We took turns. Was that marriage? Taking turns?

I'd put the photograph that Vivian had given me in the upper reaches of my closet.

I felt guilty about hiding it, but also guilty about having it. And yet, from time to time, I found myself pulling it down and looking at it and thinking of Vivian and my own mother and how my mother was keeping watch over me. But what did she want me to do? I wondered. What did she expect of me? I didn't know.

I'd decided not to bring up golfing with Elliot, hoping it was just something Peter had said to rattle me. But then one morning I was getting ready for work and Peter was in his shorts and collared polo shirt, and a pair of old saddle-shoe golf spikes — the old kind with metal spikes that clacked even more loudly on the hardwood floors.

"You're golfing today?" I asked, dousing my coffee with half-and-half.

"With Hull, like I said."

"I didn't know you were serious about that." I was a wife stirring coffee.

"Why wouldn't I be serious?" he asked. "Have you seen my watch?" Peter was terrible at looking for things. He was now standing in the middle of the living room with his hands on his hips, in a posture of defeat, glancing around.

"Try the bedside table," I said. He strode off to the bedroom. I called out loudly, "Where did you get those golf shoes? They look ancient."

"Oh, these, they're my father's. I had to borrow them." He returned, watchless. "It wasn't there. Do you think it just disappeared?"

"No," I said. "What happened to your spikes?"

"I tried to make a shot out of the pond on the seventeen. Stumbled a little, up to my ankles. They dried all misshapen."

"Oh."

"It's okay," he said. "I took a stroke and still parred the hole." He had his golf bag now up on one shoulder. "I've given up on the watch. Let me know if you find it," by which he meant, *Could you find it for me?*

"Have fun," I said.

"I will," he said, kissing me distractedly on the cheek. "I will." Was this what marriage relied on? Gestures of love? Perfunctory repetitions of kindnesses that make up for emptiness by being plentiful and reliable? I could still hear Elliot's mother saying, "Marriage is a crock." Hadn't people lived side by side for years, drawing on these kindnesses so that they had the strength to make it through the unkind world? Didn't these small kindnesses — like the little loving jabs passed between Dr. and Mrs. Fogelman — keep people alive? Maybe people were too demanding of love these days. Too entitled to some romantic vision of it. I was raised in a kind of Great Depression of Love. I didn't go around demanding a bigger share. Shouldn't we all be more contented? Why so greedy? Why did I want to be with Elliot Hull? Why did I think about him all the time? While living my life, while observing myself living my life, I was also wondering what it would be like if I were with Elliot — in this small moment and that. Didn't I have enough? Didn't I have more than anyone should ask for? I thought: What if I were with Elliot right now? I wouldn't have to think this much about it. I could stop being a scientist — it was beginning to become a habit — a science project that was studying me.

On the way home from work, I thought of Elliot and Peter bumping along the golf course in a white motorized cart, swinging their clubs, putting on the greens. Had Elliot really not played since high school? Was he out there making a fool of himself? Was Peter showing off? He was an excellent golfer. He'd once brought home five thousand dollars in some amateur tournament with a friend from college. Mainly, I imagined them talking about the weekend, Peter inching ever-so-jokingly toward some mention of me as Elliot's pretend wife, about conjugal rights or something.

If Eila was right and life wasn't held together by anything anyway, I decided to just leave it alone. I made a decision not to ask about how the game went and that I wouldn't call Elliot about it. I'd just let it sit.

But when I got home from work — a little early due to a snafu; a couple had decided to sell their house and then to divorce and each thought the other should pay for staging — I found Elliot sitting on my sofa, drinking a beer, his foot in a bucket of ice, his pant leg cuffed to his knee. I was stunned. I hadn't known if I'd ever see him again, but here he was, in the flesh, his dark curly hair, his arched eyebrows, and sweet dark eyes. I felt guilty all of a sudden, as if I'd conjured him myself out of a pure desire to see him again.

"What are you doing here?" I asked. "What happened?"

Peter then walked in from the kitchen, holding our plastic automatic ice-maker bucket. "An unfortunate run-in with a sprinkler head," Peter said and then dumped the rest of the ice into the bucket. Elliot braced and grabbed his thigh. Ripken was being a steadfast nurse, lying at his feet, dutifully. "And bad timing on the part of a rogue squirrel."

"I flew out of the cart," Elliot said.

"Well, he didn't really fly," Peter said. "He's wingless."

I walked up and saw a gash on Elliot's shin. He lifted the leg and showed me his swollen ankle. "I never saw the squirrel," he said.

"You were looking the other way," Peter said. "He was fast. It was a knee-jerk reaction to swerve."

"Start at the beginning," I said.

Elliot looked at Peter, giving him the floor.

Peter took a swig of beer. "Well, we were traveling downhill, at a good clip. Elliot and I were just chatting it up. And he was looking off at those big fat houses. Well, you're never out there, but there are these beautiful old homes. Then the squirrel darted in front of the cart. I swerved. Elliot wasn't holding on . . ."

"I wasn't holding on," Elliot said, as if to say *How was I supposed to know to hold on?*

"And he flew out of the cart . . ."

"Even though I'm wingless."

"And he landed pretty hard, twisting his ankle," Peter said. "Then he gashed his leg on a sprinkler head. No way to see any of this coming. No way."

"Nope," Elliot said, shaking his head. "It's a mysterious chain of events. I can say that I never did see the squirrel."

"That squirrel was crazy," Peter said. "Darting out in front of me like that. Jim saw it."

"Did he?" Elliot asked.

"Yep."

"I'll get some peroxide," I said.

"No, no," Elliot said, wincing and pulling his foot from the bucket. "I'm fine. I'll fix it up at home. I'm going to go."

"Don't be ridiculous," I said. "You can't drive with a puffed ankle like that."

"It's my left foot," he said, unrolling the pant leg and picking up his shoe, the sock balled up inside of it. He could barely look at me. His eyes kept sweeping the floor. I had the feeling that he was afraid to look at me. What would happen if he did? Was there something he wanted to tell me? "I'll be fine," he said. "I drove here."

"I insisted on helping him get set up with ice, some Vicodin, a remote control," Peter said. "I feel really bad about this, like it's all my fault."

Elliot gave him a glance, as if to say, *If it's not your fault, whose is it?* But quickly followed it with, "I'm fine." He picked up his keys and wallet and limped to the door, still holding his shoe.

"You're not fine," I said. I wasn't sure what conversation had taken place in the golf cart, but I knew that Elliot hadn't told Peter anything about us. Peter was too lighthearted. "I'll help you to the car," I said, grabbing his shoe.

"Sorry it didn't work out," Peter said. "Maybe next time . . ."

"I'll be right back," I said to Peter.

"What am I going to do with all of this wasted ice?" he said, standing in the middle of the living room.

I shut the door and caught up with Elliot, who'd already pushed the elevator button.

"Wow," he said. "That sucked."

The elevator doors opened. We stepped in.

"I'm so sorry," I said, pushing the button for the lobby. "Was Peter awful to you?"

"There was no squirrel," he said. "And . . ." His sentence stalled and he shook his head.

"What?"

"I don't know," he said, closing his eyes and resting his back against the wall of the elevator. "I should tell you . . ."

"What?"

"Nothing," he whispered.

We walked out of the lobby, into the back parking lot. I was apologizing all the way — for Peter, for his friends who could also be jerks, for the lack of a squirrel. I spotted Elliot's jalopy, the one he'd bought off the friend who was in California now. I unlocked the door for him, put his shoe in the passenger's seat. He lowered himself into the driver's seat. "Gwen," he said.

"Yes?"

"I don't know how I'm going to do this."

"Do what?"

"Lose you again. You'd think that the practice round in college would have warmed me up, prepared me somehow, but it's worse this time. How could it be so much worse?"

I was standing in the open door of his car. I said, "I don't want to be lost," I said. "I have no choice."

"You do have a choice."

"I made a commitment."

"But has he?"

"What?"

"Nothing," he said. "I'm just looking for loopholes." He winced as if he'd just had a pain shoot through his ankle, then shook his head. "I love you. I just want you to know that."

I loved him too, but this was the difference between us; I didn't want him to know — not how much I felt, how strongly — the way, even in this moment, he made me feel weak and a little short of breath. "I don't want to be lost," I said again. This was as close as I could come.

A few minutes later, I was back in the apartment. Peter had dumped the ice. Later, when I went to take a shower, I'd find the hardened lump of cubes cluttered in the drain of the tub. He was talking on the phone. He was saying, "Yes, yes. Sure. Got it," talking in the shorthand you use for people at work. When he hung up, I said, "A rogue squirrel?"

He shrugged. "Jim saw it too. A rogue squirrel. He's lucky it wasn't a goose. They're all over that course and I've seen them attack a man when he's down."

"So Elliot is lucky?" I said. "So lucky he got thrown from a golf cart and ripped up by a sprinkler head and twisted his ankle?"

"Hey," Peter said. "It's a sport, you know. Golf is. Things happen."

"It's a geriatric sport," I said, staring at him, baffled.

"There's an undeniable physicality. You'd be surprised how many golf injuries I end up seeing."

"People dislocating their hip replacements doesn't really count!" We were veering way off topic. Peter was very good at this distraction technique. It didn't matter in this case, though. I was already resigned to letting it go. "I don't want to talk about it," I said.

"He's a terrible golfer. I don't know when I've ever seen someone that bad. He doesn't swing as much as he's like trying to screw himself into the ground."

"I don't want to talk about it."

Peter sat down on the sofa with a grunt. "He'd be lucky to eventually be good enough to *develop* a snap-hook. He shot a 114 and he shaved!" He was borderline gleeful now.

"I said I really don't want to talk about it!" I shouted, walking to the bedroom.

"Getting thrown from the cart is a rite of passage, Gwen," Peter explained, "and he didn't even get that part right."

I stopped in the middle of the hallway and turned and walked back into the living room. "So you threw him from the cart on purpose?" I said.

"No," he said, "not really. There was a squirrel."

"Mmhm," I said. "Okay, then I really don't want to talk about this — at all."

"Okay," he said. "I don't either, then."

"Fine."
"Fine."

CHAPTER TWENTY-SIX

Fall rolled in quickly. The days got shorter, and cool air started to tunnel into the apartment. The windows rattled with the wind. It was a gray, rainy season that seemed only occasionally punctuated by sun. My mother died during autumn, so that season always had a strange hold over me. With the cold chill and the leaves falling from trees, everything losing its greenery, it's a death-haunted season anyway. This particular fall, I felt haunted not only in part by the dim memory of my mother but also by Vivian. When she confused me for her sister Giselle, I'd promised her that I would "tell him the truth." Months had passed, and I still wasn't living fearlessly. Every day I felt like I was betraying a trust, and it just got harder and harder to ignore Vivian's goading in my mind.

I wanted to call Elliot and ask about his mother. I waited for word, but no word came, and I wondered if she was still alive or if she'd died and Elliot hadn't been able to call me or didn't want to. I wondered if he was okay. In the middle of one obsessive night, I convinced myself that his mother hadn't been dying at all, that she'd been faking it, for reasons beyond me. In the morning, I knew that was crazy, but still I considered looking up his course schedule at Johns Hopkins to watch him walk out of his class so that I could measure his expression, his gait — to make sure *he* was still alive, really. I went so far as to find his schedule online, but I avoided what would have proven to be a devastating blow to my self-respect. I resisted the urge.

I thought of Elliot every day, but I didn't mention his name. I didn't mention him to Peter and Peter didn't mention his name to me. I made sure not to ask Eila any big philosophical questions about my life — held together as it was or not. And I blatantly told Helen and Faith that I didn't want to talk about Elliot Hull. He was "off the table."

"Can we do that?" Helen asked. "Can we take entire subjects off the table? Do we even have a table? Is that healthy?"

Faith shrugged. "I'm fine with it. Consider Hull off the table as far as I'm concerned."

Helen looked at Faith and then back at me. "Fine," she said. "But one day I might want to take something off the table and I want this to be a real precedent."

"But we can't make a habit of it. It should be like the get-out-of-jail-free card. A one-time usage," Faith suggested.

"Fine," I said. "Everyone gets one 'off the table' without question. And this one is mine."

Then one day I was pulling out of a grocery store parking space and I saw him pushing his cart toward the designated drop-off. It was late. He was pushing the cart and then he stood on its ledge, under the carriage, and he rode it, gliding across the empty spaces, drifting downhill. He was straight-faced, almost solemn, but so responsible. I never returned my carts.

I thought of driving up to him. But I wasn't sure what I'd say. I'd wanted to know that he was alive. He was. I watched him stuff his hands into his pockets and walk back in the direction he'd come. He no longer had a limp. His ankle had healed. Finally, he arrived at his jalopy. There, in the passenger's seat, was a woman with a pretty face and short brown hair. Her mouth started moving as soon as he sat down. Was she someone he could have a conversation with that would last a lifetime? He was nodding, then pulling out of the spot and merging into traffic, then gone.

And I sat there, as if I'd had the wind knocked out of me. Was he seeing someone — someone he could buy a cartful of groceries with instead of just one lime? Was he over me, just like that? I wasn't over him. I wasn't any closer to getting over him than I had been on the rowboat on the lake. I eventually straightened up and shook my head and said aloud, "Good for him," but I didn't believe the words myself. I started to say them again, with more conviction, but my throat cinched. My mouth folded in on the words.

Maybe Elliot had moved on. I couldn't accept this, but I was trying. Still, I couldn't let everything about that time at the Hulls' house slip away. I decided that I had to confront my father. I couldn't let another day pass.

The following Sunday, I went to my father's house for lunch. It was a few days after his birthday.

My father hated anything that seemed close to a celebration for him. If I mentioned his birthday in the weeks before it, he issued stern warnings not to celebrate. I was always forced to ignore the actual day and do something after the fact and purposefully low-key. When Peter saw me making a German chocolate cake — my father's favorite — from a box, he'd offered to come along, adding, "Though I know it would throw him into an attack of unworthiness." This was true.

"He can barely handle a box cake made in his honor," I reminded him. Bringing Peter would make it seem almost like a party, and my father would spend the visit apologizing to us for having gone to too much trouble.

I brought the German chocolate cake. My dad made his specialty — fried salmon cakes. The salmon came from a can. I was anxious and not hungry. I watched him eat, and before he took a bite of his cake, I told him to make a wish. We didn't have candles.

"A wish?" he said. "Oh, well, I just want you to be happy."

"You're supposed to wish something for yourself," I said. "It's your birthday."

He gave me a scholarly stare that seemed to say: *That is a wish for myself, my darling little dope.* He ate his cake, pressing the crumbs with his fork.

"If you're not going to use your wish, then I will," I said.

"Feel free — you know I'm frugal and hate to waste," he said.

"Then I wish that you would tell me the truth." I stared at his plate. I couldn't look at him.

"The truth? About what?"

I felt my eyes sting with tears. "Mom," I whispered, struggling to find my voice. "What really happened? The truth . . ."

The room was quiet. The heater ticked on and hummed. My father put his hand on top of mine. "I want to show you something."

"Okay," I said, feeling a little unsteady if only because this was so unusual for him. I felt like we were in some new part of our relationship, and I was a little disoriented. He'd always been the guide — the one who led by example, his example being how to let things sit, how to avoid.

I followed him upstairs to the hallway where he pulled on the thin rope attached to the attic stairs, which unfolded from the ceiling like spindly legs.

"What is it?" I asked.

"Come on up," he said. He walked up the stairs first, the hinges tightening as he made his way, the stairs squeaking under his weight. Once he pulled the string on the bare bulb, I climbed up too. The air was cool and dry. It was a huge attic, running the entire length of the house. The fake Christmas tree stood in the corner, some tinsel still dangling from its limbs. The rest of the space was filled with boxes, floor to ceiling, packed in tight. I recognized the one marked *Gwen* in thick black marker. It contained my yearbooks, cap and gown, a few grade school report cards, likely gnawed at by silverfish, and a few odd trophies. I'd never wondered what was in the rest of them — every house had boxes. I shivered and crossed my arms against my chest.

"Watch yourself," he said. "Only step on the beams." The rest of the floor was faded insulation, which was probably too flattened to do much good.

"This is where I put all of your mother's knitting. I boxed it up and put it here. I didn't know what else to do with it."

"Which boxes?"

"All of them."

I was astonished. I let my eyes tour the room. There must have been over fifty boxes, big boxes taped up and unmarked. "All of these boxes are filled with knitting? All of them?"

"My mother's punch bowl is in that one and there are some old picture frames in there," he said, pointing. "But the rest is knitting," he said. "Jam-packed, in fact."

"But, is that even possible? There's so much!" I said. "When could she have had enough time?"

"She didn't sleep much," he said.

"Even still . . ." I walked along a beam to a stack of boxes, dragged my fingers along their dusty tops.

"She knitted a lot," he said.

"But this much? That's crazy," I said, turning a slow circle to take it all in.

"Yes," he said, quietly.

And then I turned and looked at him. He was tapping his fingertips together nervously. "It *is* crazy," I said again, seriously now.

"It is," he said.

"What you're telling me," I said, "is that my mother was crazy?"

"She was suffering," he said, clasping his hands together and bowing his head, almost in a posture of prayer. "It's different."

I thought about my mother — suffering? I hadn't ever considered it. She was dead. That had been enough for me to manage, to feel guilty about. But she'd been suffering? "In what way?"

"Well," he said, suddenly a little flustered with anger. "Crazy sounds like something she might have done on purpose, for fun!

Being wild and crazy!"

"I didn't mean it like that," I said apologetically.

"I know," he said. "I'm sorry."

"It's just that there's so much," I said, taking a step forward.

"Be careful," he reminded me. "Only step on the beams."

I secured my footing. "This just seems so sad to me," I said, picking at the tape on the lid of the closest box. "It's just that there's so much . . . suffering," I said. "Why didn't you show me this before?"

"I wasn't sure if you'd want to see it, to know. I thought it might scare you to know."

"I think I had a right to know!"

My father glanced around the room. He patted down the sparse hair on his head and then said, "You did. I just didn't want to scare you."

I wasn't sure exactly what he meant by this, but I felt like he was insinuating that I was frail in some way. "You thought I'd be afraid that I'd go crazy too?"

"I don't know," he said. "She scared you sometimes when you were little. You'd sit with your head in her lap and she would hum you to sleep, and she would be knitting so furiously the whole time. You knew something was wrong — the way kids know without knowing . . . It was in the way you sometimes looked at her. I can't explain it."

I needed facts. "She was compulsive."

He shook his head. It was clear that he still wasn't comfortable talking about her problems. "She suffered."

"Was she depressed?"

"Yes," he said, buttoning up his cardigan. "She was anxious and depressed, both."

I looked at the boxes again. It seemed like they were pressing in from all sides. "I want to go through it all," I said.

"The boxes?"

"Yes."

"No, don't," he said, looking teary-eyed. "It's too much. It's all packed away. Let it stay packed away."

"I want to go through it all," I said again. "I'm going to." I turned and looked at him. He stood there, his hands clasped together in a gesture I didn't recognize. Supplication? "What did you expect?"

"I don't know," he said. "I thought you wanted me to tell you something about her. This is what I had to offer."

"I'm going to go through it all," I said.

"The boxes are cumbersome. I'll help you bring them down," he said. "Let me help."

I started out quickly, frantically, in fact. I

worked for hours rummaging, picking things up, making piles of folded blankets, sweaters, mittens, and socks. After I had some kind of order, I spread one of my mother's blankets on the floor. I knelt down on it, my eyes blurred by tears. It had tassels on the ends of it, and I remembered their wooliness from my childhood in a vague way. The volume of knitting — scarves, pillowcases, hats, sweaters — told me one story, but I decided to study one blanket in particular, only one, deeply, to see what I could learn about someone from her knitting alone. I knew very little about knitting. I'd only gone through a short phase of it myself, in college. It had reminded me of my mother at the time. I'd only known that she'd knitted things for me as a child. I had no idea that it had been an obsession. I ran my fingers over the stitches as if trying to read Braille.

My father brought me a cup of tea, and would occasionally amble in to ask, in a quiet voice, if I wanted any more.

"No, thank you," I'd say.

He would pause there, waiting for me to tell him what I saw or, at least, what I was looking for, but I had nothing to offer on either count. He would always say, "Okay, then. Let me know if you need anything," and he would retreat to his notations at the dining room table.

One of the things made immediately clear was that my mother was not compulsive about the perfection of her work; far from it. There were rows that were taut and fretful, too close and knotted, and then some evenness might be regained for a while, but the small knots would invariably appear again. And then there were loose patches, as if done in a period of distraction. I assumed that I was the distraction.

At the bottom of one of the boxes was a set of oversized paperbacks on knitting. The pages were dog-eared. She'd circled certain patterns and lessons with a blue ballpoint, and at one point, a purple crayon, which I assume was what she'd had handy. But the other stitches — lace, cable, ribbing — never showed up. She seemed to stick to the basics.

I knelt down on the blanket, which was stretched out on the floor. I could see the pattern of a few days — the intricate flow of emotions, a fraught desperation that gave way to a wandering despair, the lilt of anxiety and depression. I called my father into the room. He came quickly as if he'd been hovering just on the other side of the doorway. His cheeks were flushed, his eyes expectant.

"I have a question," I said, and I stood up so suddenly that I felt light-headed. I still held on to the blanket with one hand, squeezing a woolly tassel.

"Yes?" This was my father, standing in the doorway, duck-footed, his cardigan buttoned up, his cheeks soft and tinged pink, his unsteady eyes.

I wanted to cushion the questions somehow, to make it easier for him, but I didn't know any way to disguise it, and, as much as I wanted to protect him, I was tired of protection — his protection of me and mine of him. I was tired of hiding things. "Was she suicidal?" I asked.

He froze for a moment then nodded. The room went silent. In the distance, I heard a leaf blower. His eyes welled up and then he shook his head again. "She wouldn't have tried to kill herself with you in the car. She never would have done that."

"Where was she driving that night with me in the car?"

He sat down in an overstuffed armchair, rubbing his chin as if he wanted to stop it from quivering. He looked small and frail. "She was leaving me," he said in a quick exhalation of air.

"Leaving you?" I sat down on the couch

and stared at all of the piles of knitting, the stack of books, the emptied boxes. "Why didn't you tell me?"

"She would have come back," he said, although his voice revealed more than a hint of doubt. "I know she would have."

"Did you have a fight?" I didn't remember my parents ever raising their voices, no squabbles, no shouting. When I was younger, I wished they'd been more volatile so that I could have had memories — even bad ones were better than a vague nostalgic memory that left me nothing to hang on to.

"No," he said. "She was too fragile for that. She didn't have any fight in her. She wasn't that kind of person. It was an erosion, she told me. She felt eroded, and she needed to be away from me to see what that feeling meant."

"Where was she going?"

"To a friend's house, a girlfriend from her Mount Holyoke days."

"How did the wreck happen?" I asked.

"I'm not sure," he said. "The roads were wet. There was construction. She was exhausted. She hadn't slept in days." I imagined her tugging the wheel in a sleepless haze, the damp air, the flashing lights — maybe they were disorienting rather than clarifying. Maybe she was already asleep.

"But someone came in and saved me."

"Yes," he said. "A man named Martin Mendez. A stranger. He and I had coffee once."

"You had coffee with him?" This stunned me. Martin Mendez and my father — two men in a diner, talking about what, exactly? Did he describe the accident site, the skidding car, my mother's death?

"I felt like I needed to know as much as I could," my father said quietly. "He was a good man. He died a few years ago."

"What did he say?"

"He said that he saw the accident. He watched her car careen into the water. The car started to fill." My father stopped for a moment. "He said that the water was cold. But when he went in, he saw you thrashing and she wasn't. And so he saved you first. By the time he got out, someone else was there. He went back in and pulled out your mother, but she was already gone. She likely died on impact."

I turned and looked out the bay window at the weedy lawn, the crumbling sidewalk, the rusty mailbox, a boy walking a terrier down the empty street. "If you'd told me earlier, I could have asked Mendez these questions myself." Martin Mendez was dead. I'd never get to hear his version for myself, to help me rebuild my memory.

"I'm sorry," my father said, but I didn't want his apologies.

"I want to see the bridge," I said, standing up, suddenly furious. "What kind of car was it? I want to talk to the paramedics. They came, didn't they? I want to talk to them!"

My father stood up. "No, no," he said. "It's over. It's history."

"I want to talk to the paramedics!" I shouted.

My father walked to me and touched my shoulder. I shrugged him off, and he let his hand fall to his side. "Sweetie," he said. "Gwen."

"Look at all of this," I said, pointing to the ransacked boxes, the piles of sweaters and hats and mittens, the stack of knitting books, the blanket on the floor — this secret that my father kept all of these years, boxes and boxes of secrets, and now unpacked, let loose. I wondered why he'd needed to hold on to the secret so tightly. "If you'd told me earlier," I said. "If you'd only . . . I would have been able to put it together for myself. All of these boxes, it's all so unhealthy, so poisonous, packed up there for all of these years and years. How did you live? How did you live and breathe with all of those heavy boxes up there in the attic collecting dust, just up there, over your head all the time?"

"It's over," he said again.

"Why didn't you just tell me that she was leaving you? All these years, I blamed myself in so many stupid ways . . . Why didn't you tell me the truth?"

He stared at his hands. "I thought I was shouldering all of the blame," he said. "I thought I was sparing you."

"No," I said. "You were wrong." I picked up my pocketbook and walked to the door. "You were completely wrong."

CHAPTER
TWENTY-SEVEN

I don't remember the drive home, only that when I walked into the apartment, Peter was making a casserole — one of his mother's recipes — and I knew that I'd forgotten some plans that included a potluck. He always made this for potlucks. He was wearing his thick white chef's apron, the one he wore when making this meal.

I'd come to some not yet fully formed notion of the role of secrets in our private lives. I couldn't have articulated how pointlessly dangerous they often could be. My father showed me my mother's knitting. He let go of his secrets, finally. This changed everything. My mother's knitting, the attic so weighted with all of her sorrowful and frenetic stitching — it was too much. I only knew that I'd decided not to live with secrets any longer.

I put my keys and pocketbook on the dining room table. I walked into the kitchen.

Peter looked up from topping the casserole with bread crumbs. I stared at him for a moment. I knew that I was about to change everything, and I wanted one last look, one last glimpse of this man. I loved Peter in this moment — the apron, his quick hands, his broad shoulders. I loved the way he glanced at me and smiled, like a little boy who's proud of himself for being so grown up. I felt sorry for him because I knew what was coming. I wanted to spare him. I would have if I could. I'd have transported him to some future when maybe the two of us could be friends — like comrades who'd been soldiers side by side in these pretty trenches we'd dug for ourselves. I would miss this life, this apartment, this steamy kitchen, this man. But I knew that he would never be enough. I knew the truth, and it was time for me to start saying it.

I said, "I'm in love with Elliot Hull."

He paused, put the canister of bread crumbs on the counter. He didn't look at me. "What?"

"I'm in love with Elliot Hull."

"Did you sleep with him? Are you having an affair?"

This response infuriated me. It seemed recklessly territorial and demeaning, and yet came so naturally. "No," I said. "It's worse than that."

"No," he said. "Having sex with him would be the worst. Trust me."

I didn't respond. I didn't move. I just stood there.

"Are you leaving me for Elliot?" he asked, and then he kind of laughed, as if this were absurd, and I suppose all of this must have seemed absurd.

"No," I said. "I think he's seeing someone."

"So you're in love with someone who's seeing someone else," he said, as if he were trying to cast this off as a matter of my stupidity instead of betrayal.

"I'm not leaving you for Elliot." I hadn't yet gotten very far in my thinking, but an odd calm settled over me. I said quite logically, "But I don't think I can be married to you and in love with someone else."

"Please," Peter said. "People do it all the time." He picked up the casserole, put it in the oven with an angry jab, and set the timer.

"Do they?" I asked. Was this his definition of marriage? How could we have been together for so long and I didn't know that he held this belief? And he'd said it with such steadfast conviction that it shocked me.

"Sure they do. Of course. Don't be naive. You'll get over Elliot. And that'll be that." His tone was casual now, and again, I couldn't help but feel like I was being patronized. *I'll get over Elliot? And that will be that?* I was infuriated, but at the same time, I knew that I couldn't push him. He was responding the way he knew how. But still, I was confused by what he was saying. What was he saying exactly? What did he mean people do it all the time — stay married to one person while in love with someone else?

"Have you been?" I asked.

"Been what?" He got a beer from the fridge and was opening it on his apron.

"Have you been married to me and in love with someone else?"

"No," he said, shaking his head and then wagging a finger at me admonishingly. "Not at all. This is your problem. Don't turn on me." He pulled his apron off roughly over his head and stuffed it through the handle of the fridge. "Fix it," he said. "That's what I'm saying here. Just fix it." He walked to the living room.

I stood there for a moment, alone, and then I said, "Peter, I don't know how to fix it." I walked back to the dining room table, picked up my pocketbook and keys.

"Are you walking out?" he said, finally

showing some real anger. "You can't walk out on a fight."

"Are we fighting?" I asked.

"No," he said, shaking his head. "Of course not. You tell me you're in love with someone else and we're not fighting! That's what we're *not* doing!"

"I'm going out for a while," I said, feeling sick. "We're not making any progress here. I have to think. I need to be alone."

"We've got a potluck tonight," he said. "At Faith's. Did you forget?"

"I've got to go," I said, and I left.

I drove for an hour or more, running over the argument in my head, seeing my mother's taut, then lulling stitches in my mind's eye. I imagined her driving, like I was, as the dusk settled in and then night. I'd walked out on both my father and my husband. I felt outside of myself, detached, and invisible. No one knew where I was or what I was doing or what I was going to do next. I didn't either.

Eventually I wondered where I should go. I needed to talk to someone, didn't I? I couldn't wander forever. Faith would have been my first choice, but she'd be preparing for guests and then guests would be arriving. That left Helen, who understood men

323

and relationships and love with her own particular brand of insight. I knew she probably wouldn't go to Faith's potluck, claiming it was the married clique — not to mention too clichéd to bear. It was a Sunday night. I hoped that she was home.

I knocked on the door of her apartment. I heard her bustling within. Helen's body seemed to have its own entourage of restless gestures that followed her everywhere. "Who is it?" she called out.

"It's me," I said. "Gwen."

The bustling stopped for a moment, and then the door swung open. She looked at me, and I wondered what I must have looked like — wide-eyed, disheveled, pale? "Gwen," she said. "What's wrong?"

She ushered me in, sat me down on the long white sofa. I didn't say anything. I didn't know where to begin.

"Okay," she said. "Hold on." She brought out a bottle of wine and two glasses. She filled a glass and handed it to me. "Au Bon Climat, 2005. Pinot noir. Have some."

I took a sip, closed my eyes, let it fill my mouth. It was smooth and good. When I opened my eyes, I nodded. "It's really good."

"So start talking," she said.

And I did. I talked and talked and talked.

She didn't interrupt. She sat back. She nodded. She sipped her wine. I didn't cry. I didn't even tear up. I simply reported the last few months of my life — Elliot Hull, his mother, his sister, Bib and the nesting eagles, the golf outing, Elliot in the grocery store parking lot, the woman in his car, my father's confession, my mother's knitting, her accident, my argument with Peter, everything. I said it all quickly, almost breathlessly, but with a certain serenity too. I narrated all the way to this moment, on her couch, with the wine. And I looked over to her. "That's why I'm here," I said.

I looked at Helen and realized I'd told this story while staring off, glancing around her apartment, not making eye contact. Basically, I told the story while living in my own head. I was surprised now that her face was flushed, the pale skin of her neck blotchy. Her wet eyes were scanning the room. "I don't know what to tell you," she said.

"You always have something to tell everyone."

"Not this time," she said. "You should call Peter. You should talk to him."

"That's it?" I sat back and stared at her.

"Call him," she said. "He'll be worried about where you are. He loves you." She stood up and said, "Excuse me. I have to go to the bathroom."

I sat there a moment. I wondered if this was the reason Helen had never gotten married, if she was incapable of insight when it was needed most, if she shut down on her men, in just this way, in the crucial hours.

But too, I decided she was right. Simply put, she'd told me what to do. Peter would be worried. He did love me. I dug in my pocketbook for my cell phone and then realized I'd left it in the passenger's seat of my car. Helen's cell phone was on the coffee table. I picked it up and dialed Peter's cell number.

It rang, but only once, and then there was Peter's voice, and I could immediately tell he was drunk. I didn't say a word. He said, "Hey, why haven't you called? I've been waiting for your call. Did you get my messages?"

For a moment, I was relieved that he'd gotten drunk because I'd left and that he'd been desperately waiting for my call, but the moment quickly disappeared. I didn't answer — because this was Helen's phone, not mine. Peter thought *Helen* was calling, not me. *Hey, why haven't you called? I've been waiting for your call. Did you get my messages?* His voice was so intimate and private and urgent. My heart started pounding so loudly that I heard it in my ears. My stomach felt light as if filled, sickly with air. I shut the phone.

Helen walked back into the room. She looked so simple now. Helen. She was a traitor. All of her gauzy dresses, her flapping and bending, her wild gesticulation, it was all a cover-up. For what? This simple woman with simple needs. She was a brute, a thief. I imagined all of us as animals suddenly. *That's all we are,* I thought. *Animals.* "Did you call him?" she asked.

I nodded, but it was only the slightest jerk of my head. I put her cell phone down on the coffee table.

She looked at the phone and then at me. "Did you . . ." she took a step toward the phone and then stopped. She clasped one hand with the other, as if one were trying to keep the other from making the wrong move. "You used my phone," she said.

I put my pocketbook straps on my shoulder and stood up.

"Wait," Helen said. "What did he say?"

I walked to the door.

"Gwen," she said, and then she relied on her flurry of gestures, all of which meant nothing. She said, "It wasn't premeditated. We ran into each other in a bar, after he'd played golf with some buddies. He walked me home in the rain and it just happened." I thought of his waterlogged spikes. "We tried not to see each other again, but . . . listen. I've shut it down. For good. It's over."

And this was the confirmation. She and Peter had been having an affair. She sighed. "I don't blame you for hating me. I hate myself." And then she reached out to touch my arm. I held up my hands to stop her. I opened the door and walked quickly down the hall, the patterned carpeting moving swiftly under my feet, the yellow walls sliding by.

"Gwen!" Helen shouted. "Gwen!"

When I got outside, there was snow. It was only early November so I felt disoriented, and it was easy to imagine that I was in a different world now. It had dusted the ground and my small Honda, and it was still coming down, swirling and gusting.

I got in my car, turned on the engine, the wipers. The snow was light and dry. I put the car in drive and eased onto the streets. Peter and Helen had been carrying on an affair — this stood as a fact in this different world. I could still hear his drunken voice: *Hey, why haven't you called? I've been waiting for your call. Did you get my messages?*

Was this something Peter had done to get back at me? I remembered the way he'd leaned onto Helen's lap and bitten her corsage. Didn't he dislike Helen? He'd said she laughed like one of those old toys that when you press the bottom, the toy collapses. I remembered how she'd forced us to be thankful, to be appreciative during our last lunch. I wondered now if Helen was punishing me for not being thankful enough.

I drove deeper into the city. The apartment buildings rose up on all sides. And then my cell phone, sitting exactly where I'd left it in the passenger's seat, started to ring. I picked it up and looked at the caller ID.

It was Elliot Hull.

What in the hell could he want now? Did he know? Had he sensed something was wrong? I was willing to believe almost anything now. This different world had different facts and different rules.

The truth was that I was relieved that he was calling, grateful. I wanted to hear his voice to erase the echo of Peter: *Hey, why haven't you called? I've been waiting for your call. Did you get my messages?*

"Hello," I said, pulling over into an empty parking spot.

"I know I'm not supposed to call, but Peter is hitting golf balls at my house." I heard him clattering around. I heard a muffled, "Holy shit!" And then his voice came through clearly again. "And he's got a pretty fucking good swing!"

"Golf balls? Into your house?"

"Shit!" Elliot said, amid more clattering. "Yes, golf balls! He's completely lost it. What the hell?"

"I'm so sorry," I said. I'd seen Peter get drunk many times, and every once in a while drinking brought on a snide tone that could then turn verbally hostile. Although I'd never seen him act on it, I wasn't surprised that he'd broken down. Golf balls, though? Hitting golf balls into Elliot's house? This was my fault. Elliot shouldn't have to get involved. I wondered if the woman was with him, if he'd been trying to have a nice evening with her alone and had been forced to explain this insanity. "I'll come get him."

"Any ideas on why he might want to put all my windows out?" Elliot asked. "Two, by the way, so far. He's gotten *two* windows."

"I told him."

Elliot was quiet a moment. "What exactly did you tell him?"

I took a deep breath and spoke as quickly

as possible. "Look, I know that you're seeing someone right now and that you've
moved on, just like last time, with Ellen
Maddox, or backwards, in that case."

He immediately started saying, "Wait,
wait. Slow down a minute." But I didn't
even pause. I talked over his protests.

"You know, you moved back to Ellen
Maddox, really. But what I'm saying is that
I told him that I'm in love with you, but not
because I want to be with you. No. No.
That's not what I meant. But only because
I don't want secrets. There are too many
secrets in the world. People are hoarding
them everywhere. And I had to tell him.
That's all. This is about me and him. Not
you. I'm so sorry. I'm hanging up. I'm not
giving you a chance to talk. I'm just hang-
ing up now because this is my problem with
Peter, not yours, and not about you and me.
So I'm hanging up. I'm coming over to col-
lect Peter, but that's it. I won't bother you.
I'm hanging up."

He was protesting more loudly now.
"Wait, wait. Don't hang up!" But I did
anyway. I had to.

I would learn later, much later, a sketchy
version of what happened in between the
time of Elliot's call and when I arrived at

his house. Peter started yelling obscenities. He sliced a ball and it popped off one of the neighbor's shutters. The neighbor called Elliot on the phone and told him that he was going to call the cops if he didn't get the maniac to settle down.

Elliot went out to talk some sense into Peter. When he reached for the club in Peter's hand, Peter threw a punch, and soon they were wrestling in the snow.

That's where I found them.

The fight was vicious. Peter was drunk, but more athletic than Elliot, but Elliot was taking advantage of Peter's sloppiness. Both were getting in some quick punches. Their bodies were rolling and pitching in a blur of motion, the fog of their breath bursting up from their mouths into the cold night air. Peter's golf bag had tipped over. The golf clubs were splayed on the white lawn. A box of balls had tipped too, and the balls had rolled to the sidewalk where they sat like lost eggs. The angry neighbor was on his front stoop now, glowering at them in a sweatsuit with the hood's drawstrings tightened up around his meaty face. A few other neighbors were peering out of lit-up windows. The snow was coming down faster now, the flakes bigger and wetter.

I got out of my car and just stood there

on the sidewalk, watching in stunned silence. Did I want Elliot to beat Peter up? I did, I think, for sleeping with Helen. But I didn't mind Peter getting in a few jabs of his own — on Elliot who'd moved on to someone else so swiftly. Was that why I was frozen there? It was possible, but also I'd absorbed so much in one day. I was no longer living in the world I'd woken up in. I didn't know what was expected of me here, how to act, what to say.

Elliot finally got Peter's button-down pulled up and over his head so that his arms were trapped and his chest bare. His skin was pale but reddened with spots that looked like they'd form bruises overnight. Elliot then pulled Peter in close to his body, his shoes slipping in the snow, and put him in a headlock.

"You need to go home!" Elliot said breathlessly. "Just stop and go home!"

"No truce!" Peter was shouting, reverting to the language of a sixth-grader. "No truce! I do not give up!"

"Someone's going to call the cops!" Elliot said, and he scanned the street, as if wondering if someone already had, and that's when he saw me. Elliot loosened his grip and Peter jerked free and stood up. He tugged his shirt down violently, as if he were fighting himself now. They both stared at me. Elliot already had a puffed eye that was sealing shut. Peter had a little blood trickling from his nose.

"Gwen," Elliot said.

"Tell him you love me!" Peter shouted.

"Gwen," Elliot said, walking toward me. "I'm not seeing anyone else. I don't know what you were talking about on the phone." I wasn't sure I could trust him or anyone. Nothing made any sense.

Peter caught up to him before he could get too close and shoved him. "Get your own goddamn wife!" he said. "You lousy fucker!"

"Hey," Elliot said, putting his finger in Peter's face. "Don't start again."

"You slept with Helen," I said to Peter. This was a simple sentence, all that I could manage. He was about ten feet away and I was speaking softly.

"What?" he said. "Helen?"

"You slept with her," I said.

"Did she just say that?" He laughed and spun around.

"It's true," I said. "Admit it."

"I'm not admitting to that!" he said. "That's horseshit." He started to pick up his golf clubs then, but lacked balance and fell to one knee. He staggered quickly back up.

"Just tell her the truth," Elliot said, staring at the ground, his arms folded on his chest.

I looked at Elliot sharply. "Why don't you sound surprised?" I asked him.

He looked up and then back down at the ground. "Because he told me," he said.

"You knew? For how long?"

"He doesn't know anything!" Peter said, holding a club by its foot and pointing its handle at Elliot. "You don't know anything, do you?"

"He told me that day in the golf cart," Elliot said.

"Why didn't you tell me?"

"How could I?" he said. "I would have just been the old boyfriend who was trying to break you two up. He'd have denied it. It would have been his word against mine. It was a trap. Plus," he said, "it wasn't my secret to tell."

"You should have told me," I said, wiping the wet snow angrily from my face. "I feel like an idiot."

"It isn't true anyway," Peter said, walking toward me, his golf bag on one shoulder. I noticed he was wearing his father's spikes again. Had he put them on for this occasion? "I didn't sleep with Helen. I don't even like Helen. I love you." He started walking toward me. "Tell Elliot you love me," he said in a slurred whisper. "C'mon, sweetie. Tell him now and we can all go home."

I stared at the two of them.

"Gwen," Elliot said. "I wanted to tell you, but I couldn't."

"You should have thrown yourself into the trap!" I shouted. "You should have told me! What's the matter with a little honesty?"

I jogged to my car and got in. My hands were shaking as I shoved the key into the ignition. Finally, I managed to get the car in gear and drove off, leaving them standing there. In my rearview mirror, I saw Peter listing to one side under the weight of his golf bag, and Elliot, who turned around and punched him, one last time, in the stomach. Peter folded at the waist. And Elliot stuffed his hands in his pockets and walked toward his front door in the steady snow.

CHAPTER
TWENTY-EIGHT

I drove to my father's house. It was late. The house was dark. I had no key and so had to knock on the front door, like a stranger, and maybe that was fitting. I suddenly felt like I was surrounded by strangers and that I was a stranger to myself. I saw my father's bedroom light turn on and then the porch lamp. He opened the door with the old-fashioned chain still in place. When he saw it was me, he quickly shut the door to unlock it, and then opened it wide.

"Come in, come in!" he said, peeking out at the snowy yard at my back. He was wearing a blue flannel bathrobe that looked ancient. It struck me as a widower's bathrobe. Wasn't that something that wives bought husbands when they'd worn out the old one? No one had told my father it was time to retire this one. It seemed intimate to see him like this — his skinny legs and bare feet sticking out from beneath the robe.

I thought about saying that I shouldn't have disturbed him, excusing myself, and leaving. But where would I have gone?

I walked into the living room. It was just the way I'd left it — the boxes with their popped-open lids, the stack of knitting books, the blanket on the floor. I didn't explain why I was there, and my father didn't ask. Instead he said, "Do you need to spend the night?"

I nodded.

"Do you want something warm to drink? I can make hot cocoa. I have some packets somewhere. Are you hungry?"

"No," I said. "I just want to lie down. I'll just sleep on the sofa."

"Why not in your old room?" he asked. "Let me strip the bed and get fresh sheets on it for you."

"No," I said, sitting down on the couch. "Here's fine. It's all I can manage." I lay down and curled up.

My father stood there not sure what to do. Finally, he bent down and picked up my mother's blanket and draped it over me.

"Will you be warm enough? I'll turn up the thermostat."

"I'm fine," I said, pulling the blanket's tassels up to my chin. "I'll be okay."

I called Eila in the morning. "I'm so sorry to leave you in the lurch. I'm sick," I said.

"Don't bullshit me," Eila said and I knew she was alone. This was her Sheila voice. It was too early in the morning to be Eila. And I was relieved. I wanted a real person. I was tired of fakes.

"I'm sorry," I said. "Everything's gone to shit. How about that for not bullshitting you? I left my husband and then found out he's been having an affair with my best friend." I wasn't crying, and it seemed strange to be able to say all of this so coldly. I could tell, though, that I would probably start to cry at some point and I might not be able to stop once I did.

"Ah, hell," she said. "I'm sorry."

"You told me that lives don't come apart, but I have to say that this certainly feels like things have come apart."

"Oh, you can't listen to me when I'm trying to be philosophical. I have no idea how the world works. I live with a Pekinese. That's all I can muster." She sighed. "Is there anything I can do?"

I sighed. "Yeah," I said. "I'd like to know something about you. Something that's true. Not this Eila stuff. Something about you."

"Something true. About me." She thought about it a minute. "My father was a son of a bitch. My mother worked as a secretary at a dentist's office. I was an ugly kid and people used to mistake me for a boy. That's three things. Does that help?"

"Weirdly, yes," I said, and it did.

"How much time do you need?"

"I can't afford too much."

"Take a week," she said. "Okay?"

"Yes, thanks."

After I hung up with her, I dialed Faith at work. I needed help. I asked her to get a few of my things from the apartment.

"Do you want to talk about it?" she asked in a hushed voice.

"No."

I refused to talk to anyone. I put on one of my father's T-shirts and a pair of his sweatpants. Peter left messages. He figured I was at my father's and called the house phone there too, but I'd already told my father that I didn't want to talk to anyone. I heard him on the phone in the kitchen, telling Peter exactly this. "She'll call you," he said, "when she's ready." I wondered when that would be. It felt years away. I had nothing to say to him. I spent much of my time replaying our relationship, but now casting everything in doubt and suspicion. I wondered if Helen was his only affair, if he'd ever expected to be committed to me even as we were taking our vows, if he'd ever really loved me. I was no closer to my definition of marriage, and looking at my life as a scientist, that little experiment seemed to have failed. Nothing was clearer.

The voicemail on my cell phone was cluttered. There were multiple messages from Peter, Helen, and Faith. I deleted their messages as soon as I heard their voices kick in. It was a reflex. *No,* I said aloud to no one, *don't talk to me. Don't try to explain.*

There was only one message that I listened to.

It was from Elliot.

He said, "I'm not going to hound you with phone calls like I did the last time. I'm only calling this once. Nothing has changed for me. I'm in love with you. I have been for a very long time. It's the kind of love that won't stop, although I've tried to make it stop." He sighed. "I don't know why you think I'm seeing someone else. I'm not. But you were right. I should have thrown myself into the trap. I should have told you even if I thought it was going to doom any chance we might have had. I should have opted for the truth. But I was too scared of losing you." He paused again. "There's more. There's a lifetime's worth more to say. But that's all for now. That's all I'll bother you with."

And then he hung up.

That's when I started crying. Something seemed to tear open inside of me and I couldn't shut it. I didn't think about Elliot or Peter or Helen or anyone specifically. I just cried, breathlessly and raggedly, with no end in sight. Even when I caught my breath, the tears kept coming.

My father canceled his classes for the day so that he could stock up and keep an eye on me. While he was at the grocery store, I picked up a pair of my mother's knitting needles. I opened the box that was packed with yarn. I'd knit that one blanket in college. I wasn't sure I'd remember how, but my hands remembered, kinesthetically, the way to make the stitches. The tears kept rolling down my cheeks, beaded on the yarn, dotted the sweatpants.

My father came home and, carrying grocery bags to the kitchen, he saw me knitting. He paused for a moment, as if he was going to say something — and what would that be? Would this image scare him? Would he want to warn me? I didn't look up, and he moved on.

I was mourning, but what I was mourning, exactly, wasn't clear to me. At first at least, it didn't need to be clear. Mourning felt restless and the knitting relieved that restlessness in some small measure. I thought that I was mourning my marriage, and I was in a way, but I wasn't sure that it was mine to mourn. Had it ever been a marriage that I existed in completely as myself? I knew that the painful answer to that question was no. It had come to define me, though, and although I'd never become completely comfortable with being a wife, I walked through life as a known quantity. I had a safe and insular title. I was a wife. I had to let that go.

And letting that go, I had to let Peter go too. I'd been practicing this, I know, in many various ways. My decision to become Elliot Hull's pretend wife, the kiss in the rowboat, and then, upon my arrival back into my own world, my decision to observe my marriage as a scientist was a decision to disconnect, to step outside of it. Hadn't I known that I was putting off the lessons that Vivian had taught me even then? That I was trying to postpone living my life with courage and honesty? Although that was the first time I'd done it so purposefully, I was beginning to understand that I'd been standing back, just a bit, for some time. I'd been doing it in the ice-cream shop, even, when I ran into Elliot. I knew, equally well, that Peter's affair wasn't entirely his fault. I'm not saying that I should have worked harder to keep him interested. To hell with that! It isn't any one person's job in a marriage to hold the other's attention to keep him from straying. I've never bought that old saw. But, in a broader way, his affair grew out of a marriage that I'd chosen, that I helped create, one that I'd never really ever fully demanded enough of, one that I found comfortable instead of engaging, one that I'd never allowed myself to jump into with full vulnerability.

Even though he'd wanted me to be Elliot's pretend wife and said he was okay with it, he may have known there was something deeper. This didn't make his affair with Helen forgivable, but I wasn't innocent myself. I remembered, too, his intimate, drunken voice — "Did you get my messages?" — on Helen's cell phone. Peter wanted to keep the affair going. Even as he was building to a drunken, jealous rage, he had the wherewithal to speak to Helen in a seductive voice. And, too, I knew that he thought he'd been hung up on by Helen, and maybe that, too, fueled his anger that snowy night.

And let's not forget Helen in all of this. For some strange reason, I felt more betrayed by her than by Peter. Part of this is because I don't think of men as being as strong as women, and so I could allow myself to chalk a tiny bit of Peter's actions up to something particularly male. But Helen? I couldn't give her this infinitesimal leeway. This was old-fashioned, outdated thinking, and I knew it. I wish I were a better feminist. For this reason, though, her betrayal seemed more calculated, more personal, more vindictive. I kept going back to the way she'd explained the affair. "I've shut it down. For good. It's over." She was saying that if it were up to Peter, the affair would have gone on and on. Was she trying to make herself look good — some hero! Or was she really getting in another jab? Either way, it seemed cruel. My friendship with Helen was over. I could imagine a time years from now — maybe decades — when we might be able to have a conversation that seemed normal, almost like great friends, but the trust was gone, permanently. I was the lucky one, though, because I knew that Helen was suffering, that she'd continue to suffer because she couldn't really trust herself on a very basic human level.

On all of the intellectual levels, I knew that my marriage was over, that I couldn't ever really go back to Peter, that I would have to relinquish this role that I'd come to use as a passage through the world.

And I didn't have Elliot as an excuse.

This was my own doing and undoing.

This should have been emotional on its own terms, in a clear way, but it wasn't. Every time I thought of Peter, I felt a loss that was more deeply rooted in my life. Every time I thought of Peter, I thought of my mother, her death, my lonesome childhood, *that* loss. I couldn't understand why except that you don't get to choose the time when mourning hits you. Some people mourn before a loss — knowing that it's coming. Some people mourn suddenly, in public, as if the reality of their loss is only brought into sharp focus when confronted with a group. Some people mourn for years, decades — the loss keeps coming, like a leaking faucet that stains a spot of rust into the tub. I was mourning my marriage, Peter, these years of my life, but they were dredging up the past. I was mourning something that I couldn't have mourned as a five-year-old girl, something I couldn't have understood or had the language to come to terms with or the context.

How do you mourn what you might have had?

And that brought me to Elliot, always Elliot. I blamed him for not telling me about Peter cheating on me. It wasn't his place, no. But he should have told me anyway. Could I trust him now? Was he really not seeing anyone? Who was the pretty woman in his car?

I wasn't sure that it was at all possible to find my way back to him. Could we start again — at the beginning or the middle? Was everything too impossibly muddy? I was in love with him. That's all I knew. I was in love with him, and I had to mourn the possible end of that too.

What did the mourning feel like? Imagine flying, the landscape changing beneath you — shifting between deserts, jagged mountains, gorges, and long, twisting bodies of water. I was unprepared for this kind of grieving, how quickly it turned to anger then love then an embattled pride. I felt foolish, wounded, and then unbearably tough. Then for a stretch, without warning, I would feel empty, but soon it would start up all over again.

That evening, Faith knocked at the front

door. I looked at her through the window. She was holding a container of homemade cookies and, propped next to her, was my rolling suitcase. Something about her stoic figure made me feel steely and rigid, which I knew wasn't fair. She'd come to help. She was being a good friend.

My father walked into the living room. "Should I get it?" he asked.

"You can let her in," I said.

He looked hugely relieved, and I realized how much he'd hated his role as gatekeeper. He must have despised the conflict and having to disappoint people.

I was still knitting, though I had no idea what I was knitting, exactly. A scarf? A shawl? A blanket? I was just practicing, small stitches, large stitches, making rows. I'd gotten faster — the knitting needles slid over each other, the yarn slipped up and over, on and back off, the needles making pleasing little clicks like claws.

I listened to Faith and my father exchange pleasantries then whispers — talking about me and my possible mental state, no doubt — and then she walked in and parked the suitcase. I didn't look at her. I glanced at her and saw that she was looking at the room, which was still piled with my mother's knitting and the empty boxes. I couldn't bring myself to repack them, and I could tell now that this might look like another sign of my instability. Did I look like a crazy person? Knitting amid all of this knitting?

She opened the container of cookies and put them on the coffee table in front of me.

"No, thanks," I said.

"Oh, Gwen," she said, "I'm so sorry."

I knitted faster. "Please don't say that. Don't give me your sympathy. My husband cheated on me with one of my best friends. Nobody died. So let's not be melodramatic."

She sat down, not sure what to do now. She'd come prepared to give her sympathy, but I'd refused it and now it was just an unopened box sitting between us. "What are you going to do?" she asked.

"I don't know."

"Are you going to talk to him? I know he'd love to talk to you." I assumed that this was part of her mission. Had she talked to Peter at length? Was he trying to turn this whole thing around?

"I'm in the middle of a conversation that has suddenly come to an end," I said.

She stared at me, unsure of what this meant exactly. "Helen would like to talk to you too," she said, but she was more sheepish about this. I assumed that Helen had made her promise that she'd give me this message, but she wasn't so sure that Helen deserved it.

"Tell Helen that for his birthday, I suggest she get him a pair of suede buck golf shoes. That's what he needs."

"I don't think they're going to be exchanging birthday gifts."

"Why not?" I said, not sure if I was being as sarcastic as I sounded. "They should make a go of it. They're perfect for each other."

She sat back in the cushions and sighed. "I just can't believe it," she said. "It's so awful. It's so ugly and unnecessary. What the hell were they thinking? Why are they such selfish idiots? I'm just so furious." She punched the sofa cushion with her fist. This got my attention. I looked at her, really, for the first time. She looked like hell. Her eyes were red-rimmed, like she'd been crying. All the makeup had been wiped away except for two soft gray smears around her eyes. I felt sorry for her, sitting there in her coat, her oversized pocketbook on the floor between her boots. "I don't deserve to be pissed, not like you do. And I'm not trying to take one single ounce of that anger away from you," she said. "But I am so pissed — at both of them."

I realized that this must be hard on her,

truly. It had to have upended some of the things that she believed about marriage, or at least made her lose her footing. I was never sure how confident she was in her own marriage — a marriage that had always seemed to me to be a pairing of opposites. I found myself in the strange position of comforting her. "It's going to be okay. Don't worry. We weren't ever that strong."

"Really?" she said. "You had me fooled. I thought you two were so tight, such a unified force. I always admired how easy you made it look. Not like my marriage. We're always fuming and bickering . . ."

"We didn't have enough to fume and bicker about. Maybe that was the problem." I thought of Elliot's mother, the way she'd told me that marriage was a crock, but love wasn't. I said, just as she had, "I was a damaged girl. I made a damaged decision."

Faith leaned forward. "What do you mean?"

"I shouldn't have married him in the first place."

"Do you really believe that?" she said.

I nodded.

"You two were happy. You were best friends."

"We were friends, but not confidants."

She took this in, maybe wrestling with the

question of whether she and Jason were friends or confidants. What was their level of intimacy? Were they in danger? She stood up and walked among the piles of clothes and blankets. She reached down and picked up a stack of sweaters, let her hands run over the uneven stitches. She put the pile down in one of the empty boxes, and then picked up some mittens and wedged them into the box as well. This made me bristle, but I didn't want to tell her to stop. She had nervous energy. She was trying to help.

"Peter and I had portions of our lives that were roped off from each other," I said, trying to explain. "It didn't just start with the affair with Helen."

"Do you think he had other affairs? He swore to me that he didn't."

"No," I said, frustrated. "That's not it. We were cordoning ourselves off. We didn't share what we were thinking. We made little decisions every day to keep parts of ourselves separate. We roped off one area and then another and then another until we had lovely banter. Banter that could go on and on."

"You were so funny together," she said. "I loved your lovely banter."

"But finally we ended up living side-by-side lives. That's what made it possible for him to have an affair."

She stuffed a few tassel-topped hats into the box. I knew that I would take everything out of the box as soon as she was gone, but I let her feel useful in this small gesture. "I just didn't know. I guess no one can really know another couple's relationship."

"I don't think Peter and I knew either, if that's any consolation."

She'd packed the box tight then walked to her bag. She pulled out a picture frame and handed it to me. "Here," she said.

I let the knitting fall to my lap and I took the photograph. It was, of course, the photograph that Vivian had given me as a gift — Elliot, Jennifer, and Vivian in the yard, the gauzy curtain. I'd forgotten that I'd told her about it, but I had, in the creamery, while I was trying to really explain what had happened, and had failed.

"You said it made you feel better, stronger. It made you feel watched over. I thought you might need that right now."

I wasn't sure what to say. I looked up at her. "I can't believe you remembered," I said. "Thank you."

"I hope it helps," she said, and she picked up her bag, readying to go. "Are you in love with Elliot?" she asked, and then she held up her hand. "Don't answer. You don't have to answer that. That's just what Pete said, but I didn't come here for that."

I didn't answer. "Did you come for some other reason than dropping off my things?" I asked.

"To make sure that you were okay."

"Am I okay?" I asked.

She patted the box's lid. "I don't know."

"Neither do I."

CHAPTER
TWENTY-NINE

The snow came and went, leaving muddy ice frozen in shady patches on the front lawn. I sat in the flickering glow of the television, but I didn't watch it. I knitted, and while knitting sometimes the yarn would go blurry, and a tear would roll down my nose onto my busy fingers, and I would cry for a while, but keep working.

Why did I keep knitting? I felt oddly useful, like a small machine, and though my heart felt rather dead, my hands didn't. They kept making, creating. The skeins of yarn took shape one stitch at a time.

And the photograph sat in its frame propped on the end table. Sometimes I stole glances at it. Sometimes I'd pick it up and take in the details again — the rippling water, Jennifer's plump baby face, Vivian's long, elegant legs, Elliot's bowed knees and swim trunks, the muddy fishing rods. But usually I simply knew it was there, keeping watch. The photograph was mine now. It had not only found me through Vivian's generosity and Faith's thoughtfulness — love and friendship — it had also seemed to come home.

My father made my meals — his usual inelegant dishes. He watched television, sitting beside me on the sofa. At one point he told me that I looked flushed. "Do you want to take your temperature?"

I shook my head.

Sometimes he would point to the TV screen and make some benign comment like, "Will you look at that?"

I'd look up and stare and nod, but not really absorb it. I was tired, mainly, exhausted, as if I hadn't slept for years.

One afternoon I fell asleep, and woke up to a knock at the front door. I called my father, but he didn't answer. I looked out the bay window. His car was gone. Instead there was a blue pickup truck parked at the curb and a man I'd never seen before standing on the stoop. I looked back at the truck. A small figure was moving in the passenger's seat, but I couldn't make out the person. In the back of the truck, there was what looked to be a cello in a black case.

He knocked again then stood back from the house with his hands in his pockets and looked at the upper windows. He started walking back to the truck, but then the passenger froze, then rolled down the window.

It was Bib.

Her bony frame and small pinched face appeared. She stuck her body out of the open window and waved to me. She'd spotted me there, watching. My heart swelled. Bib! I was so glad to see her I felt like shouting her name and running out into the yard.

The man turned back around, and I decided this must be Sonny, Jennifer's husband, the drummer. Why was he toting a cello? I wasn't sure. But Bib took my breath. Bib was here. Bib had appeared and was now kicking open the passenger door and swooping toward the house, arms outstretched, like one of those nesting eagles she was so afraid of. Maybe she would lift me off the earth, not like a twenty-pound sheep to eat, no. Maybe she would lift me right up off the earth, to save me! Just like that!

I ran to the door, opened it wide, and stepped onto the cold stoop in my bare feet. The sun blinded me. Bib was tripping toward me. She hugged me around the waist so hard I had to grab the wrought-iron handrail.

After a moment, she said, "We've got an

invitation for you. You have to come! It all went to sleep!"

"What went to sleep? What are you saying, Bib?"

"It all went to sleep! The bad stuff is sleeping!" she said.

"She's trying to tell you that Vivian is in remission," the man said.

"That's amazing!" I said, and I thought of Vivian, revived, sitting up in her bed, her cheeks pink. Was she eating again? Was she reading now to herself, books she loved? I felt more than a wave of relief. I was flooded with it. "Is she doing well? How does she look? Is she still weak?"

"She's gaining back her strength, slowly but surely. She's stunned all the docs. They're not sure what to do."

I shook my head. I was speechless. I thought of how she believed in miracles, but only because, as she put it, she didn't have a choice in the matter. I imagined her in a field with an enormous rake of her own, her own brand of bravery.

"The doctors are embarrassed because they were wrong!" Bib said.

Sonny introduced himself, striding forward, hand outstretched. He was barrelchested, bigger than I'd expected, but handsome and warm.

We shook hands. "I figured it was you," I said. "I'm Gwen."

"I know," he said. "I've been sent on a mission to find you."

"And we did!" Bib said. "We did find you!"

"Actually, Bib did," Sonny said. "Elliot said you might have gone to your dad's house, but he only knew that he lived in town, and he's not in the phone book." He glanced at the front hedges, as if he knew he was getting close to a subject about which he shouldn't have known as much as he did — how I left my husband and retreated. I was surprised to hear Elliot's name, though I shouldn't have been, but some part of me clung to his name — I loved hearing it on someone else's lips. "Bib remembered everything you told her about growing up — the name of the street you grew up on and the color of the house and the name of the neighbors, who had their name on their mailbox, which helped. The Fogelmans."

"Wow, did I tell you all of that?" I asked Bib.

"When I was crying," Bib said. "To make me think of something except crying."

"Nice house," Sonny said.

"Do you want to come in?" I asked, hop-

359

ping from foot to foot to relieve the stinging cold on my feet.

"No, no. That's okay," Sonny said. "We don't want to intrude —"

Bib cut him off. "We have an invitation for you!" Bib said. "To the lake house! We're having an un-funeral."

"An un-funeral?"

"Vivian's idea," Sonny said. He pulled a white card out of his jacket pocket then. "She wanted to make sure this found its way to you."

"So you're on a mission from Vivian?" I asked. I'd assumed that Elliot had sent them.

"Yes," Sonny said, reading the hint of disappointment in my voice. "But I know Elliot would love to see you there."

"Come! You have to come! We're having un-lilies and un-cake and un-eulogies! It's going to be un-sad!"

I looked at the invitation, turned it over in my hands. *Elliot. Elliot.* "Thank you," I said. "I'll think about it. I'll try."

My father came home, carrying a stack of papers under one arm and his ancient leather briefcase — another widower's item, like his bathrobe, something a wife would have replaced a decade ago — and found me sitting on the sofa, holding the invitation and its white envelope.

I knew that I couldn't let myself go to the un-funeral. Not yet. I was still sorting through loss. I knew it would take a long time. But right now, before I took another step forward in my life, I needed to find the deepest loss, to unearth it, hold it up to the light, in the open air, to see what I could find there.

"I want you to take me to the bridge," I said.

He sensed my urgency. "Now?" he asked.

"Yes, now."

We drove for about fifteen minutes out of town and finally we were winding along back roads. We were silent in the car. My father has always been respectful of grief, in his way.

Eventually I saw a stone bridge up ahead, the river running beneath it. My father pulled over onto the shoulder so deeply that my side of the car was blocked by brush. It was impossible to use the door. He left his door open and I slid across the seat and got out that way.

It was bitterly cold. A wind was whipping up off the river, which was choppy under the bridge's lights. I waited for some feeling to overtake me — some memory of that night to rise up in stark realism. I waited to feel closer to my mother, to understand her, to have some sudden insight.

None came.

I looked at the bridge's sturdy pilings and the water below. "How was it possible?" I asked. "It's all so impenetrable now. No one could possibly drive into the water."

"They've made it quite safe, haven't they?"

I stood there, staring down into the water then up at the sky. My cheeks were stiffened with cold. "Your theories on love are all about safety," I said.

"My theories on love? I don't have any theories on love," he said modestly.

"Yes, you do," I said. "You loved her and you lost her, and from then on, you decided to be careful with love. You couldn't ever really hand it over with an open heart, not even fully to me. You closed up shop," I said.

He looked out across the river, his eyes shining with tears. "I wish I'd done better by you," he said. "You just reminded me of her so much . . ."

I knew it must have been hard. I knew it even then when I was a child, which is why I'd never pushed him before to talk about any of this. I'd never pushed him before I met Elliot, in fact. It was beginning to dawn on me how much Elliot had changed me, how he'd opened something up inside of me, and now I needed answers. "You taught me to only be able to accept love like that, in small doses. You taught me to be afraid of overpowering love — the kind that, if you lose it, that loss can destroy you."

He shook his head angrily. It was the first time I'd seen my father really angry in as long as I could remember. He grabbed my arm. "No, Gwen," he said. "I don't believe in that kind of love. I'd do it all again. I'd fall in love with your mother a hundred times over. The way I loved her, that was the way to love." He looked away and let his hand slide from my arm.

"But it destroyed you," I said. "Didn't it? Look at your life!"

Just like that his anger was gone. He smiled weakly and shook his head. Did he know what his life looked like to people on the outside? "I keep on loving her," he said, "because I'm afraid if I stop, I'll forget her. And I can't ever let that happen. But I don't believe in, how did you just put it? Love in small doses? I don't believe in loving safely."

There was a distant horn. We both looked up. The wind kicked up my hair. I brushed it out of my face and held it back with one hand. "What kind of love do you believe in?" I asked, in almost a whisper.

"The overpowering kind." He paused and then said, "You're right. I do have theories on love, but I never told you them."

"I assumed them, and I was wrong." We were lit for a brief moment in the headlights from an oncoming car. It passed. "I got all of them backwards."

"I guess so," he said, shuffling one of his shoes in the roadside gravel. "Are you really in love with Peter?"

I shook my head. "No," I said. "He cheated on me and I hate him for that, but it was always love in small doses with him. From the beginning."

"Are you in love with someone else?" I knew this was a nearly impossible question for him to have asked. He would consider this, under normal circumstances, to be more than prying. It would seem like barging in, doors flung open wide, holding a searchlight on someone's private life. But he knew that things were different between the two of us now, and we had to ask hard questions. I didn't realize how desperately I'd wanted him to ask me a question like this, intimate and direct, until this moment.

"I'm in love with Elliot Hull," I said.

"The professor of philosophy? The thinker?" He smiled.

I nodded.

"Well," he said. "Life is a tangle."

"I guess it is."

"I suggest you not play it safe," he said.

CHAPTER THIRTY

There was a stipulation printed on the invitation to the un-funeral: *Attire: Casual, Un-black.* That Saturday I woke up early and put on a pale blue dress. I found my father working at the dining room table.

"Are the cusk eels talkative this morning?" I asked.

"You're dressed. Are you going out?"

"Yes," I said.

"You look beautiful," he said.

"Thank you."

"Are you going to talk to your thinker?"

"I'm going to try."

He got up then and hugged me. It was a great big bear hug that tipped me almost completely off the ground. It was so big that I felt like I was made of air, like I was just a little girl. It wasn't the hug of someone who gave love in small doses — but more like someone who'd chosen not to live that way anymore. I felt like I'd gotten something returned to me, something lost so long ago I didn't even really know it had once existed, but it felt right and good and mine.

The un-funeral was going to be a catered event at the lake house, starting at noon. I headed east, and in a few hours I was making my way down the same dirt roads that I'd ridden along with Elliot in the convertible. I didn't know what to expect from an un-funeral, from Elliot, from myself. I wasn't even convinced that once there, I would be able to get out of the car and walk up to the door. How would I start to tell him something if I didn't really know what that something was? Was I ready for Elliot Hull — to love him and be loved by him?

I slowed down as I approached their long driveway, which was already lined with parked cars. I was surprised by how very many cars there were, but it was a party after all. What had I been expecting? A quiet moment alone with Elliot in the rowboat? I was coming unprepared. I didn't have a symbolic rake to hold in a field, and I was desperate to see Vivian healthy, growing stronger, but I couldn't envision it.

I sped past the entrance and drove until I came to a gas station. I pulled into a parking space and, while resting my hands on the wheel, I took some deep breaths. I watched people come and go — three kids on dirt bikes, a hassled young mother with a baby who was pulling on a wisp of the mother's hair, a few construction workers, and all the while, the man behind the counter, looking at the ceiling-hung television set to Court TV.

I realized that I had unfinished business. I couldn't see Elliot until I'd talked to Peter. I didn't need permission to see Elliot — permission was no longer a part of our marriage. And I didn't need release from the marriage itself — that would take time, wouldn't it? Emotionally, it would take years. What did I need? Maybe only to hear Peter's voice — a sober admission of the truth?

I opened up my cell phone and dialed. It rang once and he picked up. "Hello?"

"Hi."

"Gwen," he said. "Are we on speaking terms now?" He sounded contrite.

"I couldn't listen for a while there. You could have spoken all you wanted, but I knew I wouldn't have been able to hear it."

"And now?" he said.

"Try me."

There was a pause. "I'm sorry."

"I am too," I said.

"Don't say it in that voice."

I hadn't realized I'd used a certain voice. "What do you mean?"

"You say it like you're sorry for the whole relationship."

"And what are you sorry for?" I asked, staring into the convenience store, its rows of shelves, packed with brightly colored junk.

"For that mess with Helen. It was stupid. It was idiotic. It meant nothing. I was just acting out."

"Acting out? Doesn't that mean you were rebelling? Were you rebelling against me?" I felt like he was casting blame.

"That's not what I meant. Idiotic and stupid. That's what I meant."

"And by *that mess with Helen,* you mean sleeping with my best friend?"

"Yes," he said slowly. "I do."

"I'm not sorry for the whole relationship," I said.

"Good," he said, sighing. "You don't know how good that is to hear —"

I cut him off quickly. "But I'm not coming back."

He wasn't ready for this. He started rambling. "Let's have lunch. Let's talk this out. We should go to therapy. Faith says that therapy can work wonders — or just lunch, if that would be easier."

"No," I said, thinking: *I'm a woman in a field with a big rake, and I'm done. It's over. I'm finished.*

"We can salvage this. We can get back to the best of what we were together."

If I was a damaged girl who made a damaged mistake, I didn't want to make the same mistake just as I was beginning to feel stronger. "I want more than the best of what we were together."

"What?" he said. "We had something great. You want more than that? We were perfect together."

"Some version of me was perfect with you, but it's not the version of myself I want to be." The man behind the counter was looking at me now. Maybe he'd been keeping an eye on me for a while, wondering if I was coming or going or casing the joint. "I've got to hang up now."

"No," Peter said.

"I'm sorry," I said.

"I refuse to accept this," he said. "I absolutely refuse."

And then I hung up.

By the time I made my way down the driveway, the cars had thinned out. Votive candles in bags lined the front walkway. A few kids in puffy jackets were running on the lawn. I found a spot and parked.

As I walked up to the door, I saw Bib, wearing a ski hat and boots. The frilly white of her dress bounced around her stockinged knees. Her cheeks were bright red from all of the chasing. I didn't want to interrupt her.

I gave a knock, hearing the clamor of voices and laughter inside. When no one came to the door, I let myself in.

The hospital bed was gone. In its place were a few people holding glasses of what looked like cider. Sonny was among them, as was the woman that I'd seen in Elliot's car. I startled at the sight of her and took a step backwards. Was he still seeing this woman? Had he lied to me? I felt flushed. I had my hand on the knob ready to turn back. It wasn't too late. No one had seen me, not even Bib in the yard.

But then I heard my name.

I looked up and saw Sonny charging over. "I wasn't sure you'd come."

"I wasn't sure either."

"Miranda," he called to the woman. She looked up. She was elegant, holding her glass of cider, smiling. "Come here. I want you to meet Gwen."

"Oh!" she said.

"No, no," I whispered to Sonny. "It's

okay." I tried to edge around him.

He looked at me, confused, for a moment, but then introduced us. "Gwen, this is my sister Miranda. She's staying here for a while. She's a nurse and is between things in her life so she's been helping Vivian a good bit."

"Oh," I said. "Hi. I'm Gwen."

"I know," she said, taking my hand. "I've heard so much about you."

"Good, I hope?" I said, laughing the way people do. I was so flustered I was relying on clichés.

"Angelically good," she said.

"Let me bring you to Vivian," Sonny said, and he wrapped his arm in mine and led me into the kitchen.

Vivian was sitting on the sofa, the one I'd found so out of place in the kitchen. With some help from a woman about her age, she was holding Porcupine — who'd grown leaps and bounds. They were proclaiming his great fatness. "Look at these chins! These thighs!" Vivian was saying. "Look at this ample girth!"

"Look what I found!" Sonny said.

Vivian lifted her head, caught my eye, and smiled brightly. She showed me the baby. "Isn't he enormous! So healthy! Come here and congratulate me for being alive!"

The woman next to her took the baby onto her lap, and then stood up to show him off to the others. I walked to Vivian, took the seat next to her, and gave her an enormous hug, and when I thought the hug would end, it didn't. She kept on holding me.

"A miracle," she said. "See, when you have no choice, you have to believe in them."

She held me by my shoulders now and looked into my eyes. I started crying. I wasn't sure that I'd ever felt more like I had a mother in my life. I'd expected my mother to show up at the bridge by the river, but no. It seemed like she was here, in Vivian, in this moment at an un-funeral on a sofa in a kitchen.

Jennifer appeared in the doorway. "Gwen!" she said. "You came!" She looked around the room, for Elliot, no doubt.

Vivian smiled and then nodded out through the French doors to the backyard. "He went out for some air. There's only so much un-funeral anyone can take. Go on," she said.

I looked at Jennifer. "Go on!" she said.

I walked out the French doors, across the deck, and saw him standing there, looking out at the dock, the pair of rowboats, the lake. I was surprised by the simple and astonishing fact that he existed at all in this world. Elliot Hull — he was right here in front of me. He was a man looking out on a lake. He was the person I loved and I'd loved him since the first time I met him at the icebreaker our freshman year of college, when we were just two kids who were supposed to compliment each other's shoes.

I walked down the deck's set of stairs, stepped onto the grass, and he turned around, not expecting to see anyone, most likely, but there I was.

He stopped and smiled.

I stood completely still, not sure what to do next, but I was suddenly no longer worried about what to say. I wasn't thinking about words at all.

He started walking toward me. His stride picked up speed and I knew what he was going to do. He was going to pick up the right girl this time. He was going to pick *me* up and spin *me* around. He was almost running by the time he reached me. He fit his hands around my waist, lifted me up off the ground, and then around and around and around.

ACKNOWLEDGMENTS

I want to thank Frank Giampietro — poet extraordinaire, super-powered Insight Man, secret weapon. I want to thank my agent, Nat Sobel, who sticks by me and my whimsical whims, and my editor, Caitlin Alexander, who edits brilliantly and with a brimming heart. Thank you, Justin, for talking the talk and walking the walk. And thank you to my parents for raising me up to be all the people I can be. And, as ever, I'm thankful for my dreamy dream team — Dave, Phoebe, Finneas, Theo, and Otis. And, per usual: Go, Noles! Go, Sox!

ABOUT THE AUTHOR

Bridget Asher is the author of *My Husband's Sweethearts*. She lives on the Florida panhandle with her husband, who is lovable, sweet, and true of heart — and has given her no reason to inquire about his former sweethearts.

The employees of Thorndike Press hope you have enjoyed this Large Print book. All our Thorndike, Wheeler, and Kennebec Large Print titles are designed for easy reading, and all our books are made to last. Other Thorndike Press Large Print books are available at your library, through selected bookstores, or directly from us.

For information about titles, please call:
(800) 223-1244

or visit our Web site at:
http://gale.cengage.com/thorndike

To share your comments, please write:
Publisher
Thorndike Press
295 Kennedy Memorial Drive
Waterville, ME 04901